ALSO BY EDNA BUCHANAN

COLD CASE SQUAD

A Novel

EDNA BUCHANAN

SIMON & SCHUSTER

New York • London • Toronto • Sydney

SIMON & SCHUSTER
Rockefeller Center
1230 Avenue of the Americas
New York, NY 10020

SIMON & SCHUSTER and colophon are registered trademarks
of Simon & Schuster, Inc.

For information regarding special discounts for bulk purchases,
please contact Simon & Schuster Special Sales at 1-800-456-6798
or business@simonandschuster.com.

Designed by Dana Sloan

Manufactured in the United States of America

4   6   8   10   9   7   5   3

Library of Congress Cataloging-in-Publication Data
Buchanan, Edna.
Cold case squad : a novel / Edna Buchanan.
p. cm.
1. Police—Florida—Miami—Fiction. 2. Miami (Fla.)—Fiction. I. Title.
PS3552.U324C57 2004
813'.52—dc22
2004044992

ISBN 0-7432-5053-2

FOR RENEE TUROLLA,
world traveler, free spirit, true friend and sister

There is nothing covered up that will not be uncovered, nothing hidden that will not be made known.

—LUKE 12:2

COLD CASE SQUAD

PROLOGUE, PART ONE

FOUR A.M., MAY 23, 1992

Long legged and nearly naked, the reclining woman stared into the night, her huge eyes blank and soulless, her long hair barely covering her voluptuous breasts.

She saw everything, and nothing.

The deserted street was dark.

Her expression never changed as the sleek car on the street below turned left into a Dumpster-lined alley and crept to a halt. The driver killed the lights. He and another man in dark clothes emerged and quietly approached a steel-plated door. The passenger carried a small suitcase.

In this silent hour before dawn, they could hear the sea pounding the sandy shore four hundred yards away and smell the salt in the air. The driver punched the buzzer beside the door as his passenger nervously scanned the street outside. He looked up at the reclining woman, who smiled seductively.

"Yeah?" The static-distorted voice was almost a bark.

"It's me," the driver said.

"About time."

"Sorry about that. You know how it is."

"Who the hell's that with you?"

"My cousin, from out of town. I want you to meet him."

The buzzer sounded, locks disengaged. The driver swung the door open and gestured for his companion to follow.

On the stairs, the driver appeared preternaturally calm, his steps light as his companion stumbled hesitantly along behind him.

The nervous man reacted at the sound of a second buzzer that unlocked a heavy door at the top of the stairs.

A handsome, muscular man in his late thirties sprang up to greet them with such enthusiasm that his thick, padded leather chair continued to rock behind his massive mahogany desk.

His face was pink-cheeked, his eyes and hair dark and shiny. His watch was Rolex, his suit expensive, his winking pinky ring a diamond. He clenched a fine, unlit cigar between his teeth.

"Hey, hey, Buddy." He playfully punched his visitor's shoulder, caught him in a hearty bear hug, then stepped back to scrutinize the stranger.

"Who's this, your cousin? He could be your fucking brother. I see the family resemblance."

"Meet my cousin Michael."

"So," Chris said, "didn't know you had a cousin." He turned to the stranger, "Me and your cousin Buddy, we go way back, all the way to high school."

Chris shook Michael's hand. "So which side a the family you from?"

The stranger hesitated.

"My father's," Buddy said quickly. "His father was my father's brother."

"So where you from?"

Michael licked his lips and glanced at Buddy before replying. "Milwaukee," he said.

Chris's hooded eyes became thoughtful and he returned to sit behind his desk. A top drawer was slightly open, just a few inches. "Did you bring what I asked for?"

"Don't I always?" Buddy jerked his head toward the suitcase on the floor beside Michael. "How's about I fix you two a drink first?"

Chris nodded. "Sure."

"I'll get it, don't get up." With the familiarity of a man who had been there many times, Buddy moved smoothly behind the desk to the custom, built-in bar. "The usual, Chris?"

"Right."

"What about you, Michael?"

"Scotch, if you have it."

"Siddown," Chris told him.

Michael sat tentatively on the edge of a red plush sofa.

Ice rattled into a heavy crystal glass.

Buddy left the glass on the marble-topped bar, stepped two feet to Chris's desk, and slid a 9mm silencer-equipped Luger out of a shoulder holster. As Chris turned to take the glass, Buddy shot him in the face at close range.

Chris jerked back in his chair, his head at an awkward angle, mouth open in surprise at the geyser of blood spurting onto the front of his white shirt.

It showered onto the desk blotter as he slumped sideways in his chair. Stepping back so he would not be spattered, Buddy stretched his arm full length and pumped another slug into the back of the convulsing man's head.

The spasms stopped.

"Hated to do that, but it's the way it's gotta be," Buddy said regretfully. He turned to Michael, who sat frozen on the red plush couch, eyes wide.

"Come on, come on! It's right over here." Buddy opened the concealed bookcase safe, which was not locked.

His shaken companion, still staring at the corpse, looked up and swallowed. Hands shaking, he opened the suitcase and removed a folded supersize duffel bag.

"Fill 'em up! Fill 'em up!" Buddy demanded.

Galvanized into action by the still-smoking gun in Buddy's hand, Michael began to stuff cash into the suitcase.

"How much you think is in here?" He looked in awe at the big bills stacked tightly on floor-to-ceiling shelves.

"Maybe two million," Buddy said calmly. "Make sure you pack it—"

Both men's eyes widened at a small explosion of sound, a toilet flushing in the next room.

"You said nobody else would be here!" Michael's whisper was ragged.

The door to the private bathroom opened.

"Honey? Chris, honey?"

Smile tentative, she stepped into the room. A stripper from the club downstairs, the new girl.

She looked young, still wearing her scanty work clothes, glittery pasties and a G-string. Sparkly angel dust accented her eyelids and décolletage.

She approached them, shaky on strappy stiletto heels. One more step and she would see Chris, his blood spilling down the side of the chair, soaking into the thick carpet.

Buddy cursed. Who knew Chris would be indulging in his own private after-hours lap dance?

"Bring her over here," he told Michael.

"Ma'am," Michael said apologetically, and reached for her elbow. She took the fatal step, her painted face puzzled. She screamed, a high, shrill shriek.

"Over here!" Buddy demanded, face flushed.

Once she was dead, they filled the bags. When they were unable to cram another greenback into the duffel bag or the suitcase, Buddy yanked out a deep desk drawer, dumped the contents, and filled it with bills. He also removed the dead man's gun from the slightly open top drawer.

"What about the camera hooked up to that intercom?" Michael said.

"Doesn't record," Buddy said confidently. "Nothing to worry about."

They took the night's receipts, still stacked on the desk, put them in the safe, locked it, wiped down all they had touched, and left the way they came.

Michael was hyperventilating, breathing hard and trembling. "You didn't tell me—"

"Be cool," Buddy warned him, as they carried the bags down the stairs.

The street was still deserted.

Buddy dumped the cash out of the desk drawer into the trunk of their car. A block away he had Michael toss the wiped-down drawer and Chris's gun into the backseat of an unlocked, beat-up Chevy convertible. As Michael darted back to the car, heart pounding, he looked up for a moment at the distant figure of the reclining woman, long yellow hair aglow in the warmth of neon. She stared back, her wet, red smile seductive.

PROLOGUE, PART TWO

LATER THAT DAY

High-pitched screams and ear-splitting shrieks shattered the air. What must the neighbors think? Joan wondered.

Grinning, she closed one eye and peered through the video camera's viewfinder, slowly panning the front yard.

A bouquet of bright balloons bobbed above the mailbox, marking the party's location. Two picnic tables adorned with festive paper tablecloths stood in the shade of a huge black olive tree. The paper plates, napkins, and party favors were all in red, white, and blue rocket ship patterns. A sweating galvanized copper tub held soda cans and juice cartons nestled in an icy slush. Puffy white clouds sailed across a serene blue sky above while happy chaos reigned below.

HoHo the Clown twisted squeaky balloons into animal shapes as a rent-a-pony, led by a handler wearing a Stetson and cowboy boots, plodded docilely around the circular old Chicago brick driveway. "Giddeup! Giddeup!" bawled the rider, an impatient third grader.

The loudest shrieks came from children rebounding wildly off the bright, inflatable walls of the rented Bounce House. They sprang and ricocheted off the floors and even the ceiling in daredevil imitations of superheroes, Olympic gymnasts, and human flies.

Joan focused on her husband. Red-faced and perspiring, he manned the grill, an unruly shock of curly dark hair plastered across his forehead.

Stan wore sunglasses, oven mitts, a bib apron over his GRILL SERGEANT T-shirt and khaki Bermuda shorts as he flipped burgers and plump hot dogs that sputtered juice into the fire.

Stan winked at her and the camera, then addressed the crush of party-ers around him. "How many want burgers? Two, three, that's four. How many want cheese on their burgers? Okay. How many hot dogs?"

"Both. I want both," Lionel demanded. The husky eight-year-old was built like a gap-toothed pit bull with freckles.

"Coming right up!" Stan adjusted his chef's hat to a jaunty angle.

Lionel screwed up his face in disdain. "My dad doesn't do it that way."

"Who invited Lionel?" Stan muttered to his wife. "You know he's a troublemaker. His own mother calls him Lying Hell."

"Sssshhh. Honey." Joan rolled her eyes and lowered her voice. "He might hear you. Sally's my best friend."

"But she doesn't call her son Lying Hell for nothing. Look." He cut his eyes at Lionel, who was up to his dimpled elbows in a huge bowl of Cheez Doodles.

"Just keep an eye on him," Joan urged. "I already briefed Consuela, if she ever gets here." She checked her watch. "Where'd you put the cake?"

"On the pantry counter, still in the box from the Cuban bakery. You sure it's safe to feed them more sugar?"

As though on cue, Ryan, the birthday boy, scrambled around the side of the house. In hot pursuit were Sookie, the golden retriever, and half a dozen guests. Half of Ryan's face was painted blue, his legs churned, his cardboard crown was askew.

Joan focused on her firstborn on the occasion of his eighth birthday. It seemed only yesterday that she was being rushed into surgery for an emergency C-section. Could it really be eight years? Given his exuberance, no one would ever guess that last night Ryan had fretted, pouted, even threatened to boycott his own party. He wanted fireworks. For days he had nagged, pleaded, and cajoled. His third-grade buddies expected fireworks, he'd argued. He intended to be an astronaut, speeding in swaths of fire across the galaxy. His party theme was rockets. He *wanted* fireworks.

His five-year-old sister's birthday theme had been *The Little Mermaid*.

Her party favors, he pointed out, included real live goldfish in clear water-filled plastic bags. "She *always* gets everything she wants," he'd howled.

Joan and Stan had nearly caved. A boy is only eight once. But with memories of the barbecue debacle involving Lionel last Fourth of July, it was not going to happen.

Ryan would be king for a day, with a crown, a clown, a rocket-shaped cake—but fireworks? No. Not even a sparkler.

Consuela materialized and helped Joan refill bowls of chips and Cheez Doodles. Half-empty sodas and half-eaten food were everywhere.

Stan served up Lionel's hot dog and burger with a flourish.

"Eewwuuh. What's that?" The child poked a grubby finger at the cheese.

"Cheese. You wanted cheese," Stan said pleasantly.

"You don't have bleu cheese?"

"Nope, only American."

His freckled nose wrinkled.

"Right." Stan tossed another burger on the grill. "I'll fix you one without cheese."

Before he could reach for the boy's plate, Lionel was feeding his cheeseburger and hot dog to the golden retriever.

"Sookie likes it." Lionel beamed a cherubic smile, then frowned at the fresh burger Stan offered.

"My father doesn't do it *that* way." Sookie's plumed tail began to wag expectantly.

"Oh?" Stan's eyebrows arched.

"No. He puts the catsup on *both* sides of the bun first, *then* the hamburger." Lionel folded his arms and scowled.

"Here, Lionel, you can do the honors."

Lionel reached for the catsup bottle and scrutinized the label, his expression sour. "You don't have Heinz?"

Stan bared his teeth and made an evil monster face.

Lionel fled.

· · ·

Blue-green horseflies dive-bombed the baked beans. Joan waved them away, eager to finish feeding the kids before the semitropical sun fried their little brains. Some of the smaller ones already glowed pink despite slathers of sunscreen. She hurried inside for the pièce de résistance.

In the cool quiet of the pantry, she savored the moment away from the clamor. Comforting rows of canned goods and food cartons stood like soldiers at attention, arranged precisely by date on plastic-lined shelves. Humming "Happy Birthday," she opened the pristine white box from the Cuban bakery—and gasped.

Screams had elevated to an even higher pitch at party central. Lionel had discovered the box of matches intended to light the candles. Striking them one by one, he was throwing the flaring matches at little girls who fled shrieking.

"Stop that, Lionel!" Joan snatched away the box and confronted her husband. "I thought you were watching him!"

"I'm just trying to get them to sit down for HoHo's magic tricks—and watch the grill at the same time." Stan's long-suffering expression was that of an overburdened and misunderstood man.

"What's wrong, honey?" He removed his chef's hat and mopped his forehead.

"The cake." She studied him. The moment was tense. "Did you happen to check it when you picked it up?" The words were ominous.

"No," he said cautiously. "I still had to pick up the balloons and the hot dogs. The box was tied up and ready. Our name was on it. I have the receipt."

"Follow me." She sounded close to tears. "Why can't anything ever be just right?" She steered him into the pantry. "I described it twice. They said they understood. A rocket, I told them, with 'Happy Birthday to Ryan, Future Astronaut.' "

"Right." Stan nodded.

She lifted the lid, wrists curled as though unveiling a snake.

The words spun out in sugary blue frosting were correct: "Happy Birthday to Ryan, Future Astronaut."

But the cake was not rocket-shaped.

"A racquet," Stan finally said. "It's a tennis racquet."

"Thank you," Joan said. "I guess I'm not losing my mind."

They laughed and clung to each other until their eyes watered.

"We should get out there," she said, wiping her face on his sleeve. "Before Lionel kills the dog or burns the house to the ground."

"You don't think he'd really hurt Sookie, do you?"

"One never knows, though nothing can top this."

Most of the children were seated on the lawn watching HoHo's repertoire of tricks. Lionel was tying a dachshund-shaped balloon to Sookie's collar as though expecting it to lift the big, affable dog into the air à la Mary Poppins.

Consuela, short and compact in her white uniform, gently placed the birthday cake center front on the picnic table, then stepped back to scrutinize it. She cocked her head, puzzled, then shrugged. Long ago she'd stopped trying to understand the people who employed her. She tucked the matchbox in her pocket and turned to see what Lionel was up to now.

The boy had actually paused to watch HoHo. The clown displayed an empty glass. With a flourish, he filled it with water from a plastic pitcher. Suddenly he upended the glass. Not a drop spilled.

"That's not magic!" Lionel screeched, above squeals and applause. "I know how he did it! He had powdery stuff in the bottom of the glass. It makes the water hard, like Jell-O!"

HoHo ignored his heckler. He waved a red silk scarf above his head like a banner, faster and faster. The scarf was redder than his spiky hair and painted cheeks, as red as his shiny, oversized shoes.

Suddenly he balled the scarf in his fist. Then threw his hands open, palms outstretched. It had vanished.

HoHo's triumphant bows were interrupted by a hacking cough. He coughed again and again, then opened his mouth wide and reached down his throat. With a grand, theatrical gesture he slowly withdrew the long red scarf from way down below his tonsils.

A loud *whoosh!* punctuated the cheers and applause.

Joan glanced up from the camera's viewfinder, startled, her anxious eyes instinctively seeking out her son.

Ryan stood at HoHo's elbow, face shining.

"Fireworks!" He threw his arms in the air, victorious. "Yes! I got the fireworks!"

Across the street, the garage erupted. Smoke spiraled. Flames leaped. The children cheered. The garage door exploded outward. The pony bolted. It gave a terrified whinny, then galloped down Mariposa Lane toward the golf course, empty stirrups swinging. His handler chased him, losing his Stetson in the middle of the block. Chunks of burning wreckage catapulted high into the air and began to fall in slow motion onto the Walkers' lawn between the balloon bouquet and the circular drive. Sookie fled, tail tucked between her legs.

Car and house alarms wailed. Towering tongues of red and orange flame danced high into a brilliant blue sky. Sparks showered and sizzled amid black smoke.

"I didn't do it! I didn't do it!" Lionel's pudgy legs churned, pounding the pavement toward home.

The cheers had stopped. The children stood silent and wide-eyed, jaws dropped.

"Mom?" Ryan's voice sounded high-pitched and querulous.

"¡Dios mío!" Consuela fell to her knees and crossed herself, eyes to heaven.

"Mommeee!" "Mommeee!" children began screaming.

"Vanessa wet her pants!" a tattler bawled.

"Joanie, get all the kids inside! Call nine-one-one." Stan sprinted toward the burning garage. The heat forced him back. He peeled off his apron as he dashed to the side of the house for his garden hose.

"No, Stan! No!" Joan and Consuela were herding frightened children inside. "Don't go there! I'm calling the fire department!"

The first fire company arrived in six minutes. To Joan and Stanley Walker it seemed forever. Adrenaline-charged children shrieked at the sirens and cheered the rescue truck, the engine, the pumper, and the first squad card.

Firefighters dragged a blitz line off the pumper. They ran a second line from a hydrant. The garage was fully involved. Flames roared through a wall, engulfing the kitchen. Tendrils of orange danced along the roof line.

Firemen in self-contained breathing apparatus knocked down flames, battling to save the house. At the end of the street, police officers shouted but were unable to stop a midnight blue Jaguar that hurtled crazily around their barricades. Brakes squealing, it swerved to a stop on the next-door lawn. Leaving her baby strapped in a car seat, the young woman driver, her black hair flowing long and loose, stumbled out into the dense smoke that roiled down the street.

"My husband! My husband!" she screamed. "Where is he? He was working on his car! Where is he?"

Firefighters held her back. Suddenly she stopped struggling and sagged in their arms as the smell of something terrible wafted across the street. Something burned.

HoHo the Clown threw up on the lawn.

CHAPTER ONE

TWELVE YEARS LATER

Like all things good and bad in the world, it began with a woman.

She was a blonde, with a complaint about her ex-husband. She saw him everywhere she went. Turn around and there he was. She knew he was trying to send her a message, she said.

Problem was, the man was dead, gone from this earth for twelve long years.

Some guys just don't know when to let go.

My name is Craig Burch, a sergeant on the Miami Police Department's Cold Case Squad. My assignment is relatively new. I worked homicide for eighteen years, mostly on the midnight shift. I fought like hell to land this job. Why not? It's every big-city homicide cop's wet dream. This squad is armed with a detective's most powerful weapon: time. The luxury of enough time to investigate old, unsolved cases without interruption. I wanted that. I wanted the change. I wanted to see the faces of murderers who suddenly realize their pasts and I have caught up with them. The job has other perks as well. No daily dealing with fresh corpses or, worse yet, corpses less than fresh. No more stepping cautiously through messy crime scenes in dark woods, warehouses, or alleyways, trying to avoid stepping in blood, brains, or worse. No more trying to forget the pain-filled screams of inconsolable survivors whose unearthly cries will scar your soul and echo in your dreams asleep or awake. No more watching autopsies that suddenly and unexpectedly replay in your mind's eye at inopportune moments. And no more throwing my back out when lifting dead weight. *Real* dead weight.

This job also reduces my chances of being rocked, bottled, and/or shot at by the unruly Miamians who cluster bright-eyed and belligerent at every nasty crime scene in neighborhoods where trouble is a way of life and violence is contagious.

I quit confronting new deaths. Instead, I breathe new life into old, cold cases and track killers whose trails vanished long ago like footprints on a sea-washed beach.

Loved the concept. Still do. And I yearned for what came with it—mostly regular, daylight hours, giving me the chance to spend more time with my family before the kids are grown and gone. Made sense to me. It was long overdue. I looked forward to it. Connie couldn't have been happier—in the beginning. What's not to like? Weekends off together for the first time? The man in the mirror suntanned instead of wearing a prison pallor from sleeping days and working nights?

Now I know why people say: Be careful what you wish for—you might get it. At the moment, I live alone. Last time I called home, one of the kids hung up on me. Every job in my line of business has a downside.

This one has ghosts.

My detectives are hand-picked self-starters. They don't hear the screams, see the blood, or feel the moral outrage cops experience at fresh murder scenes. Instead, they dissect dusty files and stacks of typewritten reports as cold and unemotional as a killer's heart.

Our standard operating procedure is to reread the case files of old, unsolved murders, pass them around, and brainstorm on which have the most potential. We also field tips on old homicides from our own cops, other agencies, confidential informants, prison inmates, and the friends and families of victims.

She was one of the latter: a walk-in. Our team had just voted on whether to pursue the high-profile triple homicide of a man, his pregnant wife, and their toddler. Murdered nearly twenty-five years ago, they were presumed casualties of the time—collateral damage in the drug wars of the eighties. But one of my guys suspects another motive, something more personal. Two of my detectives, Sam Stone and Pete Nazario, were still arguing about it when the secretary steered a stranger their way.

Her hair was feathery, tousled in an expensive, wavy style intended to look natural, the kind that costs more to look as though it was never touched by professionals.

Stone sprang to his feet when the secretary brought her past my desk, directly across from theirs. He grew up in Miami's bleakest, blackest, toughest neighborhood. Sharp, edgy, young, and focused, he has a passion for high technology and is as aggressive as hell. Sometimes he's a runaway freight train and you have to hold him back.

Well dressed in blue that matched her eyes, she was your typical soccer mom with a little mileage on her.

Nazario offered her a chair. He came to Miami alone as a small child, one of the thousands of Pedro Pan kids airlifted out of Cuba and taken in by the Catholic church when Castro refused to allow the parents to leave the island. Nazario never saw his parents again and grew up a stranger in a strange land, shuttled to shelters and foster homes all over the country by the archdiocese. Maybe because he lived with strangers who didn't speak his native language or maybe he was born with it, but Nazario is blessed with an uncanny talent—it's invaluable to a detective, even though it's not admissible in court or probable cause for a warrant: He knows, without fail, when somebody is lying to him. Stone and Nazario are among the best, and I don't say that just because they work for me.

The woman in blue chewed her lower lip, her face pinched with apprehension. She looked to be in her late thirties, but it's tough to tell the age of most women. Her name was April Terrell, she said. A plastic tag identifying her as a visitor to the building was clipped to her short, crisp jacket. Her summery dress flared at the hip and quit just above a nice pair of knees. She held a little purse demurely in her lap while apologizing for showing up unannounced. I listened, trying not to look up and be obvious.

"It's about my husband," she said, then corrected herself, "my ex-husband."

They married in college, she said. She quit and worked as a legal secretary to put him through pharmaceutical school. "I thought I knew him.
The divorce caught me off guard. Our children were two and three. That
was almost fourteen years ago."

She gave the guys a sad-eyed, self-deprecating smile. "He found someone else, younger, his second year in business. He remarried right away
and started a new family."

The guys itched to hear the point. I know I did.

"It's funny." Her lower lip quivered, indicating the opposite. "All of a
sudden, after all this time, he's there. I see him everywhere I go."

Nazario frowned. "He's stalking you?"

"Our domestic violence unit has a felony stalking squad." Stone
reached for the phone on his desk. "You need to talk to one of them.
We're homicide. Cold cases. I'll call downstairs and find you someone."

"Wait." She spoke briskly. "Obviously I haven't made myself clear. I
know who you are. You investigate old deaths. That's why I'm here.
Charles was killed twelve years ago."

I looked up. Nazario and Stone exchanged glances.

"Oh," Stone said accommodatingly. "And you say you've seen him
lately?"

"Yes." Her voice held steady.

"On what sort of occasions?" Stone steepled his long fingers in front
of him, his liquid eyes wandering to a window, past the grimy streaks to a
patch of innocent blue sky above the neighborhood where he was born.

She raised her voice and her right hand slightly, as though to recap-
ture his attention. "You know what I mean. Like at the bank yesterday . . .
I saw another customer, his back was to me. He looked so much like
Charles that for a moment I forgot he was dead and almost called out his
name. The man turned around later and, of course, he didn't look like
Charles at all." She shrugged. "You know how it is. You catch a glimpse of
someone familiar but it turns out not to be them. It's happening to me
more and more. He's in my dreams almost every night now."

"When did this start?" Nazario asked, his face solemn.

"Last year. I keep asking myself why, after all this time? Why?" She leaned forward, speaking clearly, voice persuasive. "The only explanation is that Charles is trying to tell me something."

Her shoulders squared, head high in a regal pose, reacting to something in their eyes. She shot me a quick glance, suddenly aware that I was listening, too.

"I'm not crazy," she said quickly. "Please don't think that. It's just that it's made me realize that I never felt right about what happened to him. I think I always suspected, but I had two little children to raise alone, a boy and a girl."

"Did you seek grief counseling at the time?" Nazario asked softly.

The blond waves bounced as she tossed her head. "Who had time for that?" She opened her hands in a helpless gesture, pale palms exposed. "I had to take care of business and get on with life because of the children. How could I allow myself the time to obsess, to cave in to anger, bitterness—or grief? You've heard people say, 'If I only had the time, I'd have a nervous breakdown'? Our children worshiped their dad. The divorce was tough enough on them, on all of us. He and his new wife had a baby. Their dad's death was the final crushing blow. They'd never see him again, call him on the telephone, or spend another weekend or vacation together. Now that they're older and asking questions, I realize there are no answers. The whole thing didn't make sense . . ."

"Sometimes," Nazario gently interjected, "when you suppress a traumatic incident and don't deal with it, it comes back to trouble you later, when you least expect it."

She shook her head forlornly, staring down at her naked fingers for a moment. She wore no rings.

"Can you at least look into it?" she said, raising those blue eyes.

"Into what?" Stone's brow furrowed.

Lieutenant K. C. Riley, our boss, suddenly appeared, slamming an office door, lean and mean, a folder in hand, expression impatient.

"He burned to death." April Terrell's voice rose, quavering slightly. "In a flash fire. It was horrible. They had to have a closed casket. There wasn't enough . . ."

Talk about timing.

K. C. Riley reacted as though slapped.

This can't be good, I thought.

"My ex-husband, the father of my children," April told the lieutenant without introductions. "His death was no accident. I'm sure he was murdered."

"When did this happen?" Riley's pale lips were tight, arms crossed.

"Twelve years ago, May 23, 1992. It happened on a Saturday." Charles had confided the last time he'd dropped off their children that he and their new stepmother of just a year were not getting along. The brief marriage, a bumpy ride, was already off track. Natasha, wife number two, spent extravagantly. And there was, of course, a big life insurance policy.

She had since lost track of the widow, she said.

"That sort of accident was totally out of character for Charles. He was skilled and competent, precise and careful about everything he did."

Riley lapped it up, never missed a beat. "Thanks for coming in, Ms. . . . ?"

"Terrell, April Terrell."

"I'm K. C. Riley."

The two women shook hands.

"It's certainly worth looking into," Riley said. "My detectives will get right on it. Right, Sergeant?"

Three jaws dropped as one: mine, Stone's, and Nazario's.

CHAPTER TWO

"Charles Terrell is no candidate for us!" Stone fumed. "Riley knows that. We don't investigate accidents. We solve murders."

"We've got enough ghosts to deal with," Burch said.

"Bad timing," Nazario said.

"The lieutenant should have stayed in her office, red-eyed and brooding with the door closed, as usual. You know the reason she dumped this on us," Stone said. "No doubt about it."

"She's got her own ghost, and she's taking it out on us," Nazario said.

"I'll try to talk to her," Burch said.

Stone and Nazario beat it out of the office. Stone viciously jabbed the elevator button as Nazario gave Burch a soulful glance back over his shoulder.

• • •

"That woman and our lieutenant are both nuts." Stone continued to vent, striding toward their unmarked Plymouth deep in the dimly lit police parking garage.

Brilliant shafts of sunlight pierced the gloom, descending wandlike through ornamental cut-outs high in the concrete walls.

Nazario rolled his eyes. "The lady wasn't lying."

"You're right," Stone agreed. "She obviously believed every damn thing she said, just like all the others who hobnob with apparitions and hear voices we can't. They are absofuckinglutely true believers."

"She's no lunatic," Nazario said mildly. "Her story should be easy to check out. Gimme the keys."

"No way, my turn to drive, *amigo.*"

"Like hell," Nazario said. "You're the one who's nuts."

"Maybe, but insane or not, drunk or sober, I drive better."

"What the shit you talking about?"

"Admit it, Naz. If you weren't wearing a badge, they'da yanked your license like a bad back tooth years ago. You always drive like something is chasing you."

"Maybe something is."

"Cubans are lousy drivers." Stone shook his head and slid smoothly behind the wheel.

He put on his Foster Grants as Nazario settled reluctantly into the passenger seat. Squinting in the glare, they rolled out onto sun-blasted North Miami Avenue. Nazario called their sergeant, hoping they'd caught a break.

Fat chance. Burch said he'd tried to reason with Riley. No luck. Charles Terrell's fire death was top priority. Burch had checked for the police file but found only a case number. The paperwork on accidental deaths is purged after seven years.

With a grunt of disgust, Stone wrenched the wheel into a sharp U-turn.

"Meadows is your problem." Nazario was glum. "That case has you so wound up that it pisses you off to take five minutes to go to the bathroom. Meadows can move to a back burner for a day. Her case is already twenty-four years old."

"My point precisely." Stone jabbed an index finger in emphasis. "That's exactly why it shouldn't get any older. The son of a bitch is still out there, stalking somebody else's grandmother.

"You *know* why Riley's doing this," he said again, as they left the unmarked outside the Miami River front building that houses fire head-quarters.

"*Sí.*" Nazario was stoic.

Riverside Center sprawls in the stark shadow of an expressway overpass. Dark-tinted windows stare down at the river like blind eyes.

"She was always hard to work for," Stone said. "And that temper doesn't help."

"She's hurting."

"Not our fault. Why does that shit always run downhill in our direction? I like her better locked in her office nursing her hangover."

"I don't remember her drinking before it happened."

"Right. What we need is a shrink and a support group for her and that Terrell woman." Stone flashed his badge at lobby security.

.   .   .

Arson investigator Jack Olson's tenth-floor office overlooked the slick, silver ribbon that snaked below. The Miami River is a working waterway, alive with pleasure boaters, foreign freighters, illicit cargos and smuggled immigrants. Beneath its surface lie sunken secrets and the constant cross currents of international intrigue.

Olson drew a blank on the name, but seeing the file sparked a memory rush.

"Oh, yeah." His bushy eyebrows lifted and he licked his lips. "I remember that one. Was out there that day. Nice neighborhood. Relatively young guy, tinkering with his Thunderbird. The primo, 'fifty-seven hardtop, you know, with the portholes. Super V-8, double acting shocks, Fordomatic drive. Classic. Love a set of those wheels myself. Though nobody 'ud recognize it by the time we saw it. What a waste. But I digress."

He scanned the original report. "Here we go. Yeah. Couple hours before it happens, the victim borrows a line wrench from his neighbor across the street. Repairing a faulty fuel line, he says. Those T-babies are prone to that. Flakes of rust off the gas tank clogging the fuel lines. My brother-in-law restored one of 'em. Paid ten g's for it, spends a couple years on the project, and sells it for fifty."

He thumbed through supplements to the final report. "Here's how we figure it goes down. He's under the car using a portable trouble light when Bingo! The car slips off the jack and pins 'im to the garage floor.

Bad news. Worse, when the car drops on 'im, the jack stand punctures the gas tank. Poor bastard's hurting, busted ribs. Probably conscious, but even if he sucks up enough breath to yell, nobody's home to hear 'im.

"He's trapped, and leaking gasoline is splashing onto the hot bulb of his work light. Poof! Damn thing ignites. Instant inferno. He's ground zero. The fuel feeds the flames until the tank explodes. Fatal freaking accident."

Olson nodded in recollection.

"We were lucky to save the house. Hadda jack up the car to free 'im—what was left of 'im. Here, see for yourself."

He spilled the eight-by-ten scene photos out of a manila envelope onto his desk.

Nazario winced.

"Damn." Stone picked one up.

In the gutted garage, beneath the car's blackened shell, were the charred remains of a man, his fists clenched in a pugilistic position. Devoid of flesh, muscle, and tendons, the exposed leg bones resembled broomsticks. His jaws were wide open as though frozen in a silent, agonal scream.

"His own mother wouldn't have recognized 'im," Olsen said. "What's up? What's your interest in this one now?"

"Somebody thinks it was no accident," Nazario said.

"After all these years?" The arson investigator looked skeptical. His voice rose in indignation. "How come they didn't speak up sooner?"

Stone ignored the question. "Anything strike you as suspicious at the time?"

Olson raked his fingers through bristly salt-and-pepper hair, then shook his head. "Looked cut and dried to me. One a your guys was out there. Didn't spot no red flags. Homicide detective, medical examiner, a fire inspector, and me—we all came to the same conclusion.

"You're welcome to a copy a the report." He shuffled papers. "Next of kin, the wife, said he's in the garage working on his car when she leaves to go shopping and run errands. She's gone a couple a hours. We're already on the scene when she gets back. A real babe, beautiful girl, shook up big time. Had an infant in the car."

"Who called it in?" Stone asked.

Olson's thick index finger roamed down the fact sheet. "Dispatch history shows a flurry a nine-one-one calls right after the garage door blows off. Whole neighborhood musta called in. But looks like we listed the reporting persons as the neighbors across the street. The Walkers, 424 Mariposa Lane. Hadda kid's birthday party in progress. Yard fulla rugrats saw the whole thing.

"Nobody seen leaving the garage. No strangers, no getaway cars. Accidental. This kinda thing'ud be pretty damn hard to rig." The arson investigator shrugged. "You can't believe all the crazy ways people manage to accidentally off themselves.

"Then again, you probably can. You guys see it all the time. Rescue Seven caught a doozy yesterday. Guy wants his Hungry Man TV dinner. His microwave oven won't work. He tries to fix it and gets zapped. Missed his last meal—it was the one with the roast beef, potatoes, and gravy. Poor guy died hungry."

· · ·

"Lookit that." Nazario pointed to the river below and a rusting freighter limping toward open sea while they waited for Olson to copy the file. The top deck was stacked with hundreds and hundreds of bicycles.

"So that's where they all go. Been a rash of bicycle thefts in my neighborhood, off front porches, outta garages, driveways, backyards. Thieves snipping the locks of bikes chained outside the gym and the shopping center."

"They're headed for Haiti now," Stone said.

· · ·

"Told you," Nazario said in the car. "This Terrell caper ain't gonna take us a whole lot of time."

"From your lips to God's ears." Stone swung into the parking lot at their next stop.

The imposing three-building complex straddled three acres. With its raspberry-colored furniture, potted palms, and smiling receptionist, strangers might mistake the softly lit lobby for that of a resort hotel— unless they read the mission statement above the front desk at One Bob Hope Road.

"To provide accurate, timely, dignified, compassionate and professional death investigative services for the citizens of Miami–Dade County . . ."

Every year more than three thousand people arrive there too late to read the words. They're unable to appreciate the photos and paintings of scenic Florida. Dead eyes can't see the images of golden dawns, blood-red sunsets, and turquoise blue water displayed throughout a building that neither looks nor smells like a morgue. Electronic air scrubbers erase the odors of formaldehyde and decomposing bodies, a concept borrowed from airports that never smell like jet fuel.

A bronze cannon guards the entrance. The ancient weapon salvaged from the *Santa Margarita,* a Spanish galleon sunk with all aboard by a killer hurricane off the Florida coast nearly four hundred years ago.

"He had broken ribs where the car was resting on him." The chief medical examiner had pulled Terrell's file for the detectives. "No evidence of other trauma, no drugs or alcohol in his system."

The chief didn't sign off on the case himself. He'd been out of the country at the time, keynote speaker at a conference in Zurich. A deputy medical examiner, Dr. Vernon Duffy, handled the autopsy.

"The victim had a lethal level of carbon monoxide in his blood, evidence of smoke inhalation, consistent with death by fire."

The chief squinted at handwritten notations. "Hmmm, interesting. Normally, identification would have been made through dental records. It wasn't in this case."

"How's that?" Stone asked.

"This fellow had no dental X-rays. Apparently he had perfect teeth, no caries. No reason for X-rays if you never have any restorations." He continued through the report. "The jaw was badly burned. The upper front teeth were flaked apart due to the heat."

Stone read over his shoulder. "The doctor noted that the victim had an unusually fatty liver. Isn't that a sign of chronic alcoholism?"

The chief nodded. "A prime candidate for cirrhosis, had he lived long enough."

"So how *did* they positively identify him?" Nazario asked.

The chief medical examiner readjusted his reading glasses. "It appears that the victim had lost his right ring finger in his youth. In a water-skiing accident, it says here. The fellow who died in the fire was missing the same finger. In addition, the victim was last seen by his wife, working on his car, alone in the garage. He was also seen there by a neighbor and the regular letter carrier, who knew him by sight. The deceased was wearing the victim's wedding ring."

Stone snorted. "So much for Charles Terrell, precise and careful, skilled and competent. Isn't that what the first wife said? Proof again that love is blind. The guy was really a hard drinker who lost a finger and blew up his car. Man was an accident waiting to happen. Must have been a thrill a minute having him around."

"DNA wasn't in extensive use then." The medical examiner pondered the pages and frowned. "Today I would have run it. As a precautionary measure, just to be sure."

"Come on, Doc, don't give us heart attacks here." Nazario shifted uneasily in his seat.

"You're not saying you doubt his identity, are you?" Stone asked.

The medical examiner shook his head and closed the file. "But one can't be too careful. In a case out west a few years ago, the crew of a passing freight train reported seeing a burning car on top of a hill. The police found a charred body, presumably the owner, in the still-blazing vehicle. But an hour later a seriously burned man showed up at the local emergency room. He gave the doctors a cock-and-bull story about how he was injured. Investigators soon learned that he owned the car, was deeply in debt, and had taken out a big life insurance policy. Pathologists decided to take another look at the burned body found in the car and noticed gas bubbles indicating that at the time of the fire, the body had already begun to decompose.

"The car's owner had picked up a bum somewhere and locked him in the trunk, where the man suffocated. The next day he drove the car to the hilltop and propped the dead man behind the wheel. He doused the corpse and the driver's seat with gasoline. His plan was to ignite it, then roll it down the hill to crash into the passing train. It would look like a spectacular, fiery accident.

"But as he sat in the passenger seat waiting for the train, he absent-mindedly lit a cigarette. The gasoline fumes ignited and the car burst into flames. By the time the train arrived, he'd fled, badly burned."

"Mighta worked if he hadn't been a smoker," Stone said.

The chief nodded. "Had he not shown up at the hospital seeking treatment for his burns, no one might have looked more closely at the microscopic slides from the charred corpse."

"Why didn't they see it the first time?" Stone said.

"Because," the chief said, "too often, our observations are based on what we expect to see due to our training and experience. Expectations modify our observations. In other words, we see what we preconceive. The indications that the body was beginning to change due to decomposition were there. Initially they saw them, but failed to observe them. They observed the fire instead."

"We see what we preconceive," Stone echoed.

.   .   .

Uncharacteristically quiet en route back to headquarters, Stone didn't even protest when Burch told them it would take more to satisfy K. C. Riley and April Terrell.

"You don't have to be a shrink to figure this one out," Burch said.

"Right." Nazario shuffled through messages on the receptionist's desk. "Hey, Sarge, you got a stack over here. Call your wife."

"Toss 'em in the round file," Burch said casually.

"You sure? You got one at one-thirty, another one at one thirty-seven, another one at one forty-two . . . could be important. Here's one at two-thirty. The—"

"I get the picture," Burch said coldly. "My voice mail is full, too."

"—last one at four-twenty."

"Look, I already talked to Connie three times today," Burch said, "but there ain't no talking to her. She's really pissed. I think it's hormones. She just wants to bust my chops. And I'm no glutton for punishment."

"Ain't love grand?" Stone said.

"God bless America," Nazario said.

"Look," Burch said. "It ain't like she wants me back between the sheets or to join her for tea. All she wants to know is where I'm staying, so she can come over and cut up what's left of my raggedy clothes."

He sighed. "I'm calling it a day. You pick up and it's her, don't let it slip where I'm staying. I'm lucky to find the place I got and I don't need her coming over to trash it."

He left, but reemerged from the elevator fifteen minutes later. Nazario was on the phone. Stone glanced up from his computer keyboard. "What, you checking up on us, Sarge? Thought you left."

"So did I. Could one of you guys gimme a lift?"

"Sure, Sarge." Nazario hung up. "Where's your car at?"

"Who knows?" He sank wearily into his desk chair, his expression resigned.

Stone whipped his chair around and lowered his voice. "Repossessed?"

"Nah, the Chevy's paid for."

"Somebody steal your Blazer?" Nazario said, voice rising. "Outta the police garage?"

Emma, the middle-age secretary at her desk outside Riley's office, glanced up curiously.

"Keep it down, would ya?" Burch muttered.

"You report it?" Stone asked.

"Nah. I know who copped it."

"Not Connie," Nazario said. "She wouldn't steal your wheels."

"Hadda be. This is guerrilla warfare and Connie is the guerrilla queen. And don't say it," he warned them. "I've tried talking sense to her. Won't listen. Turned the kids against me, too. Wouldn't be surprised if my oldest wasn't the wheel man. Jennifer, the sixteen-year-old drama queen, just got her license. My big mistake was teaching that kid to drive. Connie didn't have the patience."

"What does she want?" Stone said.

"Me, miserable. So far she's doing a helluva job. I saw Maureen Hartley again when we solved her daughter's case and Connie blew it all outta proportion. Wish to hell I was having the party times she thinks I am."

"Let's go look for it, Sarge," Nazario offered. "We're detectives, ain't we? We can find your wheels. You always tell us to think dirty, like the perp. Who knows this suspect better? Think dirty. Where you think she'd park it?"

"In her state of mind? The bottom of the bay."

"You in, Stone?"

"Sure," the tall black detective said, as he keyed his radio to somebody trying to raise him.

"Hey, Stone." It was unit 236, Homicide Detective Ron Diaz. "You wanted a heads-up on elderly women murdered in their bedrooms? We just caught one, over in Morningside. I'm headed there now."

"She live alone? Any sign of forced entry?"

"Keep your shirt on, I ain't even there yet."

"What's the address?" Stone waved off Burch and Nazario, who left without him.

"That I can tell you. Two seventy-two Northeast Sixty-third Street."

"Meet you there."

. . .

Stone often wished he had investigated the Meadows murder from jump. Would this be his chance, at last, to follow the killer's fresh tracks, instead of hunting a shadow from a twenty-four-year distance?

He had pursued the case of Virginia Meadows with initial optimism, intent on finding the man who killed the seventy-seven-year-old widow. What he found, instead, were nine identical murder cases in cities across America.

Meadows was no isolated killing, as he first believed. In Detroit, Boston, Chicago, Philadelphia, Memphis, Cleveland, and Paterson, New Jersey, there had been other lonely elderly women. Like Virginia Meadows, they lived alone. Like her, they were strangled and tucked into bed.

All looked strangely peaceful in death, as though sleeping. How many others, he wondered, had been wrongly classified as natural causes?

The killer was still active. Stone had found the most recent case in Paterson, seventeen months ago. After linking the cases, he had been temporarily assigned to an FBI task force formed to find the serial killer. But the task force became an early casualty of the war on terrorism. One by one the federal agents were pulled off the pursuit for assignments involving national security.

Only Sam Stone was left.

As he drove, he noted the time, the weather conditions, and the traffic, both vehicular and pedestrian, in the neighborhood. The scene, a typical South Florida home, one-story CBS construction, painted white, with green shutters. The wooden front door in the center of the house was also painted green. It stood open.

Two patrol cars and a detective unit were parked out front. The crime scene van was arriving, just turning the corner.

The front yard, bordered by a hibiscus hedge, was slightly overgrown. A uniform was stringing yellow crime scene tape between two palm trees.

A heavyset woman in a housecoat, her hair in big pink curlers, stood in a side yard with a patrolman. One hand covered her eyes.

Make the scene talk to you, Stone thought, as he always did, then stepped into the house.

The living room was unremarkable, a comfortable couch on the east wall, a television set on the west wall. To the north, through the living room, was the dining room. There he turned left, following the voices to the bedroom.

Diaz was pulling on a pair of latex gloves. "So, whattaya think, Stone, she one of yours?"

The room was a bloodbath.

The frail victim lay supine on a queen-size bed, a halo of blood around her head. She wore only a nightgown, which had been pulled up around her neck. Blood had spattered across the headboard and the wall. Her wrists and hands were covered with congealed blood, probably from defense wounds she had suffered. A bed sheet was wrapped around her left leg. There appeared to be bite marks on her buttocks and right shoulder.

A trail of blood led from the bed to the bathroom. Streaks and spatters were on the walls, sink, and medicine cabinet and bloody shoe prints tracked the white tile floor. The tub was half full of water.

"Musta happened this morning," Diaz said.

It appeared as though she had been about to bathe when surprised by the killer, who attacked her there, then dragged her into the bedroom and onto the bed.

On the wall between the bathroom and the bed, a picture frame hung askew. An old wedding photo was visible behind the cracked, blood-smeared glass. The woman petite, the man tall and handsome in uniform, circa World War II. Someone injured had fallen against it during a struggle.

"No," Stone said quietly. "This is too messy. Way too messy. It's not him."

"Hell, I was hoping you'd want to take it off our hands."

"Got anything?" Stone asked.

"She's a widow. Neighbors say there's a grandson, late teens or early twenties, might be into drugs. A new handyman did some repairs around the house last week. The victim's car, ten-year-old blue Ford Taurus, is missing. We put out a BOLO."

"Did you find the knife?" Stone asked. "Is it from her kitchen? Any burglaries, rapes, or attempts in the neighborhood lately?"

"I just got here," the detective said.

Stone's eyes roved the room one more time. The clothes she had planned to wear, a dress and fresh undergarments, were draped across a chair back, freshly polished shoes placed neatly in front. She had plans, he thought, somewhere to go, people to see.

"Looks like you've got his DNA, footprints, probably even fingerprints. Hope you find him fast."

"I'm on it," the detective said. "Good luck with yours."

Stone left, relieved that the elusive killer he was seeking hadn't struck again. Frustrated, that like the killer in this new case, he was still unknown and free out there somewhere.

• • •

The photo lab was deserted after 6:00 P.M. Stone spread the eleven-by-fourteen enlargements he'd ordered across a long conference table, studied them, reread the reports, then studied them some more.

Most of the images were in color. Each crime scene had been photographed repeatedly from different angles.

Stone peeled off his jacket, loosened his tie. Arranging each set of photos in sequence, he posted the most similar shots from each scene on a large cork bulletin board that ran the length of one wall.

All spinsters or widows, the victims ranged in age from seventy-two to ninety-three. All were scrupulously clean, as though washed. Their hair had been trimmed, their nails clipped. The earliest victims were dressed in fresh nightgowns, the more recent were wrapped in white sheets. The killer had posed them in similar fashion, face up, sheets covering their bodies, hands positioned as though in prayer. The only contradictory clue was a small amount of dirt, less than a handful found under their heads, in their hair, on their pillows. Analyzed, it matched nothing in or around their homes. It did not appear to have come from their own yards. No evidence of forced entry into their homes. None had been raped. The killer had left no DNA or fingerprints.

The first victim, Tessie Bollinger, age seventy-four, died in Paterson. So did the most recent, Margery DeWitt, age eighty-seven.

He killed Gertrude Revere, ninety-one, in Cleveland. Jean Abramson, of Chicago, was ninety-three. He strangled Estelle Rudolph, age seventy-seven, in Detroit, and Patricia Lenoy, age seventy-two, in Boston. Erna Dunn, in Philadelphia, was seventy-nine. Della Golden died in Memphis at seventy-two.

Their homes had not been ransacked. Nothing seemed to be missing. All the killer took was their lives. A sick son of a bitch, Stone thought, but so clever that it took all these years before anyone became aware that the cases were linked and the work of a single serial killer. He was unique. Few serial killers successfully continue their deadly odysseys for so long. Time will mellow a murderous rage. But this man was still killing. If he began in his teens he'd be in his forties by now. He could be older. He could be anybody.

Geographic profiling didn't work. The man was a shadow. He covered the map, his victims separated by many miles, jurisdictions, and years. There wasn't even proof he was a man. But female serial killers are most often black widows or baby killers.

Stone opened his notebook to read again his list of what the victims shared in common. Alone, they were lonely. Trusting and too friendly to strangers. The task force had discovered little else. There seemed to be a breakthrough when they learned that the late husbands of two of the women were retired military. But no others had military ties except for one who had lost her only son in Vietnam.

Bollinger, in Paterson, was first, Meadows in Miami was second. Number nine, the most recent, was again in Paterson. What if the killer was retracing his steps, repeating his pattern? Miami would be his next stop. He could be here now, Stone thought.

Energized by a sense of urgency, the detective paced back and forth in front of the pictures, studying them.

He finally took them down and posted the next set.

He liked working alone, or with Pete Nazario. He had never felt comfortable with the FBI. And they clearly weren't comfortable with him. He'd been given the courtesy because he had linked the cases. But the agents mistrusted Miami Police, disliked sharing information, and showed little respect for him because he was only twenty-six and lacked experience.

The lack of respect was mutual. He'd been skeptical of their famous profiling techniques. Of course the murderer was a loner. Serial killers don't operate in crowds, not successful ones anyway. Of course he had problems with women. He was killing them.

What do you expect, he thought, from bureau profilers who had described the Beltway Sniper as a lone white man, when the shooters proved instead to be two blacks?

Stone found a coffeemaker on a corner table. Bitter dregs in the bottom. He discovered cups and supplies in a cabinet, brewed a fresh pot, and filled a flowered mug with JANICE painted on it. He restudied the pictures and reread the reports as he drank.

He'd even researched the phases of the moon in search of a ritualistic link. Nothing. The timing seemed random. He had killed on every day of the week but Saturday.

Head aching after his third cup of coffee, Stone felt a nagging yet elusive hunch, something he couldn't quite put his finger on.

He switched photographs again, to long shots from across the victims' bedrooms. He walked by them, paused to look back at the Paterson picture on his right, then at the Detroit photo to his left. He set the coffee cup down harder than intended. A wave of the scalding brew slopped over the edge and onto the counter. He didn't notice. He was checking the bedroom shots in Cleveland, Boston, and Miami.

"Damn. Why didn't I see that?" He reached for the telephone. "Hey, Naz, it's me. I need you to come down here and look at something."

"What time is it?" Nazario sounded fuzzy, as though he'd been asleep.

"I don't know." Stone glanced impatiently at his watch. "Three o'clock?" He sounded surprised.

"Oh, Jesus. Where're you at?"

"The photo lab at the station."

"Did you go home? You still there? Up early? Out late? What the hell are you do—"

"How quick can you get here?"

"That's me behind you, walking in the door."

.   .   .

Nazario was wearing khakis and a rumpled white guayabera.

Stone looked startled. "How'd you get here so fast?"

"Not much traffic at this hour, and I floored it."

"No doubt something chasing you again. You find the sarge's car?"

"Yeah. Just in time. He's embarrassed, so don't broadcast it. Looks like Connie took the FOP symbol off the tag and parked it in a loading zone. So they were about to tow it. Hope you didn't wake me up to ask that." He squinted at Stone. "What the hell are we doing here?"

"Look. Look at these." Stone motioned to the photos. "Tell me if you see what I see."

The nine enlargements were shot from across the rooms toward the foot of each victim's bed.

Arms folded, Nazario studied each in turn, thick brows furrowed.

His eyes narrowed on the third pass. "I'll be damned. I see it! *¡Dios mío!*"

CHAPTER THREE

EARLIER THAT EVENING

The shadows of the long driveway are cool and fragrant and I am grateful to be home, even if it is temporary. The quiet only seems lonely because I'm accustomed to domestic chaos, Connie, the kids, their friends, even Max, the big, dumb sheepdog. I welcome this solitude and time to think.

Thank God for Nazario. Connie would not have answered a question from me. So he called to politely inquire if she had "borrowed" my Blazer. She said she didn't know what he was talking about. He thanked her, said goodbye, and turned to me, his spaniel eyes sad.

"She took it," he said.

He then called the private number of Jennifer, the drama queen, and only other family member old enough to drive. My daughter answered the same question the same way. He said goodbye, and turned to me.

"She had nothing to do with it."

So, we deduce that unless one of Connie's girlfriends is an accomplice with enough chutzpah to snatch a car out of the police parking garage, my wife is most likely the lone perpetrator. She would have driven her own car downtown. It's not easy for one person to jockey two automobiles around. That involves some legwork, and Connie is an unlikely pedestrian in Miami's summer heat. We might get lucky. Maybe the Blazer isn't all that far away.

Hotshot ace detectives like us are trained to seek justice, scoop dangerous killers off the streets, and otherwise preserve the peace. Instead, we are on the trail of my wacko wife.

We check dead-end streets within a half-mile radius of the station. On the third or fourth try, there it is, backed into a loading zone, a ticket on the windshield and a tow truck driver about to hook it up.

Nazario is a good man who won't blab this around the station. I owe him.

My new address is this stately Miami Beach mansion, Casa de Luna. Old Spanish-style architecture, elegant and graceful, built in the twenties. Renovated, updated, restored, and refurbished, inside and out, no expense spared.

Wealthy residents inclined to travel and concerned about home security sometimes offer a policeman free lodging in servants' quarters, a guest cottage, or garage apartment. As the old mansions give way to high-rises, hotels, and loft apartments, such deals are hard to find and much coveted by cops who are separated, single, or about to be. The homeowner enjoys peace of mind and the policeman enjoys a free pad, the key word being free because cops in my situation are usually stone broke or about to be.

Bullets, bribes, and brutality allegations are not the only occupational hazards in police work. Booze, broads, and busted marriages are just as common. I teetered at the brink a time or two but never thought I'd fall, or that if I did I'd have the luck to land in one of these cushy deals.

The Blazer is emitting a peculiar odor, so I leave the windows open a crack when I park. Probably the submarine sandwich I picked up on the way home.

I take a deep breath and stand in the driveway drinking in the soft air, enjoying the salty breeze off the sea just across the Intracoastal Waterway and Collins Avenue, and wonder what it's like to be the man of this house.

The owner of this multimillion-dollar chunk of real estate is W. P. Adair. He's Wall Street rich, robust and full of life for a man in his sixties. He stays on the go, skiing, mountain climbing, and sport fishing. His young wife is his third or fourth, and a knockout.

I met them the first time I came here, to ask some questions about the murder, now solved, of an old business associate. As we talked, Adair's tall, tanned young wife, Shelly, sauntered by in a white thong bikini, headed for the Olympic-size pool.

"My kids give me hell," he said, offering me a drink, "but can you picture me with a woman my own age? I can't. They're old ladies, for Christ's sake! They don't want to ski, sail, or go deep-sea fishing. I don't feel a day over forty. I need somebody to raise hell with."

We drank to that. The man likes to play. He can afford to pay. More power to him. They left two days ago to spend the summer in Italy.

Of course, there is no free lunch. The devil is in the details. Strings are attached. I ride herd on the landscaper, the twice-a-week maid, the car washer, and the man in charge of keeping the infinity-edge pool pristine. And, should a hurricane threaten, God forbid, my job is to secure the place. All a small price to pay for secret sanctuary from a wife gone wild.

I climb the tiled stairs, use my key, and punch in the alarm code. Originally built for a live-in housekeeper, my apartment is above the four-car garage. A rear staircase connects it to the kitchen of the main house.

I take off my gun, stash it in the top of the closet, set the paper bag containing my meatball sub on the table, grab a beer from the fridge, and carry it back downstairs to give the grounds the once-over. This place, on nearly two acres, is one of the biggest private residences in Miami Beach, where real estate prices are in the stratosphere. My plan is to walk Casa de Luna's north forty morning and night to be sure nothing is amiss.

I circle the house first. Doors and windows all secure. Night birds sing, fountains bubble, and the pool gurgles as I walk past the night-blooming jasmine to check out the garden. Suddenly I am startled by a furtive move. I am not alone. Glowing eyes in the dark watch my every move.

"Hey. Who the hell are you?" I ask. "What are you doing here?"

He leaps gracefully down from the latticework, runs toward me, and presses his face to my shoe.

"Get outta here." I shake my foot free.

Instead of retreating, he coils himself around my ankle. "Cut that out!" I'm annoyed, until I realize he's obviously at home.

He murmurs, trying to get my attention.

"Holy shit, they didn't tell me about you."

Damn. Adair and his bride neglected to mention this member of the household.

I continue on my rounds. He leads the way, tail straight up, busily skirting the pool, past the fountain, along the north wall, through the garden, down the driveway, then back to the house. He scampers ahead and bounds up the stairs ahead of me.

"You must be hungry."

I frown as he springs onto the table to investigate the bag containing my sandwich.

"Come on." He follows me across the hall and we descend the back stairs to the high-tech granite and stainless steel kitchen of the main house. My search of cupboards, pantries, and cabinets yields nothing.

"Some detective I am," I tell my companion. "How's about you showing me where they keep the cat food. Fetch! Go on, fetch." Instead, he watches me and waits, tail twitching.

.　.　.

He sits on the table eating his half of my meatball sandwich from a saucer while I sit in a chair at the other end with mine and the *Miami News*. He's not crazy about the tomato sauce but tears into the meatballs and cheese.

I watch him eat and wonder how he lost the tip of his left ear, hoping he hasn't been maimed on my watch. This could be a valuable, pedigree show cat, an exotic breed worth big bucks.

"What happened?" I ask. "Trouble with a broad? I know how that is." On closer inspection the injury appears old and well healed.

He drinks water daintily from a cereal bowl, then jumps down to start the figure eights around my ankle again.

I never liked his kind. Me, I'm a dog person, at least I was until we got Max. Connie and the kids always wanted an English sheepdog. He's got pedigree papers and everything. But he's not like a real dog. The big, worthless shaggy monster has a face so full of hair he can't see in front of him. He costs a bundle to feed and is too damn dumb to even raise his head when you call him. Only thing he ever barks at is a cat. He wouldn't bark at a burglar unless the son of a bitch brought a cat with him.

I sigh, let this cat out, and get ready for bed.

I put my wallet on the nightstand and remove the latest picture of the kids. Jennifer is sixteen, her brother, Craig, Jr., thirteen, and their sister, Annie, just turned eleven. I made it to the delivery room for the first two but missed the last one. Caught a triple homicide that night and was tied up until the next morning. I prop the snapshot against the lamp. Jenny is wearing her red-and-white cheerleading uniform, her smile bright and confident. Just like her mother's when we met.

Alone in the double bed, I wonder again how it came to this. Did the job destroy my family life? Or did I? Were we always doomed? Is Connie alone in our bed right now, thinking in the dark, asking herself the same questions? Is there a way to make it up to her? Or is it already too late?

Connie always had her quirks, they were part of her charm. I played left end on the varsity football team at Miami Senior High. She transferred in from Homestead High in her sophomore year, made cheerleader right away. Short with shiny dark hair and bright brown eyes, exactly my type. We were inseparable from day one. The guys were all jealous. Later she pinned the badge on my uniform when I graduated from the academy and stepped into the whirlwind. Tough time to be a cop in Miami. Opposing armies in the cocaine wars invaded the city. We had the Mariel boatlift, Rastafarians, Santería, and the cocaine cowboys. They all came together like the perfect storm, bringing riots and the highest murder rate in the nation. More than 630 men, women, and children murdered in a single year, more than a quarter cut down by automatic weapons.

Scores of cops were lost to bullets, stress fatigue, drugs, or corruption. A lot of people were killed. Some are still walking around. Money and temptation were everywhere. Guys from my academy class were arrested for everything from drug trafficking to rape to racketeering and murder.

Writers said Miami was like Dodge City, the Wild West. They were wrong. Dodge City was never as violent as Miami.

I couldn't have survived it all without Connie. Once I got into homicide, I was never home. A few times we talked about taking the kids and getting the hell out. But we hung in. We are natives. I loved the job. We loved Miami and each other. Then, seven years and three kids into the marriage, I caught a case that changed it all. Teenagers abducted on a first date. Both shot in the head. Sunny, the girl, about the same age my Jenny is now, was raped. She barely survived. Ricky Chance, the boy, died. For weeks I went home only to shower and change.

The case consumed me. So did a woman. Her name was Maureen, a major wreck on my highway to happiness.

Maureen Hartley, the wounded girl's mother, isn't even my type. Tall and blond with classic features, she dresses and moves like the top model she once was. She is as cool as Connie is hot. But something about her touched my soul.

I cared.

Her daughter's pain hurt her. So did her marriage to a rich and manipulative man. I wanted to save her. At the very least I wanted to solve the case, to give her and her daughter peace of mind. I couldn't even do that. I tried to drink away the frustration of my failure.

I didn't find the killers, didn't get the girl, and nearly lost my marriage.

She and the case haunted me, until a twist of fate fourteen years later. I was assigned to the Cold Case Squad, living a normal family life for the first time in years, when a reporter's tip reignited the old investigation. This time, against all odds, we solved it. When I saw Maureen again, the feelings were still there. She left her husband for a time. I didn't know where it was all going but never had the chance to find out. Like so many abused wives, she went back to the son of a bitch. Maybe he brainwashed her, or maybe she likes the lifestyle and the big bucks.

Connie went ballistic, totally haywire, imagining far more than ever happened.

A year ago we had talked about act two, anticipating our lives when the kids were grown up and out.

Now I'm the one who's out. Without my job, I'd have no reason to wake up in the morning. My job matters, it's important, it makes a difference. Or does it? Is it seeking justice for others and saving my sanity or is it ruining my family?

I rewind history as I toss and turn.

Connie is different these days. I'm beginning to suspect menopause is an aggravating factor. She's only in her forties, but her mother went through the change early. I've heard them discuss it enough. Witnessed a few of her mother's outbursts and hysterical tantrums. If that isn't it, I must have caused my wife a helluva lot more pain than I realized all those years. Or is it Miami madness?

I never used to think it affected us natives, but there could be exceptions. People come to Miami and bizarre things happen. The temperature soars, the barometric pressure drops, the full moon rises, and people who are normal and otherwise rational start to use poor judgment, really poor judgment. They suddenly conclude that outrageous, dangerous, and deadly schemes are excellent plans.

Take the student helicopter pilot who made his first solo flight into a high-security prison to rescue a notorious murder suspect. Or the guys who tried to smuggle drugs into Miami in a surplus Russian submarine. Sure. Or the Cuban exiles who believed they were sending Fidel Castro an important message by firing a bazooka at a Polish freighter docked at the Port of Miami.

The chopper crashed, breaking the pilot's ankle and the escaping convict's front teeth. The Russian sub was seized. So were the exiles when a taxi driver ruined their getaway by refusing to allow a bazooka in his cab.

I lie wide awake in the dark, checking off a mental list of other cases of Miami madness. None I can remember affected natives. Eventually it occurs to me that this is not putting me to sleep, which I desperately need. I pad out to the kitchen for another beer as a lonely wail shatters the night.

He runs inside when I open the door, jumps right onto the bed, and curls up, purring. I resign myself to his company. Then I must have dropped off because the next thing I know, the feathery branches of the wild tamarind tree outside the window are drenched with sunshine, occupied by screeching birds, and I am late for work.

CHAPTER FOUR

Nazario sipped a *cortadito* from a tiny paper cup as Stone accessed the Miami–Dade County marriage license database.

"Damn waste of time," Stone muttered.

"Hey, we got to keep the boss happy."

"Impossible with that woman."

"Women always complain more," Detective Joe Corso said from an adjacent desk. "Why do you think they call it bitching?"

"Lie low, Corso," Stone warned him, punching computer keys. "Don't let her drag you into this one. She in yet?"

"Don't see her." Nazario craned his neck. Riley's office looked empty and the civilian secretary, at her own desk, was happily chatting on the phone. "Nah, Emma looks too relaxed."

"Got a hit." Stone chortled. "Here's the widow. Whoa. Once, twice, three times."

"What's her story? She a serial bride?" Nazario peered over his shoulder.

"Must keep trying till she gets it right." Data flashed across the computer screen. "Here we go. Marriage license issued to Natasha Tucker, twenty, and Charles Vincent Terrell, thirty-four, almost fourteen months before his flame-out in May of 'ninety-two. The widow Terrell, now twenty-two, and a Martin Asher, age forty-one, apply for a marriage license on November twenty-seventh, 1992."

"Six months a widow. That's all?" Nazario wiped a fleck of coffee foam from his mustache and leaned over Stone's shoulder. "Thought that arson investigator said she took it hard."

"Must have bounced back. Maybe she doesn't like living alone. Look at this one. Natasha Tucker Terrell Asher, twenty-five, and Daniel P. Streeter, fifty-four, issued a marriage license on January fourth, of 'ninety-five."

"She digs older guys. This broad ever get a divorce? Or do they all spontaneously combust?"

"We'll see in a sec." Stone's fingers flew.

"Wouldn't that be something?" Nazario said. "The lieutenant keeps yapping for results. How cool would it be to give her a black widow?"

"No such luck." Stone scrolled through new data. "Husbands two and three must have safer hobbies than tinkering with old cars. Two divorces on record. *Nada* in the marriage department since 'ninety-nine. She must be footloose and single these days. Let's check property records. Whoa, the Streeter house was assessed at two point six mill. Looks like she kept it, then sold it for three point one. Shows a Gables by the Sea address now. Same as her current driver's license.

"No wants, no warrants," he said, accessing records. "Some traffic. Speeding tickets galore. Likes the fast lane. Hmmm. Busted. Twice. Both retail theft, shoplifting. Saks and Neiman Marcus. The little lady's got sticky fingers."

"Sells a house for more than three mill and she's boosting from stores?"

"Fast lane, what can I say? Risk taker, klepto, or just a thief. I'll get copies of the reports."

"Hey," Nazario said. "Look who finally showed up. Where you been, Sarge?"

"Call your wife," the tiny middle-age secretary sang out.

Craig Burch looked pained. "Yeah, right away," he said.

"What's that smell?" Stone asked.

Nazario's nose wrinkled, his eyes narrowed.

"Jeez, you smell it, too?" Burch said. "My effing Blazer stinks. Made my eyes water driving in. Started last night, but it's worse now. Like something died in there."

"You check under the hood?" Nazario said.

"Nah, but I pulled the seats out, checked the floorboards. Thought I musta spilled something from the fast-food joint. Don't know what the hell it is."

Nazario rolled his eyes. "Uh-oh, you think . . ."

"Wait till you hear what we've got on Meadows." Stone tore himself away from the computer monitor. "Crime scene photos from all the cases . . ."

"Meadows?" Burch lowered his voice. "I thought you two are supposed to be busy on Terrell, so we can get Riley off our asses."

"We're on it, Sarge," Nazario said.

"Uh-oh," Stone muttered.

Riley stood over her secretary, outside her office door. She wore a crisp tailored shirt, fitted beige slacks, a matching jacket, and a frown. "Would you call public works and find out what the hell is going on in my neighborhood? Ask if there's a boil water order."

"Tap water brown again?" Emma pursed her lips and reached for her city phone directory.

"No, pink this time." Riley sighed. "Ran a load of wash this morning and my sheets and underwear all came out pink."

"What color were they before?" Burch grinned.

"Pale pink or flamingo?" Nazario winked. "Inquiring minds want to know."

Riley didn't smile back. "Step into my office, and bring the Terrell file. Is that it? Is this all?" She plucked the folder off Nazario's desk. "Never mind. I'll look at it myself."

She took it into her office, hung her jacket on the back of her chair, and settled behind her desk flipping slowly through the contents.

Occasionally she raised her eyes to the framed photo atop the bookcase next to the door. Two people aboard a boat. Blue sky above, liquid sky below. She was wearing cut-off shorts, a bathing suit top, and sunshine in her hair. Laughing as she held up a puny grouper. Kendall McDonald grinned beside her. He wore a Florida Marlins cap. His right hand rested on her shoulder. Had she ever really been that happy?

"What?" she snapped, as Emma cracked the door open.

"Public works," she said. "Red dye. They used it in routine tests, but somehow it seeped into one of the water plants. Three-quarters of a million households south of Okeechobee Road affected. Not harmful, according to them."

. . .

Riley looked pale beneath her tan as she waved the detectives into her office. Burch, with the most rank, took the only chair. Stone and Nazario slouched against the wall near the door, arms crossed.

"We'll talk to Terrell's widow, the second wife, today and check the neighborhood for witnesses who still live there," Stone said.

"Good." Riley toyed with a paperweight, a metal replica of a hand grenade. Her eyes looked red.

"The guys are also making progress in Meadows."

She raised an eyebrow.

"Stone's been all over the crime scene photos." Burch cocked his head at the lanky black detective.

"Right," Stone said. "The victims were all found in their beds. Sheets stretched tight at the bottom, precisely folded over. All were identically made up. The way they teach the military or hospital workers to make beds."

Burch shrugged. "Maybe the vics were all good housekeepers following Martha Stewart's rules."

"Stewart wasn't a household word when he started killing, Sarge. And no senior citizen makes their bed like that. It's damn uncomfortable, especially for the elderly. Too tight, it cramps up their feet. I used to visit my grandfather in the hospital. He and his roommate were always asking me to loosen up the sheets.

"It's also obvious that the guy hung around, felt at home, cleaned up."

"You mean he washed up, took showers after the murders?" Riley frowned.

"Maybe that, too. But I mean the scenes, the victims' bedrooms. Spit and polish, just like the beds. The photos show the rest of the rooms, except for the kitchens, cluttered, a little messy. Typical of older folks.

They accumulate things over the years, hate to throw anything out, and no longer have the strength and stamina for heavy-duty housework."

"And the kitchens?" Riley asked.

"Spotless. You could eat off the floor. Most seniors, especially the women, focus more on the living room once they're frail. They like to keep that nice, in case company comes."

"True." Nazario nodded. "You see that on so many DOA scenes."

"He might even have cooked a meal. In the last several cases, where the garbage hadn't been collected yet, there were fresh eggshells."

Riley looked impressed. "So, in addition to wiping down whatever he touches, he may cook and clean house?"

"Looks possible."

"When you find him, bring him over to my place before you book him," she said. "My terrazzo floors are a bitch to polish."

"Sure," Burch said, "but the deal is, he has to kill you first."

"Nice try, but I'm not his type. Not on Medicare yet. Good work. But make Terrell top priority," she added, "until we know what we have there."

"But if this guy is repeating his pattern," Stone protested, "he might be back. He could be in Miami now."

"Pure speculation on your part. Humor me," Riley said.

Nazario left with Stone, still smoldering but silent.

Burch remained seated.

"How's it going on the home front?" Riley asked.

He shifted uncomfortably in his chair. "It's not, at the moment."

"Too bad. Guess it's an occupational hazard." She tried to muster up an encouraging smile but failed. "Hope you work it out."

"Me, too. You okay?"

"Sure."

"Through with that?"

She gave him the Terrell file without meeting his eyes.

•   •   •

The temperature was ninety-six degrees as Nazario gingerly lifted the hood of Burch's Chevy Blazer. "Well, there's your problem, Sarge."

"What the hell is that shit?"

The aroma from a gooey, molten mass atop the engine made them step back.

"I'd say Limburger." Nazario crossed his arms. "Sarge," he said after a long pause, "it's none of my business, but you gotta make things right with the little woman."

• • •

The new city directory listed the Walkers, who first called 911 in the Terrell case, still at the same address on Mariposa Lane. A surprise in Miami, where the wandering population moves on the average of once every three years.

Nazario squinted across shaded Mariposa Lane at a towering behemoth of a house painted in the latest decorator color, a distressed mustard yellow. "That's gotta be the Terrell house, but it doesn't look right."

Burch agreed. "It's nothing like the crime scene photos. Where the hell's the garage? Should be right there, where those two thick columns are. Sure we got the right address?"

"Probably remodeled after the fire," Stone said.

They rang the Walkers' bell. A yapping Jack Russell terrier bounced as though on a trampoline around the feet of the fortyish woman who answered the door. Of course she remembered that day.

"Who could forget it?" she said cheerfully, and let them in. She expertly caught the Jack Russell on a particularly high bounce and tucked him under her arm. "I'll call my husband."

She pressed a button on a wall-mounted intercom. "I told you I was busy, I have to finish this today," an edgy voice responded.

"But the police are here, sweetheart. Detectives."

She flipped off the switch and smiled at the detectives. "Betcha that got his attention."

It did. Stan Walker bounded into the room moments later. He'd been working on an annual report from his home office at the back of the house, he said.

"Detectives?" He looked concerned. "What's wrong? Where are the kids?"

"Fine. Vanessa is at Gillian's. I think Ryan's in his room."

Burch explained.

"Is that the Terrell house across the street?" Nazario asked. "It doesn't look the same."

"Don't get us started on that," Stan said in disgust. "Just look at that eyesore."

"Natasha had the place repaired after the fire," Joan said. "But I don't think she ever spent another night there. Who could blame her? She—"

"—rented it out," Stan said. "It wasn't so bad at first. A young couple, good tenants. They took care of the place, but then he got transferred back to—"

"—California, I think," Joan said. "It was an absolute nightmare after that. She listed it as a short-term rental, and we never had a real neighbor there again. They'd come and go, sometimes every week. European tourists who partied in South Beach all night, then came back to continue the party. Music would blast us right out of our beds at four A.M. Sometimes two dozen people were living there, some—"

"—for only a weekend," Stan said. "That's illegal. The city doesn't allow short-term rentals in a residential neighborhood. But she was a widow—"

"—with a baby," Joan said. "Nobody wanted to turn her in. But her tenants were speeding up and down our street where children play. It wasn't their neighborhood. They didn't care."

"She put the place on the market back in 2000, after real estate prices skyrocketed," Stan said. "We were relieved."

"We looked forward to real neighbors again," Joan said.

"But it got worse," Stan said. "She sold the place for a huge profit to a contractor who builds those damn McMansions on spec. That should be against the law. Look at that monstrosity." He pulled the drapes back and stared in disgust across the street.

"Dwarfs everything around it. Completely out of scale and out of place. Destroys the character of the neighborhood. More than seven thousand square feet of house on a nine-thousand-square-foot lot! Eight bedrooms, eight baths, plus maids' quarters. The next-door neighbors feel like bugs under a microscope. All those tall windows looking down at them in their traditional, typical one-story South Florida twenty-two-hundred-square-foot house. The ceilings in that eyesore are so high that—"

"—it must be like living in a post office," Joan said.

"They build lot line to lot line," Stan complained. "The politicians sold us out to builders and developers whose sole purpose is to pave over as much green space as possible."

"I cried when they cut down the shade trees," Joan said. "Two magnificent live oaks, a kapok tree, and a baobob. You should have seen their gorgeous canopies."

"Isn't there an ordinance against that?" Burch peered out at the offending structure. "I thought they were protected."

"They are," Stan said. "You need a permit and a good reason to remove them. We reported them to the tree police, you know, DERM, the Department of Environmental Resource Management. They took action, but the penalties are a joke. They bought after-the-fact permits and paid small fines." He shrugged. "The penalties aren't stiff enough to be a deterrent. The builders are too rich to care. They consider it the price of doing business.

"Meanwhile Miami has fewer trees than ninety percent of American cities," Stan said. "That's the reason it's so damn hot. All the concrete and asphalt."

"They may regret cutting those trees down," Nazario said. "Santería worshipers believe that the kapok and baobobs house spirits who will bring harm to those who destroy them."

"Hope so," Stan said. "That same builder's putting up another concrete monster around the corner."

"Did you notice the color of this one?" Joan wrinkled her nose. "I don't know if any of you detectives ever changed a diaper, but it's the same color as baby poop. Who on earth would paint a house that shade?"

"People with more money than sense." Her husband let go of the drape, which fell gracefully back into place.

"Who lives there now?" Stone asked.

"Good question," Stan said. "Latinos bought it two years ago, and to tell you the truth, I couldn't even tell you their names or what they look like. They drive in. They drive out. Their SUVs all have dark-tinted windows. In a neighborhood where we all used to know each other and all the kids, dogs, cats, and kissing cousins by first name."

"You ever hear from Terrell's widow?" Burch inquired.

Joan shook her head. "Natasha remarried, I think, a man who was in business with her late husband. Terrell was a pharmacist, you know, owned that big corner drugstore on Coral Way. The place had been there forever, a landmark. They had the best soda fountain."

"It's gone, too," Stan said.

"Natasha sold the business as well," Joan said. "They put up a high-rise bank building on the site."

"That second husband," Stone said, "that would be a Martin Asher?"

"Sounds familiar," Joan said. "Hope you don't mind me asking, but why are you looking into the fire again after all these years?"

"We're checking out a report that it might not have been an accident," Burch said.

"Oh my God! Murder? Stan, did you hear that?" She turned to her husband, excited. "Honey, imagine. A murder mystery right on our block!"

"It's only a routine inquiry," Stone said quickly.

"How did the Terrells get along?" Nazario asked. "How well did you know them?"

"They hadn't been here long," Joan said, her voice animated as she led them into the comfortable living room. "They were newlyweds, she was pregnant when they moved in. It was his second marriage. He had an ex-wife—and kids. The children sometimes came for a weekend. Poor things. One was about Vanessa's age. They came over here to play a few times.

"I got the impression that their stepmother wasn't too crazy about them. Natasha was young. The most gorgeous thing you ever saw."

Stan nodded solemnly.

"She liked to be the center of attention," Joan went on. "Didn't want to share the spotlight. The two of them had a couple of big blow-ups.

"*Whoops.*" She clapped her hand over her mouth. "Sorry. Wrong choice of words. But you couldn't help but hear the arguments. Once when he tried to leave during a fight, she ran out after him and threw herself across the hood of his car."

"The day he died," Stan said solemnly, "the fellow came over here and asked to borrow a line wrench. Never did get the thing back. Part of a matching set. Said he was working on his Thunderbird. I'd never seen him work on the car before. I told him to bring his kids over to Ryan's party later, but he said it wasn't his weekend for visitation."

"See anybody else over there that day?" Stone asked.

Joan shook her head. "I was way involved in the party. I mean, it was absolute bedlam here, two dozen kids and not much help."

"Where was the party?" Stone asked. "Here inside the house, your backyard . . . ?"

"No, out front in the shade under the trees. The kids saw it all," Joan said.

"Traumatized." Stan nodded grimly. "For life."

"Take any snapshots?" Nazario asked.

Joan shook her head. "Who had time?"

Nazario tucked his notebook back into his jacket pocket. Stone checked his watch. Burch got to his feet, hoping to wrap this up today. How much more would it take to convince Riley that there was nothing to find?

"I was too busy shooting the video."

The detectives exchanged glances.

"You have a tape?" they chorused.

She cocked her head. "Probably in Ryan's room with all the others— unless he taped a rock music concert over it. I'll see if I can find it, and him. He won't want to miss this. He always says it was the biggest birthday blast he ever had. I'll be right back."

Burch sat down again. "How long have you two been married?"

Stan paused for a moment. "Our twenty-second is coming up."

"Nice," the detective said. "What's your secret?"

Stan hitched his shoulders. "Dumb luck, I guess. We were young, stayed the course, and that was it. You know how it is."

"Yeah," Burch said. "But—"

"I found it! I found it." Joan danced down the stairs, waving a video cassette. Her son loomed behind her.

Taller than his parents, he wore an oversized red T-shirt emblazoned with LINKIN PARK, blue jeans, and a silver stud in one ear.

"He starts his junior year at FSU this fall," his mother said proudly.

"That day was so cool," Ryan told the detectives. "My friends never forgot it. So weird. I wanted fireworks, so when it happened, I thought at first that they got them for me, that it was all part of the birthday trip."

"I'll make popcorn." Joan backed toward the kitchen. "It'll just take a sec in the microwave. Don't start the tape without me. We haven't seen it in years. What does everybody want to drink?"

・　・　・

They gathered around the blond wood entertainment center. Bowls of popcorn and half a dozen soft drinks on the coffee table. Nazario and Burch on the couch, Stone slouched in a leather chair. Stan, Joan, and Nipsy, the Jack Russell, shared the love seat. Ryan inserted the tape into the VCR and sprawled on the floor.

The detectives watched silently.

"Ohhhhh," Joan crooned, as a golden retriever loped through a gaggle of children. "There's Sookie. How I loved that dog. And look, look at Vanessa, she was only five then."

"Consuela looks so young," Ryan said.

"We all do," Stan said. "I had more hair and less stomach."

"We have to show this to Consuela on Tuesday," Joan said. "Look at you, honey!" She patted Stan's knee. "Whatever happened to your chef's hat?"

"There's HoHo!" Ryan said.

"And the cake!" Joan laughed aloud. "The racquet, not the rocket! I forgot about that!"

Stone leaned forward in his chair, wondering on some vague level why people were laughing. He slid onto the thick carpet next to Ryan. "Can you stop it? Back it up. There. More, more."

Ryan handed the remote to the detective.

"Okay, what is that?" Stone asked.

"What?" the Walkers chorused.

"Passing on the street, in the background."

"That reddish blur?" Stan asked.

"Right."

"Traffic of some sort. A car, I guess." Stan chewed his popcorn thoughtfully. "We didn't have much traffic on our street back then. What do you think, Joanie?"

"Remember the Camachos? You know. Four doors down, in the old Tate house? Sissy, their teenager, had a red Mustang back then. That might have been her coming home." She shrugged. "It could be anybody."

Stone flicked the remote and the tape resumed.

"Look, look," she cried. "There's Lionel!"

"Where?" Burch squinted at the tape. "Who's Lionel?"

"Right there. That's him." Joan gasped. "What's he doing to Sookie? Look at Consuela trying to stop him!"

"That boy grew up right on this block," Stan said proudly. "We should save this footage, Joanie. I always knew that kid would go places. This tape might be of historic value someday."

"Who is he?" Stone asked.

"The next Bill Gates," Joan said. "A millionaire by the time he was eighteen. Software. He invented a whole new computer language. Got a full scholarship to Princeton."

Ryan rolled his eyes.

"What's that?" Stone stopped the tape and rewound.

"HoHo's act," Stan said.

The clown waved a red silk scarf overhead like a banner.

"Something else going by. Looks like it stopped for a minute," Burch said. "Hard to tell between the trees, with all that glare from the sun."

They continued to watch.

"Hey, there it is again." Nazario leaned toward the screen.

HoHo reached deep into his throat and dramatically withdrew the long red scarf.

"Now watch this," Ryan said. "Here it comes. The big baboomba!"

Cheers, applause. A loud *whoosh*.

"Fireworks!" A glowing eight-year-old Ryan, arms raised in jubilation, birthday crown askew.

Jerky camera movements. Smoke and flame. An explosion, empty sky, treetops, a pony bolting, a man chasing after him. Chunks of burning wreckage falling like meteors. Sookie scrambling, tail between her legs.

Car and house alarms wailing. Flames, orange and red against brilliant blue sky. Pudgy legs churning. Stan sprinting. Children screaming. The screen went dark as the camera hit the ground.

"I dropped it," Joan said in a voice thin with remembrance. "Or threw it down. I can't remember which."

The room stayed quiet for a moment.

"Should have kept shooting, Mom. You could have sold it to *America's Funniest Home Videos.*"

"You're a sick kid," his father said.

"Can we borrow the tape?" Burch asked.

. . .

"God bless Americans and their video cameras," Nazario said in the car.

"Nice people," Burch said. "Real nice. Notice how they kept finishing each other's sentences?"

"Yeah. Sometimes you forget there are still families like that. We heading over to see the widow?"

"Yeah. I gotta stop on the way to pick up cat food."

"I've got some personal business, too. Something I need to take care of," Stone said. "For about an hour. Okay, Sarge?"

"A little afternoon delight, huh? Oh, to be young and single. Just make sure you stay single. And stay by your radio."

They dropped him off at the police parking garage.

"So the young stud has a sweet young thing waiting for him somewhere."

Nazario nodded. "Guy has a way with the women."

CHAPTER FIVE

Stone used his own key. He knew she'd be in the bedroom.

"Hey, where's my girl?"

She felt like a frail bird in his arms as they hugged.

"Did you eat without me?"

"No, I waited, jus doin' a little mendin' until you got yourself here." A cotton skirt, its hem ripped, lay across the arm of her recliner.

She seemed slightly unsteady on her feet, and he took her arm as they went into the kitchen of her tiny Overtown cottage.

"Why aren't you watching TV?"

She waved away the idea, lips pursed. "All that soap opera foolishness? Everybody lyin' to everybody else, everybody sleepin' with everybody else, swappin' husbands, tradin' wives. Who cares 'bout that trash? And those crazy talk shows? Where do they find those poor white trash?"

He grinned. "How about a movie? The History Channel or Animal Planet? I know you like that."

She looked away, headed for the stove.

"Gran, you still have the cable, don't you?"

"Who needs four hundred channels? It costs too much. Somebody 'ud have to watch night and day to make it worth the money. I don't watch that much, jes' the news."

He looked exasperated. "But you don't have to worry about the bill, Gran. I gave you the cable for your birthday, remember?"

"You do too much already, Sonny. Shouldn't spend money on me. You work too hard for it, you could do lots of other things with it."

She frowned in front of the old-fashioned four-burner gas stove. "You here for breakfast or supper, Sonny?"

He tried not to be alarmed. A minor short-term memory lapse. That's all it was. She still had total recall of events that took place forty years ago. If you misplace your keys, the doctor said, don't worry. Worry when you find them but don't remember what they're for.

"It's lunch, Gran. I think you already fixed it. Something sure smells good."

"Oh, that's right." Nodding, she opened the oven door. "I was jus' keepin' it warm."

His grandmother had always been the smartest, hardest-working, most resourceful woman he'd ever known. She didn't let Sam get away with a thing while raising him. For a long time he'd really believed she had eyes in the back of her head.

"Set down and read the newspaper, Sonny, and I'll fix you a plate."

He took the still-folded *Miami News* and sat in the small living room. Years ago they'd shared the same old armchair as his grandmother told him stories and showed him yellowed photos: Overtown nightclub owners, businessmen with marceled burr cuts, and show business stars. Overtown was a mecca for black entertainers, top stars who sang, danced, and did comedy at fancy Miami Beach clubs and hotels but were not permitted to eat or sleep there. They all stayed in Overtown and starred in late-night performances at its lively clubs and theaters, in the days before the white establishment gutted the once-vibrant neighborhood to build the expressway. She'd shown him photos of a woman called Diamond Tooth Mary and of his great-aunt Marva, a well-known schoolteacher and church organist.

He felt relaxed and at home in that room where his parents smiled from a picture frame on a shelf. Next to it was a photo of himself at age five. Wearing a navy blue suit, saddle shoes, and a tie, he peered uncertainly at the camera from in front of a vintage television set.

His eyes wandered back to his parents' faces, their smiles frozen in time, much the way he remembered them.

His father had labored over the fire, barbecuing juicy ribs, pork chops, shrimp, and chicken, while his mother waited on customers at their tiny take-out restaurant.

They worked side by side, thirteen hours a day, seven days a week.

His parents would drop him off at school and go on to work. After school, Sam walked home, let himself in, and did his homework until his grandmother arrived from her housekeeping job in Miami Beach. She would stay until his parents came home at night.

His mother said all the hard work was for the future. It would not be forever, she had assured him.

She was right.

He was eight years old when their future ended.

They had been robbed twice before. His father bought a gun for protection. He kept it on a shelf over his barbecue stove.

He never had a chance to reach for it the night it happened.

Sam was working on his math at the kitchen table, hoping that the hard rain falling meant his parents would be home soon. Rain always made business slow. When the knock at the door came, he thought it might be them at first, but it was a policeman. His grandmother sent Sam to his room, but he ran back to her when he heard her scream.

The policeman picked him up, held him in his arms, and said everything would be all right, as his grandmother wailed.

The next time Sam saw his parents, they lay in matching caskets, side by side.

He never forgot the policeman whose name he never knew. After Sam pinned on the badge, he watched for the man, certain he would still recognize him. But he apparently quit or retired, never knowing he had motivated Sam to follow him into the department. Sam worked hard, won honors in patrol, and persistently applied to join the Cold Case Squad. When the time was right, after he had proven himself, built some seniority and respect, and had enough clout, he would persuade the team to pursue the case that had changed his life forever.

"Hope you're hungry, Sonny. Come set down while it's hot."

She'd filled his plate with ham, sweet potatoes, collard greens, and pole beans. His iced tea was the way he liked it.

"I'll be by Saturday morning," he told her, as he slathered sweet butter on a slab of warm cornbread. "Time to mow the lawn, take the coconuts off that palm tree. Shoulda done it sooner. It's hurricane season. They'd be cannonballs in a storm."

She nodded. "I'll fix you a nice breakfast Saturday. How is your case comin', honey? The big one, 'bout all those women?"

"Good, Gran. Coming along. Really good. But the lieutenant is driving us crazy. Sending us off on a wild-goose chase just when I start making some headway."

"What on earth is wrong with that woman?"

"Long story, Gran."

She leaned forward, eyes bright. "Well, whacha got that's new?"

He put his fork down and grinned across the table at her.

He and this tiny woman had been a team; when he was a child she took him everywhere. They rode buses all over Miami. Even to places where they weren't wanted. They went to the Historical Museum, to South Beach's Art Deco District, to old Coconut Grove, Orchard Villa, Lemon City, and other historic Miami neighborhoods. They went to the library and to Saturday afternoon matinees. They watched TV detectives—Charlie Chan, Sam Spade, and Sherlock Holmes—matching wits with the sleuths. She even took him to Miami Beach and taught him how to swim in the ocean. Back then he was the only child in his inner-city neighborhood who knew how to swim. Some grew up never having seen the ocean, just a short drive across the causeway.

She always told him, "You can't be what you can't see."

He didn't know then what she meant by that. He knew now.

"The killer stays with the bodies, I think, probably overnight. He puts them to bed and folds the bedclothes really tight at the bottom, military or hospital style. I think he cleans their kitchens and bedrooms. So far he's killed on every day of the week but Saturday."

Arms folded, she listened intently as he rattled off the details.

She seemed to be a tower of strength when he was little. The more he grew, the bigger and stronger he got, the smaller and weaker she'd become. He'd always wanted to protect her from the crime, drugs, and weirdness that lurked in the dark. She was all he had.

She tapped her chin with an arthritic finger and pursed her lips thoughtfully. "Jewish," she said, and nodded. "Sounds like Jewish, Orthodox."

"Who?"

"The killer."

Sam laughed. "What makes you say that, Gran?"

"Don't you laugh at me, Sonny. I been around longer than you and I still know a few things. Sounds Orthodox."

He still grinned. "How so?"

"The things he does. I worked for the Waldmans long enough to soak it all up. Why, I always prepared their seder, helped those children study for the bat and bar mitzvahs. Chopped the chicken liver, fixed the gefilte fish. Braided the challah—that's bread, Sonny. Wasn't nothin' to learn, jus' like plaitin' hair. Grandma Waldman taught me all of it in her kosher kitchen. Had two sets of pots and pans, two sets of dishes, two sets of everythin', even glasses and crystal and dishtowels—even two dishwashers—and they can never be mixed up together. I know all about it." She sternly wagged a gnarled index finger. "So don't you talk no smack to me."

He remembered the Waldmans. For more than thirty years she'd worked for generations of that large and warm family. She'd taken him to their big house in Miami Beach. He had played with the children, the first boys he'd ever seen wearing yarmulkes. When he mocked their skullcaps later, she'd lashed out, indignant. "Jus' remember, Sonny, you never hear of anybody gets mugged by a boy in a yarmulke."

When the family patriarch, Rabbi Saul Waldman, died, she had taken him with her to the funeral.

"I'm not doubting you, Gran." He fished his notebook from his pocket. "Okay, which things are you talking about? Let me write this down. Maybe you can help me solve the case." He spoke half in jest, but his curiosity was piqued. "Maybe you'll make officer of the month, Gran."

"Don't you play with me, boy. I know what I'm talkin' 'bout here. The man you want doesn't work on *shabbat,* the sabbath. They don't work on Saturday." She shook her head, then sipped her tea.

"They have rituals for the dead." She put down her glass. "The women, their eyes and mouths closed?"

He nodded, seeing again the blown-up photos forever etched on his mind's eye.

"They never leave the dead alone. Somebody sets by them all the time, readin' the Psalms."

"I remember that," Sam said. Two years earlier, after a Jewish police officer was killed in the line of duty, a fellow officer, a fellow Jew, had remained with the corpse in the medical examiner's morgue overnight.

"But people who observe Orthodox customs are religious," he said, thinking aloud as they always did when trying to solve a mystery before Sherlock Holmes.

"Everybody's capable of murder, Sonny. You say that yourself. Religious people kill each other every day. How 'bout that rabbi in New Jersey who murdered his wife?"

"New Jersey?"

"I watched some of that Court TV," she said grudgingly. "Wasn't bad."

"But burial has to be within twenty-four hours, right?"

"There's exceptions, like the sabbath or relatives comin' from a distance. Other things."

"Well, thanks, Gran. I'll look into it."

"And for the first meal afterward, the mourners eat bread and hard-boiled eggs."

Eggshells in the garbage. Crazier things had happened.

He stood up, stretched, and, ignoring her protests, carried the plates into the kitchen.

"Hey!" He noticed something. "Gran, your back door's not locked!"

"Oh." She shrugged. "It keeps stickin' and gits hard to open."

His lunch curdled in his stomach. "But didn't I tell you a hundred times? You have to keep the doors locked. Where's the WD-Forty?" He foraged for the small, nearly empty can in the toolbox in the kitchen, then squirted a few shots of oil into the balky lock. He snapped it back and forth several times. It still felt stiff and out of line.

Exasperated, he ran his hair through his hair and glanced fitfully at his grandmother, placidly rinsing dishes in the sink.

"Keep this locked at all times. Promise me, please, Gran. When I come on Saturday I'll install a better lock, an inch-and-a-half dead bolt. Promise me."

CHAPTER SIX

"Now, this is what a Florida house should look like," Nazario said. The elevated Key West–style home, with spacious verandas and multiple sets of French doors, was long and rambling. Pale yellow, with white trim, it stood alone on several acres with a dramatic view of the wide bay.

"Looks like the widow lives large," Burch said.

A big green landscaping truck and several cars were parked in the driveway but no one was in sight. They climbed the wide front stairs and rang several times before a uniformed maid came to the door. She was in her thirties with dark hair tied back in a ponytail. Her rubber gloves were yellow, her expression impatient.

She scrutinized Nazario's business card. The lady of the house was home, she said in guarded, heavily accented English, but busy at the moment.

"You can tell her we're here," he said politely.

"No me." She looked amused as she wagged her head.

He persisted until she replied in Cuban-accented Spanish that they could tell her themselves and directed them to a cabana area behind the house. She smirked as she closed the door.

They followed the wraparound veranda, past comfortable white wicker porch furniture, to a wide back staircase descending to the water-front pool, cabanas, and dock area.

The *Natasha*, a graceful three-masted sailboat, was moored at the dock. No one was in sight.

The bay was magnificent, sea birds studding the sky where clouds and water converged. A splendid day, despite a forecast of thunderstorms.

"Think she sent us back here on a wild-goose chase?"

"No, Sarge. Listen. You hear what I'm hearing?"

Burch paused, then slowly grinned. "Sounds like Stone beat us here."

The rhythmic unmistakable sounds of passionate sex in progress came from behind the louvered doors of the largest of three cabanas.

Burch rapped loudly on the polished wooden door. "Police Department."

The rhythm stopped, replaced by scrambling sounds and angry mutters.

"We're looking for Mrs. Streeter," Burch called out loudly, and rapped again.

"Been years since I did this," he said sotto voce to Nazario.

After several more moments, the door abruptly swung open.

"It's Ross now, Mrs. Milo Ross."

She stood on one impossibly high-heeled sandal. The other was in her hand. Lush shiny black hair tumbled long around her sleek bare shoulders. Her strapless bikini was a brilliant peacock blue. A sheer wraparound skirt in the same peacock color was tied like a sarong around the suit's minuscule bottom.

A thin gold chain glittered around her slender waist.

"You looking for me?" The green eyes were cool and inquisitive, despite the scarlet flush coloring her chiseled cheekbones.

Embarrassment or passion? Nazario wondered.

"Please." She reached a crimson-tipped, well-manicured hand out to Burch for support, though Nazario stood closer. Clinging to his arm for balance, she attempted to slide the Manolo Blahnik sandal onto her slim, bare foot.

Burch was impressed. She'd sized them up instantly, instinctively sensing which man was in charge. She's good, he thought. Very good.

She slowly wriggled her polished toes into the strappy shoe, exposing her tanned legs longer than necessary, then clung to his arm for a few more beats.

"Ross?" Burch asked. "You've remarried."

"Is that a crime?" she asked lightly.

"In many cases it should be." He smiled back at her.

Nazario was focused on the man in the cabana. He was no Milo Ross.

The first clue was the name NELSON stitched over the grass-stained pocket of the landscaping company work shirt he was hastily buttoning with thick, fumbling fingers.

Tall, dark, and shaggy haired, he was handsome in a savage way, his current expression sullen.

"This is Nelson," Natasha Ross said, "and you are . . ."

The detectives introduced themselves.

"We can continue to discuss the new plantings next time," she said, briskly dismissing Nelson as he emerged, blinking, into the fierce sunlight.

She cocked her head at the detectives. "We're planning a more elaborate garden on the north side. Big beds full of color. What do you think?" She led them toward the house, leaving Nelson to wander off back to his truck.

"Color. Color is good." How uncool am I? Nazario thought, embarrassed by his own words as he spoke them.

She showed them into the cool, air-conditioned entry, through a great room with two huge fireplaces, and past a life-size marble statue of a half-naked woman reclining on a chaise longue.

"Paolina Borghese," Natasha said, running a polished finger along the woman's cold, stone arm as she passed. "Napoléon's sister. Italian, eighteenth century.

"I'll have Norma bring you some coffee," she said, ushering them into a bright yellow and white sunroom. "It's so hot out there," she said, excusing herself. "I need to get out of these sticky clothes."

"No surprise they're sticky," Burch muttered, as her heels clicked away on the marble floor. They watched her pause for brief words with Norma, the maid who had answered the door.

The latest stock market quotes from New York, London, and Hong Kong scrolled continuously on a large plasma television screen. The room was full of potted palms and color. Bowls of bright fresh flowers were on every table, and oil paintings, landscapes, still lifes, and seascapes, in ornate gold-leaf frames, hung on the walls.

"No dogs playing poker?" Burch said in mock disappointment.

"Personally, I'm partial to Elvis on black velvet," Nazario said. "And panthers. Big jungle cats stalking their prey."

"I think we just met one."

They were still speculating on the value of the room's artwork when, in a surprisingly brief period of time, she rejoined them. Her white wrap-around dress accentuated her deep tan and her thick hair was piled loosely atop her head in a style similar to Napoléon's sister, still guarding the entrance to the great room.

Norma wheeled in a coffee service and poured.

Natasha settled in an upholstered wing chair with clawed feet and armrests hand-carved into the heads of eagles.

As Burch explained the reason for their visit, her eyes changed. Her lips parted.

"Charles Terrell." She repeated the name slowly, with a hint of wonder, as though trying to recall where she had heard it before. "You're here about Charles Terrell?" Her lashes swept down, masking her expression.

Burch caught only a glimpse. Relief? She thought they were there for another reason.

"Why would you come to me to discuss him?" Her eyes wandered to the scrolling stock quotes.

"We're checking out his accident," Nazario said easily.

She seemed skeptical. "But that was a hundred years ago," she murmured.

"We're still interested," Burch said. "How did you and Charles Terrell meet?"

She sighed deeply, then leaned back and crossed her legs, as though resigned to humoring them.

"I applied for a job at his drugstore," she said, her lush, protuberant lips in a perpetual pout. "Fresh off the bus from Iowa. A farm girl, if you can imagine that."

"Hard to believe," Burch said mildly. "Your parents still live there?"

Something flickered in her eyes for a moment, then disappeared. "I'm not sure," she said easily. "We're not a close family. I felt like a displaced person, born at the wrong longitude and latitude. Didn't like that life. I didn't belong in Iowa, so I left as soon as I was old enough. Off to seek my future. My fortune." White teeth flashed, her smile radiant. "The moment I saw it, I knew that Miami was the place. There's something about it."

"You're so right," Burch agreed.

"I needed a job. I walked into a store not far from the Greyhound bus station. Charles was the owner. I got the job. The first time we saw each other . . ." She shrugged.

"Wasn't he married then?" Nazario asked.

Her unnaturally vivid green eyes met his. "His marriage was apparently in trouble.

"Eventually he divorced and we married but, I must admit, it was rocky." She smiled slightly, cautiously reminiscing from a safe distance.

"After I had our son, Brandon, Charles began to stay out late. He left me stuck with an infant. Said he was busy working, but he was never there when I called the store." She arched an expressive eyebrow. "I knew he had other business dealings, including a chain of weight-loss clinics with a partner, but he became distant." She sipped her coffee. "They say the wife is always the last to know. Not true. Never. Any woman who doesn't know doesn't want to know. He was unfaithful to his first wife, so I assumed he was being unfaithful to me. I was trying to figure out what was going on.

"He spent time with his kids, which meant seeing his ex-wife. I suspected she might be the one. She poisoned his mind against me every chance she got. I knew she hated me. Or perhaps he'd hired a replacement, some other pretty girl at the store. He laughed and denied it. I was so young and vulnerable."

Burch nodded sympathetically. Had he ever met a woman less vulnerable?

"Who knows if we would have worked out?" she said. "At the very end, I thought it might. That last night, I was asleep when he came home really late again, with no explanation. But he was in a great mood. He woke me up, in fact. I'd wanted him to take me out to dinner earlier that night. The baby had screamed all day and Charles refused to have a live-in nanny. He had a thing about strangers in the house. He'd even locked the garage door. Charles could be so anal. He'd taken his Thunderbird apart, he said, and had his tools and the schematics all laid out. He didn't want anybody in there until he finished what he was doing. I had tried to get in there that afternoon, looking for a can of mosquito spray. I was pissed off.

"But that night . . ." She sighed. "The man was amazing. He opened a bottle of champagne, a really good vintage he'd been saving, and brought it to bed. Unusual for him. It was like the first time. We made love all night."

Nazario blinked, surprised that she spoke so freely about her sex life, yet seemed so evasive.

"I wanted to sleep the next morning, but the baby was up, and so was Charles, obsessed about working on that damn car. Wish I'd never seen that stupid piece of junk. That Thunderbird was older than I was.

"I didn't like my Jaguar, either." Her pout grew darker. "I wanted burgundy, but he bought me the blue because he liked it better. I was so furious I was going to run it into a tree. But that morning he promised me a Mercedes, the convertible I wanted. I left to pick up a few things at Dadeland and then grocery-shop. But did he let me leave the baby with him? No. He said he'd be too busy working on the car." She fumed.

"In case you've never noticed, babies don't travel light. They're hell to take shopping. He stuck me with that baby all the time. Never again. Maybe," she mused, "it all did work out for the best."

"Not for Charles," Burch said.

"Well, of course." She patted her lips with a cloth napkin. "I wouldn't wish that on anyone. But I believe in destiny. Some things are meant to be."

"It must have been a difficult time for you," Nazario said sympathetically.

Surprised for a moment, she agreed. "Yes, it was." Her pout became self-pitying.

"So?" Burch asked. "Your second husband, Asher, was there to take up the slack?"

"Martin was so comforting," she said. "A partner with Charles in the weight-reduction clinics, which, of course, failed. But luckily Martin had other business interests."

Before they divorced, she'd had a second child, then a third with Daniel Streeter, husband number three.

"I love being a mom," she said primly.

Nazario had never seen anyone look less like a mom. His own mother's anguished face appeared in a sudden familiar flashback. At the airport in Havana, her palms pressed against the thick glass between them. He never saw her again.

"Where are your kids?" Burch glanced around the room as though moppets might suddenly spring up from behind the furniture. Nothing in or outside of the house hinted at the presence of children.

"Brandon's in military school, in Tennessee, I think. Isabella is at some sort of music camp in the Adirondacks or somewhere and . . ." Eyes narrowing, she bit her moist lower lip as though trying to recall. "Daniel Jr. is touring Europe with his dad this summer."

Burch thought wistfully of his own children, regretting the times he'd complained about the sounds of their happy chaos because he had to sleep during the day.

"And you're married again?" Nazario said.

"Milo and I met in Hawaii. A whirlwind courtship. We were married in Vegas last spring."

The reason Stone found no local record of the marriage, Nazario thought. "He at the office today?"

"A doctor's appointment," she said. "He's the retired CEO of Baldwin Petroleum."

"Took early retirement, huh?" Burch said.

"No, my husband retired some time ago. This all does sound like a soap opera, I suppose." She checked her gold watch. "Now, what is the purpose of this trip down Memory Lane?"

She cocked her head expectantly.

Nazario leaned forward, watching her intently. "It's been suggested that Charles Terrell's death was no accident."

"Suicide? I don't believe—" She blinked, her narrowing green eyes suddenly shrewd. "The insurance company is behind this, isn't it? Because they paid double indemnity for accidental death and wouldn't have to pay at all for suicide. Isn't there a statute of limitations? Can they just come back after all these years?"

"Probably not. But there is no statute of limitations on first-degree murder," Burch said. "We're trying to determine if his death might have been homicide."

"Homicide?" She looked confused. "That's not possible."

"Why not?"

"Or maybe . . ." Her expression morphed into something sly. "His ex-wife," she said triumphantly. "April murdered him! She's the type. Definitely! She hated him for leaving. You should have heard her when she found out about us. Charles kept promising to tell her, but never did. She had to face it, sooner or later, so I left him a message on their home answering machine about our plans for a night out. I knew she'd hear it. She showed up and made a scene. What a bitch! She's definitely the type." Natasha nodded, her expression certain. "Didn't want the divorce, but wanted child support big time."

"What would she have to gain?" Nazario asked.

"Everything!" Natasha said, eyes wide with surprise that he'd even asked. "Revenge. Payback. The oldest motives in the world. If Charles was murdered, that woman did it."

She sprang up, pacing back and forth. "It was all such a shock. I realized when it happened that the only way to survive is to look out for number one. You can't count on anything, or anybody, in this world, and nothing beats money in the bank."

She wheeled and stopped, struck by a new idea, in front of a romantic painting of a young and luminous Romeo and Juliet embracing in a garden.

"Has she remarried?" Natasha demanded.

"I don't believe so," Burch said.

"Too bad, because if she killed Charles and has any assets, I could sue her, couldn't I? A wrongful death action?" Dead serious now, she had even stopped sneaking peeks at the stock quotes.

"That's something you'd have to discuss with your lawyer," Burch said.

Natasha didn't recall any other enemies or threats to Terrell, she said. There had been a small problem with the weight-reduction clinics. "An unfortunate incident. They went bankrupt to avoid a lawsuit. A woman on the program died suddenly. No proof the pills or the diet caused it. But there were children. The husband sued. You know how people are," Natasha said, "always after the fast buck."

Burch almost spit up his coffee. Was the woman familiar with the word *irony?*

She could not recall anything suspicious on the day Charles died, but took Burch's business card and said she'd call if she did.

"One more thing," Nazario said, as they stepped out the door. "The champagne you and Charles drank that last night. You said that was unusual for him. What did he usually drink?"

"Nothing. Charles rarely drank. The man was practically a teetotaler. He was a physical fitness freak. He might join everyone in a wedding toast or on New Year's Eve, but other than that, he never drank."

"Due to a health problem?"

"No. His personality. He was a control freak. He always had to be in full control of his faculties."

Still in the doorway, they watched a chauffeured limo roll sedately up the driveway.

"Here comes my husband now." Natasha smiled.

The uniformed driver opened the door for the lone occupant, a white-haired gentlemen who ambled up the front walk, using a cane.

The bridegroom was home from his doctor's appointment.

Milo Ross glanced up and waved. Then he disappeared into the garage, where an elevator apparently whisked him upstairs. Moments later he emerged from a side hall.

"Hello, sweetheart." She lifted her face for a kiss, which he dutifully planted on her cheek.

She introduced him to the detectives. The happy couple stood arm in arm in the doorway and watched them drive off.

The landscape truck was gone.

CHAPTER SEVEN

Nelson pounded the steering wheel in frustration as the big green truck bounced over the narrow bridge to his next job at Brickell Point. Those men were police. Were they checking up on Natasha for her rich old husband?

Was she in danger? She had not seemed upset or afraid. She had faced them, eyes flashing, bold and defiant. What *brío,* what fire and spirit in that woman. Although he did not understand the words she whispered, crooned, and sometimes cried out when they made love, he knew their meaning. He had never heard such words, but he knew they meant that they would be together. Love is a universal language.

He felt hurt at how abruptly he had been dismissed. When the old man died, they would be together. *Para siempre.* Forever. Perhaps sooner, if his plans worked out.

When trimming the hibiscus hedges at the Douglas Gardens Home for the Aged, he had first seen the physical therapists in their smocks and spotless white shoes caring for patients, leading them through their exercise and rehabilitation. The grateful patients fought through pain and weakness to please their therapists. A noble occupation. Something about it fascinated him. He knew now, more than ever, that he must pursue it. For a woman like Natasha, a man needed a profession with respect, one where he did not drive a truck that smelled of fertilizer and pesticide, where he did not always have dirt beneath his fingernails. She didn't seem to mind that, in fact she seemed to revel in it, but he knew if he had a more respectable profession she would look up to him. He had to work on his English. He had to do everything in his power to impress her. He imagined himself at the dinner table with her someday in that grand house on the water.

There were problems, of course. His wife, Lourdes, and the children, in their small apartment in Little Havana. He wished now that he had not paid the smuggler all that money to bring them to Miami from Cuba. It had taken all of his savings and more, and his business was still small, but growing. But how was he to know that this rich and beautiful *gringa* would fall in love with him? The ways of true love are unpredictable and never easy.

He was surprised at first that Natasha had stopped paying the monthly bills for his landscaping and lawn maintenance after they began having sex. But he understood it would not seem right to accept money from her now that they were lovers. And she had promised to recommend his work to wealthy friends. This new job, he believed, was entirely due to her recommendation. It proved she loved him and wanted him to succeed so they could be together. He might not have much money now but, he thought, I am a millionaire of love.

He arrived at the nearly finished forty-story luxury condominium apartment building, a towering shaft in a lush green park for which he was responsible. The posh two-story penthouses in the sky had sweeping spiral staircases, lofty rotundas, and private terraces that he would fashion into exotic tropical gardens. The San Souci Towers was nearly finished. Owners would move in within ninety days. The terrace gardens, with baby orchids and passion flowers in bloom, were to be ready for their arrival. He walked through the unfinished marble lobby, still thick with dust. Tarps and blue protective plastic shrouded the installations for the front desk, security, the valet staff and concierge. Heavy brown paper crisscrossed the lobby in paths, to protect the marble floors from the feet of the construction workers.

Nelson activated the high-speed elevator that whisked him to penthouse four. Security was so sophisticated that each resident would be issued a remote, a sensor programmed to open the elevator doors at their floor only. Without the remote the elevators would descend nonstop to the lobby. But going up, no door would open on any floor without the proper signal. Nelson had his own remote now, programmed to grant him access to the entire building for his work.

When the owners moved in, the remote had to be returned and all the codes and signals changed. Nelson was amazed that people lived like this. His own protection, his security, was the rusting .45 caliber automatic in his glove compartment. But someday he, too, would live like this, he and the beautiful Natasha. He had never had a woman like her before. She was all he thought about now, her silky skin, her bright green eyes, her elegance and passion. He wished he could pay the smugglers to spirit his wife and children back to Cuba, but he knew they would refuse to go. They liked Miami, its designer jeans, its television, and its supermarkets. Perhaps he could go to the man in Hialeah to see how much it would cost to smuggle his family back to the island, by force if necessary.

The smuggler was crossing the Florida Straits anyway, his boat empty until his return trip. Why not?

For every problem, he told himself, there is a solution. Nothing must stand in the way of true love.

CHAPTER EIGHT

The kayak skittered into the water like an eight-foot alligator splashing off a canal bank. K. C. Riley adjusted her life jacket, swung gracefully down the dockside ladder, and settled into the one-seater. She felt more comfortable on the water than anywhere else in this restless and mercurial city. Water welcomed her and soothed her soul. She had always been drawn to it. Even more so now. The ancient bay gleamed and glittered as though lit from within. She used to think she could see the future by gazing into its shadows, swirls, and reflections. Now all she saw was the past.

She paddled, inhaling deeply, swaying from side to side. Her favorite hours on the water were predusk and dawn. This late weekday summer afternoon meant fewer tourists, personal watercraft, and go-fast boats.

She let the rhythm of her movements block out the concerns and clutter of the job. Unruly cops, imminent budget cuts, and threats to her unit's very existence all paled beside the chief reason she'd fled the office.

Kathleen Constance Riley was accustomed to tragedy and sudden death in all its forms. She watched autopsies, had supervised the rape squad, and stood shoulder to shoulder with other cops on the front lines at riots and disasters. Trouble was her business, human sorrow part of the job. Her emotions had never betrayed her. Until now.

Even when she knew a victim personally, she took command, knew the immediate priorities. Saw what needed to be done and did it, wrapped in her own professional cloak of invincibility. That was her mission, her salvation. A woman on the job must reveal no weakness. No one had ever seen her cry.

But the graphic photos of a dead stranger had shaken her to the core. In her mind's eye, those charred remains had morphed into someone else, another life extinguished in a fiery burst of light. She took a deep breath. Out here she felt Kendall McDonald's presence more than anywhere.

Mirror-bright water reflected mountains of startlingly pink cumulonimbus clouds adrift across a golden horizon. She glided across the crystal-clear bay, propelled by gentle currents. Small fish darted in the shallow water, just a few feet deep. Her moving shadow interrupted a small brown nurse shark stalking its prey through swaying sea grass. The long, lethal tail of a startled stingray whipped the surface as the creature wheeled and fled at incredible speed.

Riley paddled a familiar route, alert for yachts, power boats, and Jet Skiers. She and McDonald had kayaked here often, murmuring to each other, laughing and joking, their voices carrying across the water.

They'd always skirt the shoreline in water too shallow for bigger boats so the reckless speed freaks would run aground before running over them. Sandy scars left by propellers were all too visible in the sea grass and coral. She carried a small air horn in the mesh pocket of her life jacket to warn off power boaters who came too close.

She cleared the island's east end, slightly out of breath and giddy with anticipation. There it was, their favorite landmark. Inexplicable tears stung her eyes. Towering against endless sky, it was a house never lived in, yet alive with ghosts. Their whispers swirled in the southeast breeze off the sea.

She had picnicked at the foot of Cape Florida's lighthouse as a child. She and Kendall McDonald had chased each other up and down its narrow staircase as youngsters. He'd painted their initials high on its brick exterior as a teenager. The letters remained intertwined there for years, until the lighthouse was cleaned up, the graffiti erased.

Tequesta Indians fished and hunted along the same sandy stretch thousands of years ago. The campfires of ancient tribesmen still flickered in her imagination. Juan Ponce de Léon explored this very beach during his sixteenth-century quest for the Fountain of Youth.

The infamous Black Caesar camped there later, followed by more pirates—"salvage" wreckers who torched huge bonfires to lure rich Spanish merchant ships onto the reefs, where they were swarmed, looted, and sunk.

Much later came the Secret Service, political entourages, and antiwar protesters. Riley and McDonald were still children when President Richard Nixon made Key Biscayne the site of his winter White House.

The President schemed with his aides, advisers, and banker buddy Bebe Rebozo on the same beach, pacing in the long-vanished footsteps of ancient Indians, explorers, pirates, thieves, and wreckers. All of them were gone now.

So was McDonald.

They had once investigated a murder here. A pair of lovers had sipped wine and reclined on a blanket beneath the towering silver-blue Australian pines, lulled by the sounds of the surf, within sight of the historic lighthouse.

The tryst ended badly, as so many do in Miami.

When he drowsed, she removed the pièce de résistance from her picnic basket: a .38 revolver. She shot him in the head at close range, then turned the gun on herself.

McDonald was then a homicide sergeant and Riley a rookie detective. She stood at that dreamy, seaside death scene, listened to an eerie wind whistle through the dark shadows of the pines, and thought that this was not a bad place to die.

"It's the first homicide we've had out here," a veteran, no-nonsense crime scene technician announced, glancing up from his clipboard.

In sync, as always, she and McDonald had exchanged knowing smiles. Wrong, McDonald told the tech, then explained a much older case.

Irate Indians had attacked the lighthouse 160 years earlier, at the outbreak of the second Seminole War. The lighthouse keeper and his assistant scrambled up into the tower, sawed away the wooden stairs, and barricaded themselves inside. The Indians tried to burn them out. Their fire ignited oil barrels stored in the tower's base. The heat of the flames forced the trapped men out onto a high narrow ledge that ringed the tower.

Indian sharpshooters killed the assistant. The lighthouse keeper was wounded twice. Believing it to be his final act on earth, he hurled a keg of gunpowder down into the fiery shaft, hoping to take a few Indians with him.

To his surprise, he survived. Many of the Indians didn't. The gigantic explosion generated outward, extinguishing the flames. The surviving Indians fled, some on fire and screaming.

The crew of a passing schooner miles out at sea heard the explosion and rescued the lighthouse keeper a day later.

Like the other doomed lovers, K. C. Riley and McDonald would often lie on the soft needle beds beneath the silver-tipped pines. They talked about the lighthouse keeper, swearing his spirit still survived on Miami's steamy and unpredictable streets. Residents made that clear during the record-breaking crime wave of the eighties. Miamians, always an unruly bunch, fought back with axes, knives, baseball bats, guns, and machetes. Furious and fed up with crime, they took no prisoners. They killed more criminals than the police.

Sometimes street justice is the only true justice.

K. C. Riley's small craft bobbed in the surf as she gazed at the lighthouse, the beach, and the state park beyond. The huge pines were gone, all fallen like jackstraws to Hurricane Andrew in '92. Apartment and office towers rise, trees and presidents fall; only the lighthouse had withstood time, angry seas, hungry tides, and half a hundred hurricanes since 1900. The lone constant, she thought, a nail holding past and future together in an ever-changing city that forgets people and its own history too quickly. Daydreams of the past are a comfort when the present is painful and there is no future.

The wind freshened. Lightning pirouetted like a drunken ballerina across purpling clouds and a sky the color of regret. The sun sank as though controlled by a dimmer switch, and she knew she'd lingered too long.

"Did you know you made me stronger and better?" she cried. He had to hear her. But her only answer was the rumble of thunder and a series of wild, threatening lightning strikes. She clipped her safety light to her vest and pushed the button. The small red flasher pulsated like a heartbeat as she turned back, paddling against the changing current as the wind grew stronger. At home in flatwater canoes and whitewater kayaks, she felt no fear. Gritting her teeth and grunting, she dug deep with the paddle, barely able to maintain forward motion for the first hundred yards. The wind showed no signs of switching direction.

Dark anvil-shaped clouds roiled toward her. Paddling furiously, she winced at a blinding lightning strike nearby. Cracks of thunder like rifle shots split the sky. The heavens rumbled and crashed in deafening crescendos as through the gods were scoring simultaneous strikes in a giant bowling alley.

"I dare you," she screamed into the wind. "Do it! I don't care. Take me!"

The wind shrieked back, but she couldn't make out the words.

Rain pelted her face, mingling with tears as the boat ramp came into sight.

She struggled hand-over-hand up the ladder against a drenching downpour. She pushed her hair out of her eyes, dragged the forty-five-pound kayak up onto the dock, then wrestled it onto the car rack. She secured it and collapsed, breathless, in the front seat. Soaked and shivering, she wished she had a drink.

Rain cascaded like Victoria Falls down the windshield of the Rodeo as she slowly drove home, the visibility nearly zero. She sprinted to the front door, slipping and skidding on wet grass and mud. As she fumbled with the key, a tall, hooded shadow loomed suddenly among the hanging spider plants on the rain-slick patio and rushed toward her. Riley wheeled, startled, mind flashing on the gun still beneath her car seat.

"What the fuck?"

"Hey! It's me. Where the hell have you been? Poor Hooker has been barking her brains out."

Riley gasped, hand over her heart, heavy rain pelting her face. "What the hell are you doing out here?"

"Stop answering questions with questions," Jo Salazar yelped. "I hate it when you do that. Open the damn door. It's wet out here."

The women burst into the living room, dripping water. Hooker, McDonald's old hound dog, stood hopefully in their path, tail wagging expectantly, staring beyond them, out into the rainy night.

"No," Riley said bitterly. "He's not coming."

Rain streamed from her hair as she stepped to the liquor cabinet, an ornate old sideboard inherited from her grandmother, found a half-full bottle of vodka, and splashed some into a tumbler. She swallowed, eyes closed.

"What?" she croaked, opening them to Jo's solemn gaze. "This stuff gets the citizens of Moscow through cold Russian winters."

"This is a hot Miami summer." Jo shook her head, her big eyes shiny.

Riley ignored her and focused on the dog still standing stiff-legged near the door. "She always does that," she said bleakly.

"It takes a while," Jo said softly. She yanked off the hooded rain jacket she wore over a halter top and blue jeans. "They were together a long time."

"Yeah, right."

Silence hung between them, more pained than awkward.

"Let me go hang this in the bathroom," Jo said.

Riley poured another drink before letting the dog out into the back-yard. Hooker plodded stoically into the downpour, which showed no signs of letting up.

Jo returned, curly brown hair tousled, a bath towel around her neck. She tossed another towel to Riley.

"Dry yourself off at least. You look like a drowned rat." Tall and stat-uesque, with broad shoulders and hips created for childbearing, she crossed her arms like a angry parent. "Where the hell were you?"

"Took the kayak out on the bay."

"Smart move. I was afraid of that when I didn't see it here. Don't you check the weather anymore? My NOAA radio was broadcasting thunder-storm alerts all afternoon."

"It's summer in Miami, Jo. You just said so yourself. Thunderstorms are forecast every afternoon."

"You're lucky you're not a fried, drowned rat sleeping with the fishes."

"What are you drinking?" Riley sounded exhausted as she dried her face and hair.

"The usual," Jo chirped. "You got Earl Gray?" She stepped into the galley kitchen, put the kettle on the gas stove, opened a cupboard, and rummaged familiarly for the tea bags.

"I was worried," she said. "I called the station and they said you weren't working."

"Who'd you talk to?"

"Burch, the sergeant."

"Wonder why he was still there?"

"Didn't ask." Jo took two mugs down from a shelf.

"So what are you doing here? Who's watching the kids?"

"Their dad—it's Ricky's turn for a change. He's making corn dogs. They were looking forward to it."

"You want some dry clothes?" Riley pulled her drenched T-shirt over her head. Her bra was soaked, too.

"Your stuff is all too small for big healthy girls like me. By the way, have you lost weight?"

Riley shrugged, went to her bedroom, stepped out of her soggy shorts and panties, and donned a short terry-cloth robe.

"Come on, Kath. You okay?"

"Sure, never better. Not."

"You should have taken time off."

"I didn't think it would be this hard." Riley sat barefoot on the sofa, head in her hands. "I did a really stupid thing. The guys must think I'm nuts. We had a walk-in, a woman who thinks her ex-husband's death twelve years ago was no accident, that it was murder."

"So?"

"He died in a flash fire, burned beyond recognition." Riley's words were barely audible.

Jo winced and took a deep breath.

"I immediately jumped on it, ordered the guys to chase it, top priority. It's not even a homicide. It's classified as an accident. But you know who I saw when I looked at the scene pictures. They freaked me out. The guys are really pissed."

"They'll get over it. It's no big deal to check out."

"It's not fair to them. They have more important, real cases to work. They always thought I was a bitch. Now they think I'm a crazy bitch."

"So just be upfront. Say you reread the file, rethought it, and they can drop it. You're the boss, remember?"

"Maybe you're right. Stone would appreciate it. He's hot on an important case."

The teakettle whistled.

"None for me," she said, as Jo poured. Riley reached for the vodka.

"Did you eat today?" Jo deliberately poured a second cup. "Want me to fix you something?"

"No, I couldn't. I had a big lunch," Riley lied, and sipped her drink.

"Jesus, Kathy, you never used to drink alone."

"I'm not alone. You're here."

"Take some vacation time. Go away for a while."

Riley snorted. "There wouldn't be a Cold Case Squad when I came back. With all the budget cuts they're looking at, we're expendable. I have to fight for our survival every day."

"Same thing in our office," Jo said. "Sometimes I wish I was still a cop. Remember the fun we had in the academy?"

"What are you talking about, girlfriend? We were miserable, bruised, banged up, and exhausted. Remember how you almost drowned during the underwater swimming test?"

"Yeah, but it was exciting, and we made it." Jo's eyes sparkled. "We kicked ass, kid. We showed 'em all."

"Who'da thought they'd turn out to be the good old days?"

"Well, I ain't having much fun now. We've got a hiring freeze, no raises, no support from Alexander the not-so-great, and you wouldn't believe my caseload."

"How is your boss, the state attorney, these days?"

"Still an ignoranus, both stupid and an asshole."

"He keeps fucking with my detectives. He hates cold cases."

"And he's not exactly crazy about you. The man takes rejection poorly."

"He can't still hold it against me, not after all these years. He just wants every case on a silver platter, tied up in red ribbon, with a smoking gun and a signed confession. It's too risky for his record to take on old cases with witnesses who have died or forgotten and outmoded evidence-gathering methods the defense can target. The man's got no *cojones.*"

"What do you expect from a damn politician? He's hung up on his conviction rate and the next election. He has his eye on higher office. And the public doesn't give a rat's ass. We're not important anymore because the crime rate has dipped," Jo said. "Sociologists do studies trying to figure out why. Politicians brag and hog the credit, when we're the ones who really helped make it happen.

"You arrest them. I prosecute them and they ship out to the Graybar Motel. That's why the crime rate is down, because we've got more than a million scumbags behind bars, the biggest prison population in U.S. history. Ten percent of the people commit ninety percent of the crime; lock up that ten percent or close to it and voilà, the crime rate declines. Duh. No mystery there." She reached into the refrigerator, sniffed a bottle, then wheeled, her expression accusatory.

"Yuck! Kathy, the milk is sour. Damn. Can't I come over here and drink tea with milk and sugar like a civilized person?"

Riley put down her drink, leaned forward, and covered her eyes.

"Okay, okay, Kath. I'll rough it, go commando, do without. You don't have to cry about it."

She knelt next to her friend and put her arm around her shoulder. Riley leaned on her and wept.

"It's my fault." Her voice trembled. "He's dead, and it's my fault."

"You *are* a crazy bitch. You had nothing to do with it, sweetheart."

"That's the point, I did nothing. I didn't fight for him. When he told me he was in love with that reporter, I was so sure it wouldn't work that I told him to go for it if he felt that way. And he did. I was so stupid," she said miserably. "I took the high road, thought it was best, that we'd be closer when he came back. See, I was in it for the long haul. Worst-case scenario, I'd still be his friend, which was better than nothing.

"But I was so sure he'd come to his senses, that he'd be back, I let him go. I was so stupid."

"But, honey, you had no choice. You can't make somebody love you. All the stalkers in jail can attest to that."

"You can try. I should have raised holy hell, tried talking him out of it, told him all the reasons why it wouldn't work. I could have thrown myself at him, plied him with sex till he was too exhausted to even remember her name. Jo, it works for some people. I mighta pulled it off. Instead, I caved to my pride, didn't want to embarrass myself, told myself that we were meant to be, sooner or later it would happen. I counted on it. Who knew there'd be no later because the damn reporter had a friend with a crazy ex-husband?

"He wouldn't have been with her, at the wrong place at the wrong time, if I had cried, argued, fallen on the floor, and clung to his goddamn ankles, for God's sake, he'd be alive."

"Where the hell is the reporter?" Jo muttered. "Haven't seen her byline in the paper lately."

Riley shrugged. "Out of town, I guess."

"Duh. Somebody had the sense to take time off. I know it had to be tough to lose him to a reporter, the way you've always felt about them."

"Funny." Riley wiped her eyes. "I don't hate her. Wish I could. She's stubborn, hardheaded, but not a bad person when you get to know her. And she's miserable. She lost him, too, except I had a lot more invested, since second grade. I wish I could hate the man responsible, but he's dead. I wish to hell I had somebody to hate. But I don't. I just hate myself—and the city for how they've treated him.

"This year's nominations for the silver medal of valor and the gold medal of courage were posted yesterday. His name wasn't there, Jo. A fucking major on the fast track for chief, a dead hero, but they ignored him because it happened off duty and he didn't go by the book. He didn't even have a full honor guard at his funeral. That's not right. I can't stop thinking about it. Sometimes, in meetings with the brass, I just want to start screaming."

"Not a good career move, kid."

"But a violent ex-convict, high on drugs, snatches his six-year-old kid, beats up his ex-wife and his own mother, barricades himself in his mother's house, and holds the kid hostage. The kid is screaming, the father's splashing gasoline, threatening to ignite it. The place is full of fumes. He's flicking a cigarette lighter. The house could go up in a heartbeat. Kenny knew if he went by the book and waited for fire, SWAT, a hostage negotiating team, and the domestic violence unit, they'd be too late. No way the cavalry could arrive in time. So off duty, unarmed, he gives it his best shot to get that little boy out alive."

"And he did, sweetie. He did." Jo sighed. She'd heard it all before, too many times. She listened again.

"The kid said Kenny Mac threw him out the front door and yelled for him to run. He did, and a few seconds later, the whole place explodes. It kills the worthless piece of shit who started it and the only man I ever loved. Why?"

"Every life has its purpose, Kath. It's not something we can ever understand. But maybe in his life, at that moment, he'd accomplished what he was here to do.

"It's a circle. Life is a continuum. The soul is all that's permanent. Death is a rebirth. Leaves and birds come back, so does the soul. We all have a life cycle. It's nature, part of the universe, part of everything around us. The billions of stars out there, they're born and they die. In fact"—she cocked her head—"I read that astronomers see more stars dying now and fewer being born. Which means that the universe is going dark."

Riley sighed. "Thank you very much. If this is your inspirational spiel for grieving witnesses in your homicide cases, it needs work. I'd leave out that last bit if I were you." She wiped her face on her towel.

"Sorry, I digressed," Jo said, "but what I meant to say is that grieving is for us, not him. He's going forward. Staying positive will help his soul to move on."

"Bullshit, Jo. Don't try to sell me that crap, I won't even rent it. You know his name belongs on that plaque in the lobby with all the others killed in the line of duty."

"It's not important." Jo shrugged. "He didn't do what he did for recognition. He did it for all the right reasons. Maybe that was his reason for being."

"You mean his sole purpose in life was to rescue a little kid who's probably destined to wind up a bad, sad, dead druggie, like his dad?"

"We're not here to judge. That's for God on Judgment Day. Maybe that little child was saved for a reason."

"I wish," Riley said bleakly.

Hooker scratched at the back door and Jo let her in. The old dog shook herself, spraying her with water before docilely submitting to her towel. "Whose good ol' dog are you?" she crooned, as she wiped her paws and rough-dried her coat.

Riley watched, eyes pained.

"Maybe we can find her a good home," Jo offered. "I can ask around the office."

"No way."

"But every time you see her . . ."

"Kenny found her injured, lying in the fast lane up in hooker heaven, on the boulevard around Seventy-ninth Street, when he was working vice. She looked dead. Dirty and skinny, bleeding from the mouth, couldn't walk, had no tag. They wanted to call animal control. He scooped her up in his raincoat, put her in the back of his patrol car, and took her to a vet. He could have been in trouble for leaving his zone, but he did it anyway. Hooker is all I have left."

"Okay, okay. But if it's too hard, if you change your mind, let me know. I'm just trying to help."

"I know you are."

She walked Jo to her car, parked out on the street. The rain had stopped.

"I promised Ricky I'd be back by midnight. But I wish I could stay over. You worry me, Kath. I hate seeing you so depressed."

"I worry myself. Because you're wrong. I'm not depressed. I'm angry. I'm so angry, so filled with rage, that sometimes I'm afraid I'll kill somebody."

"Time to see the department shrink?"

"Sure. How swell would that look on my resume?"

"I'll call you tomorrow. Take care, Kath."

Riley hugged her friend and watched her drive away. She lingered, staring at the sky.

"They're right," she murmured to the old dog beside her. "The universe is going dark."

CHAPTER NINE

The chief stepped gingerly into his office, wincing as he eased into the chair behind his desk. Only 8:30 A.M. and his head throbbed. After words with Mildred, he'd stormed out of the house forgetting his sunglasses. The white heat of Miami's morning sun on the drive to headquarters had triggered a jackhammer behind his eyes. He cautiously touched an eyelid, certain that his retinas were blistered.

He was acutely aware that he was the fourth chief in three years. One went to prison, another was fired in disgrace, a third forced to resign. Neither his present nor his future appeared bright. So far his entire administration appeared to be a slow-motion train wreck. His solicitous aide brought coffee as the chief vaguely wondered why his command staff and aides were all men. Probably something to do with the ill-fated romance of one of his predecessors. The woman had worked at police headquarters but was married unfortunately—to a convicted drug dealer. The press had a party with that one.

He forced open a watery eye. José, his young aide, stood poised, eagerly awaiting orders, like a faithful K-9. If the boy had a tail, it would be wagging. The chief had him close the blinds, quickly, to block out the blinding sunlight and the towering steel and mirrored skyline of the city that mocked him. Then he sent José for an Alka-Seltzer. Aspirin would upset his stomach. The chief wished fervently for something stronger, some happy pill, some psychotropic drug.

He'd heard about Miami's corruption, violence, and banana republic when offered the job.

But he felt strong, vital, and still young. Three years of sterling service would enhance his resume, paving the way for his entry into the private sector as a highly paid consultant and expert witness. He had retired from the top job in Milwaukee in his early fifties, his reputation relatively intact. At least nobody had anything he could be indicted for. Ready to conquer new worlds, he felt invincible, convinced he had what it took for the job.

Most important, he had what it took to be accepted in this Hispanic city—*sangre hispana,* a trace of Hispanic blood in his heritage. His grandmother, bless her heart, after dumping her second husband, had fallen for a skinny, fiery-eyed, square-jawed flamenco dancer passing through on tour. The doomed union endured long enough to produce his father, who had changed his name from Diego Granados to Donald Green.

His son, foreseeing America's future, took back the Granados name upon entering law enforcement.

He owed his career advancement, the opportunities he'd enjoyed, and the position in which he now found himself all to the grandfather he never met, that son of a bitch, the flamenco dancer.

Bubbles from the Alka-Seltzer tickled his nose as he downed the drink.

Something afloat in the oppressively hot and humid Miami air had activated his allergies. He awoke that morning wheezing. Then he'd complained that all his boxer shorts were now pink. His wife showed no sympathy.

"I never promised to live in a foreign country," she said bitterly, apparently still upset after a bad experience the day before.

Mildred grew up in Muncie, Indiana, and was having adjustment problems. She had called him hysterically from her cell phone, hopelessly lost while driving. No one on the street, not even a letter carrier, spoke enough English to help.

The woman had no sense of direction. He had explained Miami's grid system to her a dozen times. "Think of St. Louis," he'd said. "STL: streets, terraces, and lanes all run east and west. Then remember CPA: courts, places, and avenues. They go north and south. Simple."

But it was not simple. Demented city planners, brains fried by the sun or too many Cuba Libres, allowed for too many exceptions. There were all the dead ends at waterways, canals, railroad tracks, and the bay. There were too few through streets, the confusing distinctions between SE, SW, NE, and NW, and the fact that most Miami roadways have at least three names. Street signs use only one. The name on the sign almost never matched the one on the road maps.

Her call had caught him in a crucial meeting with the mayor and city manager, huddled at a table in a dark corner of a Cuban restaurant in Little Havana. Both his bosses puffed thick black cigars. Bloated by the heavily spiced food, sinuses clogged by his allergies and the acrid cigar smoke, the chief had made the fatal mistake of answering his cell phone.

He tried to smile casually at his macho bosses while listening to his wife sob.

"Now try to remember," he said patiently. "What did I tell you about St. Louis and CPA?"

He was certain they heard her scream. "Don't you patronize me, you son of a bitch!"

He kept calm.

"Okay, sweetheart, let's figure this out. Tell me the name of the street you're on right now."

"General Maximo Perez Way."

· · ·

"Staff meeting in twenty minutes." José's pitted face peered around the door jamb. For God's sake, the chief thought, the boy suffers from terminal acne. "Alexander Rodriguez, the state attorney, will be there."

Son of a bitch, the chief thought, and licked the Alka-Seltzer's salty residue from his lips.

"Call Joe Padron," he told José. "Make sure he's coming."

Padron, their best public information officer, could put a positive spin on anything. Cops could rape and pillage, and Padron could somehow portray them as heroes. He could compose press releases that kept facts murky, revealing nothing, yet the newshounds blindly accepted them. The man had a talent.

José returned moments later. "Padron is out at a scene. Sixty-five-year-old lady and her four-year-old granddaughter shot in the cross-fire outside Miami Senior High. Our second school shooting this week."

"School hasn't opened yet."

"Right," José said. "They're in summer session."

The chief frowned and dreaded September.

"Fuck the old lady and the kid," he shouted, head throbbing. "Get Padron's ass in here now!"

The budget was giving him fits. Every time unsubstantiated intelligence warned that terrorists had targeted Miami, he was forced to boost the department's alert from yellow to orange. Each day on orange alert cost $5,000 in overtime for officers assigned to protect high-profile facilities, including the homes of the mayor and the city manager.

The publicity always generated new threats, a vicious circle.

The rank and file were close to mutiny because of the *Miami News* and their goddamn investigative piece exposing the practice of allowing police officers to drive their patrol cars home. The story had revealed the huge cost. Taxpayer groups were raising hell. The police union had won the take-home car perk, including free gas and maintenance, years ago. Patrol cars parked in officers' driveways in residential areas would be deterrents and keep the neighborhoods safer. That was the premise. Unfortunately, as the goddamn *News* revealed, most cops refuse to live in crime-ridden Miami, America's poorest city. So they commute in city cars to their homes in more affluent neighboring counties. The chief himself did not know until he read it in the newspaper that some of his officers lived as far as a hundred miles outside city limits, or that the soaring number of city cars involved in out-of-county traffic accidents was costing big bucks in injuries, damages, and lawsuits.

Disgruntled cops and their unions would go to war if he tried to eliminate take-home cars. Once given, no perk can be taken away.

Why did the blunders of prior administrations come back to bite him? And if the crime rate was down among civilians, why the hell was it accelerating among cops?

Alex Rodriguez would be at today's staff meeting to discuss cooperation in the prosecution of the latest gaggle of street cops charged with planting throw-down guns beside people they'd shot. Others had recently been arrested for stealing drugs and money from evidence, beating hapless civilians, and extorting sex from women motorists.

Other behavior, not criminal but just plain stupid, continued to generate negative headlines. Wrong house raids, the pepper spraying of tourists, and the one-legged suspect who outhopped half a dozen officers and got away.

Couldn't they make him look good? Just once?

So far his prospects for a lucrative career as a consultant and expert witness, in demand as a talking head on Greta Van Susteren, CNN, and MSNBC, were looking less and less likely.

He sighed. If only it wasn't for the damn police impersonators, home invasion robbers wearing uniforms, handcuffs, and police paraphernalia bought from the same businesses that supplied the department. Some even bought surplus patrol cars. Distinguishing the real police officers from those who were not was impossible, except that the impersonators seemed better organized.

He knew what would make him feel better, at least for a few hours. He missed Bunny. The last time his mistress had flown into town for a weekend, she had left furious after spending most of their long-planned tryst alone at their Miami Beach hideaway. Something Fidel said on Havana radio had set off impromptu civil disturbances in Miami, and the chief had spent the entire weekend pounding steamy pavement trying to placate the mayor, the city manager, the press, irate residents struck in traffic, and rabid city commissioners who further agitated the demonstrators.

Why blockade expressway toll booths and Miami intersections to protest something said in Havana? Why couldn't police apply a little attitude adjustment, then lock them up? Instead the offenders were considered patriots whose arrests would be politically incorrect.

"I never promised to live in a foreign country." His wife's words echoed through his throbbing skull. None of their neighbors spoke English, and the social functions they attended were all with Hispanic city officials and politicians.

Not easy for her, but what about him? He thought he'd seen it all, but crime was different here.

The latest trend was "the unlicensed practitioner." Unlicensed lawyers, contractors, doctors, dentists, and plastic surgeons all practicing chosen professions in which they were untrained. Self-described gynecologists conducting examinations on kitchen tables, plastic surgeons operating in cheap motel rooms. Why in God's name did patients go to a dentist who performed root canals in his garage?

In a raid last weekend his officers had arrested dozens of "dentists" caught taking dental impressions in the backseats of cars outside flea markets.

He blew his nose and wondered if Cuban coffee was a hallucinogen.

He shivered. The worst case was that of a woman who wanted a firmer, rounder butt. Her "plastic surgeon" injected her with silicone in a motel room. Unfortunately, it was the sort of silicone used to caulk bathtubs. She died and the prosecution called it murder.

"They're here," José announced.

The chief stepped into his private bathroom, splashed cold water on his face, dried it, and adjusted his cuffs. He preferred a business suit to a uniform, unlike one predecessor who had designed his own, heavy on the gold braid, with triple rows of medals, topped off by a tricornered Napoléon-like hat.

Chief Granados strode confidently into the conference room, pleased to see Padron present, his pen and yellow legal pad in front of him on the polished conference table.

There were several assistant chiefs and a dozen other men and women in uniform already seated. So was State Attorney Alex Rodriguez. He looked absolutely Kennedyesque, with his classic profile, prematurely silver hair, custom-made suit, and red silk tie.

Riley, the Cold Case lieutenant, arrived a moment after he did. She looked fit, tanned, and as sleek as a Thoroughbred, with not an extra ounce of weight on her athletic frame. Best-looking woman in the room, the chief thought, but always all business.

What would these people think, he wondered, if they knew he was wearing pink briefs? It would be all over for him in this macho, testosterone-fueled department. He would never live it down. What if a sniper chose today to pick him off? Another good reason not to wear a uniform. It was like wearing a target. What if he stumbled in the lobby and smashed a kneecap? Paramedics would cut away his trousers in front of the troops. With his bad luck, he'd survive.

He greeted the upturned faces, thinking he'd call and ask Mildred to pick up a dozen pair of the silky jockey shorts he liked. Remembering her last words that morning, he decided to buy them himself on the way home. He simply had to make it through the day without a major injury. Murphy's law worried him. What were his odds? Why were his briefs pink? Had Mildred done it deliberately? Did she suspect he was cheating?

"How are the shooting victims, Joe?"

"The kid?" He pointed thumbs down. "The grandmother?" He waggled his hand. "Might make it."

"Outrageous." The chief's square jaw jutted in indignation. "I want all our resources on this. Hopefully our people can effect a quick arrest and bring the family closure to this tragic situation." He hoped it would be in time to broadcast the perp walk on the news at eleven.

Rodriguez gave his usual status report on cooperation between the department and his office and the number of cases pending. He also named the members of his staff assigned to prosecute the throw-down cops.

The chief promised his "full support."

The state attorney saluted all and rose to leave. His eyes swept the room, lingering on K. C. Riley, who ignored him.

"The T word is killing us," said the chief, as he opened their preliminary budget discussions.

Rodriguez paused at the door. The chief wondered where the state attorney had his hair cut. The silver fox had to be aiming for higher office.

"In times like these, Chief, if you don't mind the suggestion. You have to be brutal. If this was my department, I'd pare down or eliminate specialized squads that don't produce major results. Redistributing the manpower will make the most of your resources."

Riley stiffened in her chair.

"I've said that all along," agreed Hector Diaz, the major in charge of SIS, the strategic information section.

Here it comes, Riley thought. Diaz, you fat pig, you son of a bitch. Your unit is secure because Miami's politicians need spies to compile intelligence on their rivals. Jo Salazar was right. Alex still had a hard-on for her.

She lifted her chin, smiling serenely, glad she'd worn her navy blue power blazer with the Brooks Brothers pinstriped shirt that cost too much.

"If you mean my unit," she said pleasantly, "that would be a serious mistake. The department hasn't had many success stories lately. You may recall the Sunday *News* magazine piece that featured the Cold Case Squad. We had nothing but positive reactions. The public appreciates that no victim is forgotten, that no killer can ever stop looking over his shoulder. They like knowing that, sooner or later, justice can and will prevail.

"We're just four detectives and a sergeant, no significant manpower drain. And they are the best at what they do. Dead files speak to them. If an old, cold murder case has even a faint pulse, they can detect it. They get into the minds of people they've never even met and do it better than anybody. Departments around the country have modeled similar units after ours. If anything, our team deserves more recognition and support."

"Maybe I'm missing something," Rodriguez said smoothly. "I'm unaware of any prosecutable cases brought to my office by your detectives recently. Is there something I don't know about?"

"Yes," Riley said, eyes cold.

The chief tugged at his chin. Was that stubble? He had just shaved, for God's sake. What was it those *Queer Eye* guys on TV said: A clean, close shave makes it look like a man is at least trying. What was the other thing? Something about ear hair. His right hand moved involuntarily to check.

"Well put, Lieutenant." The chief tugged thoughtfully on his earlobe. "But our current budgetary constraints—"

"The department is in woeful need of good press," she said quickly. "Good *national* press. My detectives are making headway on a major case."

Every face in the room looked expectant.

"You may remember that Detective Stone was temporarily detached to work with an FBI task force on murders that he was able to link as the work of an unidentified serial killer?"

"That task force was abandoned some time ago," Rodriguez said impatiently, "due to a priority we all face, specifically national security."

Riley ignored him and spoke directly to the chief. "Detective Stone has continued to pursue the cases and has uncovered new leads missed by the FBI. If we nail this case, we'll be closing homicides in seven other states across the nation."

Padron scribbled notes. "Stone," he said, looking up. "Isn't he the black guy?"

"Right," Riley said. "An excellent detective who grew up here, just a few blocks away. Proof that something good can come out of Overtown."

"Great story," Padron crowed. "A minority hometown boy. I can sell that. Yeah. Ya got a composite of the killer? The press eats that stuff up. It'll take some of the heat off the arrest stories."

The chief brightened.

Riley backed off. "I don't think we're ready to go public. We don't want to tip off the suspect."

"What's to tip? He knows he's been killing people for years," Padron said. "Could be time to go public. Ask them for tips. Can't hurt. The victims are elderly, right? The most vulnerable among us. Everybody's got a mother or a grandmother. It'll give potential victims a heads-up. It'll make the news in every city where this guy has killed. We'd have national coverage."

"Joe might have something there," the chief said.

"Reporters love serial killer stories," Padron said. "Our lone, homegrown detective, hot on the trail. I like it. I like it."

The state attorney checked his watch and frowned. "Odd that I'm unaware of it. You have been coordinating this case with an ASA, haven't you, Lieutenant? That is standard operating procedure."

"Of course," Riley said. "Assistant State Attorney Jo Salazar."

Rodriguez spun out of the room without another word.

"Salazar," Major Kelly, the vice commander, said. "She's good." The others nodded.

"We should schedule a news conference," the chief said.

"The sooner the better," Padron added.

Riley bit her lip. "I'll speak to the detective."

She smiled confidently at the chief and promised to get back to Padron within the hour.

She kept smiling until the elevator door closed behind her.

"Oh, shit," she muttered. "Shit, shit, shit."

CHAPTER TEN

K. C. Riley bolted from the elevator punching the buttons on her cell phone. Out in the open the cellular signals flew free and connected. "Come on, come on," she pleaded as it rang. "Answer, answer, answer!"

. . .

As she paced the courtroom of Circuit Court Judge Ellen Featherstone, indignantly arguing against bond for an HVO, a habitual violent offender, Jo Salazar felt her belly jiggle.

Before realizing it was her cell phone on vibrate, she assumed the sensation was bad vibes emanating from the defendant. He leaned forward, watching her intently, wearing the same weaselly expression as her seven-year-old daughter's pet ferret. Not fair, she thought. The ferret was more trustworthy and honest.

As the judge studied a defense motion before her, Jo surreptitiously checked the tiny phone clipped to her waistband. She recognized the number. The message: 911.

Almost instantly, it vibrated again. She recognized a second number. Her boss. Same message.

What new hells were these? Could they be related?

She returned to the prosecution table, unclipped the phone, and slipped it into her open briefcase, unseen.

"I have another point of law here, your honor." She peered into the yawning briefcase as though in search of a document. Her gold bracelets jangled as she pretended to rifle through files, while actually punching in Tom Morgan's beeper number. She prayed that Morgan, like her, ignored the judge's hard-and-fast rule that during appearances in her courtroom, all attorneys were to turn off their beepers and cell phones.

Assistant Public Defender Morgan sat alert and protective at his client's side. Not too close, however. His client, accused of kidnaping, assault, and sexual battery, was subject to sudden violent outbursts, and even his own lawyer, though he would never admit it, was afraid of him.

Studious and dedicated, Morgan blinked innocently through his owlish glasses, hands folded in front of him, waiting to object to Salazar's new point of law—if she ever found it. The ferret smiled at the prosecutor's obvious disorganization.

Morgan was ready to fight to the death to free his client on bond. If only he could succeed, he would probably never have to see the man again. He would surely flee the jurisdiction, probably back to his native Honduras.

"I'm sorry, your honor," Salazar said, clearly embarrassed. "I seem to have misplaced that particular document, but in truth it isn't necessary in order to establish that the defendant is a definite flight risk and a danger to the community. Under Florida Statute 775.084, he faces a minimum mandatory of fifteen years." Her hand snaked back into the briefcase and pushed the SEND button.

As Salazar approached the bench to continue her argument, a chair suddenly scraped back. A flurry of movement began behind her.

Morgan, no longer calm and patient, had leaped to his feet. He approached the bench, eyes wide and anxious behind the thick glass in his spectacles.

"Your honor, your honor. I beg the court's indulgence. I'd like to request a brief recess. It's an emergency."

Jo Salazar turned, mouth open in surprise at the interruption.

"Mis-ter Morgan." The judge leaned forward to scrutinize him, eyes narrowed. "Are you in violation of my strict policy on electronic devices? Must I remind you again that when you appear before me, *I* am your only emergency." She placed her right hand over her ample bosom. Her words speeded up, increasing in volume as she spoke. "I demand your full and total attention. How do you think I could possibly manage my caseload and this courtroom if every lawyer, defendant, and witness who appears before me is granted time to conduct their social, personal, and business lives on cell phones and beepers, leaving me to await their pleasure?"

"No, your honor. I apologize, your honor. I apologize." Morgan babbled frantically. "Just this one time, I promise. Please. Your honor?"

"Five minutes," the judge snapped.

The public defender babbled in gratitude as he backpedaled hastily toward the door.

Her honor glanced at Salazar, who shrugged sympathetically. The new crop of young lawyers could be so totally rude and self-absorbed.

The judge swept imperiously off the bench, secretly pleased because she had to pee anyway.

Jo Salazar made her way to the far end of the crowded corridor that resembled a teeming street in Calcutta. No question which 911 call she would answer first.

"Hey, what's going on? I was in a bond hearing in front of Featherstone."

"Jo, thank God." Riley hunched over the phone in her office. "Have you talked to your boss?"

"He called when you did."

"Did you talk to him?"

"What do you think? Duh? I called you first. What's going on? Spit it out, I have to be back in court in four, no, three minutes."

"I need a huge favor. Alex was at our staff meeting this morning. I'll explain later. Something came up. Remember the serial killings that Stone connected last year?"

"The one where the FBI assembled the task force?"

"Right."

"I mentioned some progress in the case. He wanted to know who we've been coordinating with in your office."

"Oh, shit."

"Sorry. I threw in your name. Had to. You're the only one who'd back me up. Stone hasn't got anything tangible enough to share with an ASA. He just noted some similarities in the crime scenes that may lead to future clues about the killer's identity—that's it, nothing concrete."

"Still, Alex is gonna be pissed that I didn't keep him informed. You know how he likes to be kept in the loop, especially when it comes to your unit."

"Say it's still vague, but might hold some promise, that you told Stone to come back when he had something more concrete."

"I'll cover you."

"Thanks, Jo. You were right. I'll tell the guys to drop that Terrell thing I forced on them. And you were on the mark about Alex. He's out to get me and my unit."

"Brought it on yourself, kid. A few little tumbles in the sack, the ignoranus probably would've found himself a new obsession. But oh, no, you had to smack him down and kick him to the curb. See what happens when you have scruples?"

"Who knew he'd turn out to be the most powerful man in Miami–Dade County?"

"And he never guessed you'd turn out to be who you are. He's forgetting the cardinal rule for an ambitious man: Be nice to people on the way up, because you'll meet them again on the way down. He'll get his."

"Hope we live to see it."

Jo called her boss. "You rang, sir?" she chirped cheerfully. "I was trapped in Featherstone's court and couldn't get out—you know her policy."

She assured him that there had been no major legal questions in Stone's case, promised to keep him informed, and hurried back to courtroom 12.

Tom Morgan stood outside.

"Everything okay, Tom?" she asked, concern in her voice. "Is it time?"

He shook his head, bewildered.

"It was a nine-one-one message to call home, but it must have been a mistake. A wrong number."

"Don't worry." She patted his shoulder. "It has to be any minute now. What is she, nine and a half months' pregnant? Tell Marie I said to hang in there, the first one never arrives on schedule. We better get back inside before the judge does or she'll hold us both in contempt."

The ferret snarled out loud when he saw his attorney and the prosecutor smiling and chatting together as they walked back into the courtroom.

CHAPTER ELEVEN

Burch rode in the tow truck taking his Blazer to Downtown Automotive. Nazario picked him up.

"Damnedest thing. It stopped dead at the causeway toll booth," Burch said, "like it was outta gas, but I still had half a tank.

"Almost had to arrest the son of a bitch behind me. An SOB in an SUV. Talk about road rage. Didn't back off till I flashed my badge. I'm sick of this shit. It was hot as hell out there."

"Think your true love struck again?" Nazario asked, as they hurtled south on North Miami Avenue in an unmarked Homicide unit.

Burch glared. "Nah. These things happen. Cars crap out. Shit happens. Jesus, be careful!"

Face placid, one elbow out the window, Nazario veered out of the path of a lumbering Metro bus.

"Slow down, will ya? What the hell's the matter with you?"

"Don't worry, Sarge." Nazario sounded hurt. "I'll get you there in one piece. Riley's already in. Saw her barreling into her office, cursing at her cell phone as I was leaving."

"Looks like this is gonna be one helluva day."

"What d'ya get?" Stone greeted them from a computer terminal in the Cold Case corner of the homicide office.

"Shoulda been there. Shoulda seen the widow. A *monstruo*." Nazario gave a long, low whistle.

"Guess what she's doing when we show up?" Burch said.

"You mean *who* she's doing," Nazario said.

"Banging the gardener in a cabana. Broad daylight. She's the bomb and doesn't care who knows it. Did you notice," he said to Nazario, "how her clothes all unwrap, that little bathing suit skirt, her dress? That ain't no coincidence."

"Who the hell is she?" Stone said. "That's what I want to know. I've been trying to pull up her past. Her first marriage license application lists a POB of Davenport, Iowa. The second time she gave her place of birth as Preston, Iowa."

"Maybe it's a suburb." Burch shrugged.

"Third time it was Mason City, Idaho, a whole different state. Didn't apply for a Social Security card until 1990, here in Miami. No history anywhere in Iowa—or Idaho. No background anywhere until she walks into Terrell's drugstore. Ran the prints from her shoplifting busts through AFIS. Nothing came back. It's like she just dropped outta the sky."

"Natasha Tucker Terrell Asher Streeter Ross," Nazario said. "A mouthful for somebody without a past."

"Not exactly a criminal mastermind." Stone displayed a printout. "Get this, Sarge. At Neiman Marcus she gets busted for stealing buttons."

"Buttons?" Burch said.

"Yep. Apparently she dug the gold buttons on some fancy designer suit. Didn't buy the suit, a little Chanel number, price tag forty-two hundred dollars—"

"Jeez, worth more than my first three cars put together," Nazario said.

"—but liked the buttons enough to whip out a little blade and slice them all off the jacket and the cuffs. Twenty-two buttons. They catch the whole thing on surveillance camera. When security stops her and finds them in her bag she's shocked. How'd they get in there? Threatens to sue. The judge reduced it to a misdemeanor and let her make restitution.

"At Saks, it was lingerie. Panties."

"Sounds right," Burch said. "She probably goes through 'em pretty fast. Lotsa wear and tear."

"Embroidered silk scanties, six pair, priced at—get ready for this—a hundred and sixty-five to two hundred and eighty-nine bucks apiece. That's more than Naz's good suit."

"Go to hell, you wish you looked so good."

"Said she planned to pay, but popped outside first, for just a sec, to see if her driver was waiting. Said security stopped her before she could go back inside and ante up. Security says they prosecuted because she was a repeater. They'd caught her stealing see-through nighties. Gave her a pass the first time, with a warning to stay out of the store."

"She has a chauffeur who waits while she steals undies? I'm impressed," Nazario said.

"High class," Burch said.

"The lingerie department is on the third floor. She took the goods two flights down on the escalator to exit the store. They said she was on her way into Tiffany's when they caught up with her. Funny thing, they said before she left the store with the loot, she stopped to validate her parking card."

"That's our girl." Burch shook his head. "Consistent as a heartbeat."

"The store security guys remember her well."

"Not surprising," Burch said.

"First, she's drop-dead gorgeous. Second, she never got rattled. Took the whole thing in stride. Lady shoplifters usually panic when they hear they're going downtown. But she stayed cool as a cucumber. Third, and most memorable, they said, was when a female police officer frisked her. She wasn't wearing any panties."

"Ohhh, 'splains everything," Burch said. "She needed 'em. Musta misplaced hers on the way over there."

"Should've seen the shoes she was wearing," Nazario told Stone. "Wonder if she copped them, too."

On each occasion, Stone said, Natasha carried credit cards and more than enough cash to pay for the stolen items.

"So what did your built-in shit detector say when you talked to her?" he asked Nazario. "Liar, liar, panties on fire?"

"Strange. Evasive as hell," Nazario said. "Truth one second, lies the next." He consulted his notebook. "Truthful about Iowa, lied about the farm. Charles a nondrinker? True. Nothing suspicious the day of the fire? A lie."

"Those last two worry me. We got work to do," Burch said.

"Maybe she wouldn't recognize the truth if it bit her on the ass," Nazario said. "Maybe she doesn't know when she's lying."

"See, women like that make me appreciate Connie," Burch said. "At least I always know where she's coming from. This broad looks hot as hell but she's cold as ice on the inside. Smart, too."

"Not smart enough to steal and get away with it," Stone said.

"Who knows how often she did?" Nazario said. "We only know how many times she got caught."

"Her thing with money," Burch said, "must go back to her childhood. Bet we find out she was born poor."

"Or without a conscience," Nazario said.

"Or with bad genes," Stone said.

"Marries up every time." Burch was thinking aloud. "Has a kid with each husband, a little souvenir from each marriage, to keep the poor schmucks hooked financially. She uses the kids, too. They're all shipped out. You'd never know she was a mother."

"Poor parenting isn't a crime," Stone said.

"This should cheer up the lieutenant," Nazario said. "She likes being right."

"Who doesn't?"

Joe Padron hustled past, beelining for Riley's office. "Hi, pal." He waved enthusiastically and gave a cheerful thumbs-up.

"What the hell was that?" Burch said. "Who the hell was he 'Hi, pal'-ing?"

"Stone, I think."

"Not me," Stone said.

Padron emerged from Riley's office minutes later, still smiling. "See ya downstairs, pal."

"You," Burch said. "It was definitely you."

"No way." Stone shook his head and shrugged.

. . .

K. C. Riley hailed them from her door. "You, you, and you. In my office. Now."

"She talking to us?" Stone said.

Nazario looked around. "Ain't nobody here but us chickens."

"Uh-oh," Burch said.

. . .

"Sit," she said.

The detectives rolled two more chairs into her cramped office.

"We need to talk."

Nazario rolled his eyes. "It's never good news when a woman tells you that."

"There's good news and bad news," she said. "The good news is, forget Terrell. I'll talk to the ex-wife, get her the hell off your backs."

Their reaction was not what she anticipated.

"What?" she demanded.

"You were right," Burch said. "Something stinks about the Terrell case. We're about to be all over it."

Riley planted an elbow on her desk, dropped her forehead into her hand, and sighed. "Tell me."

They filled her in at length.

"Damn . . ." She reached for the hand grenade on her desk as though it were a security blanket. "What's the latest husband like?"

"Milo Ross. Stone was just checking him out."

"He's older than dirt," Nazario said.

"Legit," Stone said. "Big bucks. Retired CEO. Bailed out of his Fortune Five Hundred company with a golden parachute fifteen years ago. Age seventy-nine. One of the richest men in Florida, maybe in the U.S. Natasha pulled off a real Anna Nicole."

" 'Cept she's way better looking," Nazario said. "That big blonde is scary."

"Whoever heard of an Iowa farm girl named Natasha?" Riley's brow crinkled.

"Ross seems in relatively good shape, unless she kills him with sex," Burch said. "He came home from a doctor's appointment while we were there. Probably got a scrip for the little blue pills. He's gotta be on Viagra."

"Maybe at that age he just likes to look at her," Nazario said.

"Sure, and the pope smokes dope."

"I copied the Walkers' birthday party video to return to the family. The original's at the lab," Stone said. "Powers thinks he can enhance the tape for a better look at traffic across the street around the time of the fire. At least one, possibly two, suspicious vehicles. A make and model or even a driver's general description might help us out."

"Tell me her story again," Riley said, "about their night together before the fire."

"You mean the sex, the champagne, the all-nighter?" Burch asked.

"Yeah. You say the marriage had problems?"

"He was staying out. Evasive. She thought he was seeing somebody, but didn't know who," Burch said.

"But that night, she said he was amazing." Nazario raised his eyebrows. "Like the first time."

Riley gave them a knowing smile.

"Goodbye sex." She leaned back in her chair. "Kiss, kiss, boom, boom, bye-bye. When one sex partner knows it's not happening again but the other doesn't. He's saying here's something to remember me by. Thinks he's being romantic or kind. Ego enhances his performance. When it dawns on her later, she's furious or crushed . . . unless her ego is equally overinflated and the thought never even occurs to her. You guys know what I'm talking about."

"Right." Burch finally spoke up when nobody else did. "Not that I ever was the goodbye guy." He paused. "But it mighta happened to me."

"Sure," Riley said. "Goodbye sex isn't gender specific."

"I'll buy that," Stone said. "Say Charles Terrell knew this was the last time they'd have sex. Was it because he was about to dump her for somebody else? And then, before he could dump her, he accidentally caught fire?"

They exchanged skeptical glances.

"Or did he know he was gonna catch fire?" Nazario said.

"Or that somebody was?" Riley said.

"He might have felt threatened, knew somebody wanted to kill him," Stone said. "You know, like soldiers going to war. The night before the big battle, everybody feels the need to get it on. A biological urge, survival of the species."

"The son of a bitch is alive," Burch said.

Riley sighed. "My other news is about a press conference this afternoon. Stone's the star attraction. You," she told him, "are taking the Meadows case public."

"We can't," he protested in disbelief. "There is nothing we can release!"

"Right." Burch looked incredulous. "You gotta be shitting us. No good reason for it. It ain't like the public is clamoring for information. What's the point?"

"I think the killer's in Miami. I can feel it." Stone shook his head. "He'd be tipped off. The FBI would be pissed off. They wanted it all kept quiet."

"The press will convene at four, in the conference room adjacent to PIO," Riley went on briskly, as though deaf to their objections. "Crime Stoppers will offer a five-thousand-dollar reward for information. You'll ask for help from the public. Say nothing that will hurt the case. Try to make us look good. Don't embarrass us."

"No way!" Stone sprang to his feet. "I won't do it."

Riley got to her feet, eyes intense, the grenade gripped tightly in her right hand. "You will do it. That's a direct order." She tossed her head. "Look at the bright side, Stone. You wanted the opportunity to work full-time on Meadows. You've got it now."

"But ask the public for tips and they inundate you with hundreds, a majority of 'em wacko, most, if not all, worthless." Burch was red in the face. "But some poor asshole in this room will have to check out each and every one. You have to be careful what you ask for or it blows up in your face."

"I'll try to get you help to sift through them. Hopefully the right one will come in. You and Nazario, keep working Terrell.

"Get your thoughts together," she told Stone. "Go talk to Padron. He's waiting for you in PIO. Everybody will be at the conference. The chief, the deputy chief, the major, the captain, ASA Jo Salazar, your sergeant, and me. So do it right. You'll be representing all of us—including the victims.

"That's all." She avoided their angry stares, returned to her chair, and gazed out her window, eyes following a sleek, silver jetliner as it pierced the clouds high above the state building.

CHAPTER TWELVE

The detectives clustered at Stone's desk, where they couldn't be heard from Riley's office. Corso joined them.

"The woman's crazy. She's always had it in for me." Stone paced wildly. "I can't do it. What the hell can I say?"

"She's lost it," Corso said. "Never had it. No good reason for the bitch to turn on you like this."

"I don't know what she's thinking, or if she's thinking at all," Burch said. "But, Sam, my man. If you want to work on this squad, you gotta do it. She's the boss. Whatever the hell is going on, it, too, will pass. Now, whacha got new in Meadows?"

"Nothing releasable." Stone collapsed into his desk chair as though crushed by a heavy weight. He stared at the floor. "There is a chance," he muttered, "that the killer is Jewish, could be Orthodox."

"I'm not even gonna ask at this point how you came to that conclusion," Burch said. "Let's see, we got about five million Jews in the U.S. Half a them are doctors and lawyers. That narrows it down. How many suspects does that leave us?"

"Gimme a break," Stone muttered. "I'm dying over here."

"Do it," Burch said. "Get through it the best you can. What else you gonna do? Try not to hurt the case, what there is of it. We'll go do some follow-up on Terrell." He promised to be back before the conference.

. . .

April Terrell and her children lived in Morningside, an old neighborhood of burgeoning redevelopment and spiraling real estate values just north of downtown Miami. The address was just east of Biscayne Boulevard, about four blocks from the bay, a charming, older building with bicycle racks out front and a pool out back.

A girlish voice answered the buzzer. "Sergeant Burch! I wanted to meet you. Come up. My mother will be home any minute."

A girl about seventeen opened the door to the third-floor apartment. Wholesome and fresh scrubbed, with blue eyes and blond hair like her mother, she reminded Burch of his own daughter, not in looks or coloring but in her manner, the way she had about her. He could see the same hopeful exuberance, the innocent energy of girls exploded into puberty, about to blast off into the world like unguided missiles. Jennifer's hunger for experience, her eagerness for adulthood, scared him. Was she all right? He missed her.

"My mom told us about you both," Joy Terrell said, inviting them in.

Girls were not that poised and self-assured when he was young, Burch thought.

The mother's influence, he decided.

"Charlie? Come say hello."

The boy, who appeared to be a few years younger, glanced up from his video game, barely acknowledging his sister or the visitors.

"They're real police detectives!" she said enthusiastically.

"We like to think so," Burch said.

The boy, about fifteen, became more interested, wandering over to join them as they settled on a comfortable couch and armchair in the warm, inviting living room. "You ever shoot anybody?" he asked Nazario.

"Nope."

"Anybody ever shoot you?"

"Charles!" the girl admonished. She and Burch exchanged knowing glances, a meeting of the minds on the crass nature of younger brothers.

"It's not like you see on TV," Burch explained. "Most cops work an entire career, then retire without ever shooting at anybody." He didn't say that those cops probably didn't work in Miami. "I've only got nine years to go myself."

"The job is actually ninety-nine percent boredom and one percent sheer panic," Nazario explained.

Disappointed, the boy returned to his video game.

When they declined the girl's offer to fix them coffee, she pulled a chair up to within a few feet of where they sat, then gazed at both men, expression expectant. She wore pink barrettes in her hair, blue jeans, and a frilly little cotton blouse with bows on the shoulder.

"We were so excited when my mom went to see you," she said happily. "She thought about it for a long time."

Burch wondered how much the mother had told them.

"Charlie doesn't remember much about my dad. But I do. I really miss him. Want to see his picture?" She sprang to her feet without waiting for an answer.

She moved with the same coltish grace as Jennifer, Burch thought, as the girl returned from another room with a framed photo.

And like Jennifer, she, too, was chatty and outgoing. "This is my favorite." She handed Burch the picture. "It was his birthday. Wasn't he handsome?" She peered over their shoulders to study it with them.

Tall, blond, and rugged, with pale eyes and strong features, Charles Terrell wore a huge grin. He stood at a dining room table, a cake in front of him.

"Nice," Burch said.

"Once when I was little, he took me shopping to buy a Christmas present for my mom. He held my hand. He took me to the circus, too. I remember him holding me way up high so I could feed peanuts to the elephant. He was really neat."

Charles made sneery sounds from his video game.

"Don't pay attention to him." She rolled her eyes at her brother. "He hardly remembers anything. Once when we went to see my dad, my mom dropped us off at the house. But Dad wasn't there, and Natasha made us wait outside until he came home. It got dark. We were hungry. Charlie was crying and had to go to the bathroom."

"Shut up," Charlie muttered.

"It's tough growing up without him." She fixed serious blue eyes on Burch.

"My mom hasn't even dated all these years. She wants to wait till we're both in college. I'm afraid nobody will even ask her then."

"I've seen your mom." Nazario winked. "You have nothing to worry about."

She smiled. "You can talk to her about most things, but sometimes, you know, it would be more comfortable to talk to your dad. Especially Charlie." She lowered her voice. "It's hard to be the only boy in the family. But I think dads are really important for girls, too. I started dating last year." She smiled shyly. "Some of my friends with fathers or stepfathers say they hate it when their dads insist on meeting their dates and telling them what time to bring the girls home. But I think it's kind of nice. Don't you? Do you have any children?"

Nazario shook his head.

"Three," Burch said.

"Do you live with them?"

"Yeah," he said reluctantly. "Sorta." Was the guilt he felt because he lied to this sweet, sad kid? Or because he wasn't living with his own children?

"They're lucky," she said. "A lot of kids in my class come from one-parent homes, like ours."

"My oldest is a girl about your age."

"What's her name? Where does she go to school? Maybe—"

A sound interrupted. A key turned in the lock and the door opened.

"Somebody, help." April Terrell juggled bags of groceries.

"Did you get the ice cream?" Charlie said.

She was surprised to see the detectives, hoped that Joy hadn't talked their ears off, and wondered aloud why the visitors had no coffee. With the kids in the kitchen, unpacking the grocery bags, she confirmed that Charles drank little, if at all. And that he had lost his right ring finger in a teenage accident.

"Gruesome," she said. "Water-skiing. His finger got tangled in the tow line."

"Any medical problems, liver, anything like that?" Nazario asked.

"No, not at all. Charles was obscenely healthy, he worked out six days a week, rain or shine."

"The condition of his teeth?"

"Excellent." She smiled. "He must have used every product that came into the store. He flossed, had a Water Pik, an electric toothbrush, a toothbrush sanitizer. He watched his diet, took vitamin supplements, and—"

"Dental work?"

She frowned and looked from one to the other, puzzled. "Right after it happened, an investigator from the medical examiner's office called to ask the same thing. Charles saw a dentist a few times in college, mostly for cleanings. He never had any major work done."

"Where was Charles buried?" Nazario said.

"He wasn't." April Terrell sighed. "Natasha had him cremated. I knew that wasn't what he wanted, but she was in charge. I guess under the circumstances it didn't make much difference, but it would have been nice to have a place . . ." Her voice trailed off.

"I had such mixed emotions about bothering you," she said after a pause. "I know you're busy with more important things, but this haunts me so."

"We're looking into it," Burch said. "Right now we're interested in learning more about Natasha, her background."

"You have to ask her, I guess. She's supposedly from the Midwest somewhere. I was always good at that, but never could place her accent. Have you met her?"

They nodded.

"Is she still as beautiful?" She sounded wistful.

Burch paused, as though he hadn't really noticed. "An attractive woman." He shrugged.

"What was the problem involving the weight-loss clinics?"

April's hand flew to her mouth. "You don't think that could have had anything to do with it?" she asked. "It was terrible. He and a business partner, Martin Asher, opened the clinics. Asher used the title doctor, but wasn't really a physician. They originated a regimen that combined diet, exercise, and over-the-counter diet pills, which were basically herbal supplements.

"They seemed to be successful until a housewife with small children collapsed and died suddenly after a month or two on the program. Her husband blamed the combination of pills and sued. Charles's lawyers argued that she must have had some undetected heart abnormality. She was also on birth-control pills and medication for a chronic condition. Asthma, I think. Maybe what she was taking wasn't compatible with the diet pills." She shrugged. "I don't know. The husband was obsessed. He'd lost his wife, the mother of his children. The clinics went bankrupt to avoid a judgment. Much later, after Charles died, a rash of cases came to light. A class-action suit was filed against the manufacturers, but I think it was too late for that family. I don't believe they ever collected anything."

Burch borrowed the photo of Terrell and promised to keep her posted.

"Please give my best to Lieutenant Riley," April said, as they rose to leave. "She's so thoughtful and understanding."

"Oh, yeah," Burch said. "One of a kind."

"You're not leaving yet?" Joy burst from the kitchen, dismayed. "I'm making cookies, chocolate chip. They only take ten minutes to bake!"

"Next time," Burch promised.

"Please, please, please!" She clasped her hands together prayerfully.

She looked genuinely disappointed when they couldn't stay.

"Nice kid," Nazario said, as they left the building.

"Yeah," Burch said. "Got a smile that could break your heart."

CHAPTER THIRTEEN

"Something ain't right here," Burch told the chief medical examiner in his third-floor office on Bob Hope Road.

"For a start, the fatty liver in the autopsy doesn't jibe with this guy's lifestyle."

"Any history of severe malnutrition, or obesity?" the puzzled doctor asked.

"He was a physical fitness aficionado. Did a forensic odontologist examine the teeth?"

"Without X-rays to match them to, probably not. But the doctor on the case would have taken a look at the jawbone."

"No indication on the chart."

"No problem," said the chief medical examiner. "We can do it."

"No way," Nazario said. "He was cremated."

"But in cases of that sort, we keep the jawbones. We can examine them now if you like."

.   .   .

Floor-to-ceiling shelves filled the windowless room deep in the bowels of the decomposition morgue, the smallest building in the medical examiner's complex. Cardboard boxes labeled with case numbers lined the long shelves. The contents were mostly unidentified skeletal remains, bones excavated by builders, human remains found scattered along canal

banks, in barrels, in woods, underwater, or in the Everglades. Police con-
fiscated some skulls and long bones from *ngangas,* the large metal caul-
drons used in the practice of Santería. Complete or partial skeletons were
packaged in larger boxes, while others contained just bits and pieces of
still-unidentified human beings, Miami's forgotten John and Jane Does, or
fragments of them, some unearthed as long ago as the 1950s.

"The ones with rotting flesh still attached are boiled clean before storage," the doctor explained. "We use meat tenderizer in the water.

"Let's see here. If I remember correctly, jawbones are over in this section." The chief medical examiner meandered among the shelves like a
librarian in search of an elusive book.

The detectives trailed him through the rows of numbered boxes.

"We could be eating homemade chocolate chip cookies with normal
people," Nazario said mournfully.

"You'd want to miss this?"

The chief double-checked the case number on the file in his hand.
"Here we are," he said cheerfully. "Ninety-two-four-seventy-six."

The contents rattled as he took down a container the size of a shoebox.

. . .

In the lab, under bright overhead lights, the doctor used a scalpel to sever
the tape sealing the box.

"It all seems to be here." He lifted the lid and carefully placed the contents on a small examining table beneath a large magnifier.

He didn't need the magnifier to see the obvious.

He paused to recheck the case number on the box.

A number of the teeth had been loose and glued back into place. He
examined one of the jawbones carefully, then put it down.

"These are the teeth and the jawbones of an individual with remark-
ably poor dental care. A great amount of decay is visible. There is evidence of several old, poorly maintained silver fillings, abscesses, and a
buildup of dental plaque."

. . .

Dr. Vernon Duffy, the assistant medical examiner who signed Terrell's autopsy report, had left the job shortly after handling the case.

"Went back to New Hampshire," the chief medical examiner said. "A good man, but he never could take the heat down here. As I recall he had other problems. His wife was very ill."

Burch remembered Duffy. Stooped and pale, with rimless spectacles, he would arrive at death scenes wearing a shapeless sports jacket and carrying his equipment in a foam-lined camera case. The detectives he'd worked with relied on his expertise and held him in high regard.

They called New Hampshire from the chief medical examiner's office.

"Vern," the chief greeted him. "How's the wife? Sorry to hear that. I have a couple of homicide detectives here in my office. A problem with an old case."

Not a prayer that the man will remember after twelve years, Burch thought, as he and Nazario picked up extensions.

He was wrong.

"What a day that was," Duffy said, from the kitchen of his home. "Hell on wheels. That was the last weekend I worked in Miami. Had to take my wife to the emergency room at four o'clock in the morning, another small stroke. I was still there when they paged me. A county car with two code enforcement officers ran a red light in the Grove, set off a three-car crash with two dead. That was top priority, until the double murder was discovered over on the beach. An organized crime figure, a mobster, killed in his strip club, along with a young dancer who worked there."

"I remember—the Club Montmartre, right?" Burch said.

"That's the one. Then your victim dies in a flash fire and two toddlers in North Miami manage to drown themselves in a neighbor's pool.

"You have to understand, I was the only doctor on duty. Solo, and we were short on technicians. The county manager and risk management were all over me about the traffic fatalities. They wanted chapter and verse. I was up to my neck in hysterical families. Miami Beach detectives wanted answers, and every reporter and news crew in town was camped out in the lobby. They refused to leave until we confirmed the identities of the strip club victims. That was a big, high-profile story at the time.

"That's no excuse, mind you. But in your case, witnesses confirmed that the man was working on his car, alone in his own garage. I believe there was another identifying characteristic present—a missing finger. When next of kin said the victim had no dental records, I was careful to establish that the burned man was missing the same finger, at the same digit. The identification seemed adequate at the time."

"Do you recall taking a close look at the jawbones?" the chief said.

"He was all burned up, charred and messy. I probably asked one of the techs to clean it up and take a look. I couldn't swear to it. Phones were ringing off the hook. TV crews pushing and shoving at the front desk. No way to even go take my wife home from the hospital. No days like that up here. Sorry if there's a problem. You know where I am if you need me."

. . .

"Where the hell is this thing taking us?" Burch said.

The chief medical examiner's only response was to take two labels from his desk drawer. He wrote *Unidentified* on one and used it to replace Charles Terrell's name on the file. Then he replaced the color-coded yellow ACCIDENT label with a red one. It said HOMICIDE.

. . .

"I coulda joined the fire department, the circus, or the CIA. Coulda been a Navy SEAL or a NASA scientist. Something easy," Nazario said, as Burch drove them toward Miami Beach.

"What if Riley goes crazy and schedules a press conference on this one? How'd you like to explain this to a room fulla hostile reporters asking questions?"

"Crazier," Nazario said. "You mean if Riley goes crazier."

"Maybe it's hormones," Burch said. "How old is she? Bet it's her time of the month."

He remembered that Miami Beach double murder, a real headline grabber.

"It was *the* strip joint back in those days," he told Nazario. "The Place Montmartre, on Collins Avenue. Local landmark. Place had a huge cut-out sign on the roof. A blonde more than ten, twelve feet tall—and that's lying down. The broad's sexy, half naked, lying on her side wearing nothing but high heels, long hair, and a come-hither look.

"Heard a story once about a sailor on a passing Liberian freighter. Horny and out at sea for months, he spots her through binoculars from two miles out. It's love at first sight, and he goes over the side. He's swimming hard for the beach until the Coast Guard drags 'im out of the water.

"Place is gone now. I think they built the new Miami Ballet conservatory on the site."

"How can it be related to our case?" Nazario said.

"Same day, few hours apart? All I do know is I don't believe in coincidences."

"Yeah, you're thinking dirty. Me, too."

Miami Beach Detective Sergeant Eddie Satin worked the case.

"He's long gone. Drank himself to death," another detective at Miami Beach Police headquarters said cheerfully. "But Tom Callahan worked it with him. He's still here."

They found Callahan at a scene, a body on the beach.

They parked in a loading zone and trudged across sandy beach toward the endless blue of the sparkling sea. A crowd of curious bystanders had clustered around a tiny makeshift raft that had been hauled up onto the beach.

"*¡Dios mío!*" Nazario whispered. The puny craft, just a piece of canvas crudely lashed between two inner tubes, had bobbed and drifted across the vast Florida Straits and arrived in Miami at last.

Too late for the lone occupant who stared skyward, feet trailing in the water.

"Mighta been dead as long as a week," Callahan said. He stood sweating in the sun, filling out his report and waiting for the morgue wagon.

"Musta died of exposure. He had to be determined. Makes ya wonder how many more are out there."

The dead man was naked, except for a single red sock on his left foot. He may have shed his clothes as the relentless sun and sea brought madness. Or he might have used them in futile attempts to flag down passing boats and planes.

If he had any food or water when he set sail, his supplies had long been exhausted.

"What brings you guys over to this side of the bay?" Callahan demanded.

He remembered the murders at the Montmartre. "Who could forget that one? What's up?"

"We're wondering if it might be related to one of our unsolved cases, a guy named Terrell the same day."

Callahan squinted across the sand. "Hey," he shouted. "Get those kids out of there!"

A patrolman waved back a gaggle of curious youngsters scampering toward the raft.

"Terrell? Nah. That name never came up. We solved ours. Got lucky. Shoulda seen it. A stripper blown away with her boss. Just a kid. Turned out she was eighteen years old. Lied about her age, said she was twenty-one to work at the club. Musta thought she was lucky to land the job—all it did was guarantee she'd never make it to twenty-one. Got her brains splashed all over the wall for her trouble. Bullet went through the palm of her hand first, like she tried to defend herself at the last minute. Musta thought she could snatch it outta the air like Wonder Woman. Wonder Woman she wasn't. Danced under the name Hurricane Allie. Saw her act a couple times myself. Did a thing with the lights and a high-speed fan. Pretty cute. At first we figured a jealous boyfriend mighta interrupted something. But it was strictly revenge, pure and simple. Guy mighta had robbery in mind, too, but he panicked."

The turquoise surf lapped gently at the shoreline as towering clouds billowed and bright sailboats darted on the horizon.

"How'd it go down?" Nazario asked.

"A couple nights before the murders, this schmo, Frankie Scheck, walks into the place. Short, skinny nerdy guy. Not slick with the women. So a couple a the girls come onto 'im and he starts buying 'em drinks. What do you expect in that kinda place? They order champagne, which you know hadda be club soda or seltzer water. The girls evaporate when the check arrives. Nine hundred bucks. He raises hell, starts yelling about being ripped off. So Chris, the owner, you had to hand it to 'im, whatever else you had to say about 'im, he always kept the place under control. Cops were always welcome, our money was no good there. He was cool, for an OC figure. Hired a lotta our guys for off-duty jobs. Chris warns Scheck, who keeps ragging about the bill. Next thing you know, the bouncer roughs 'im up and tosses 'im out on the street.

"He comes down to the station next morning and makes a complaint. Claims they took his wallet, his money, and credit cards during the scuffle." Callahan shrugged. "He's still steamed when it doesn't go anywhere. A couple nights later, he takes it into his own hands.

"Goes back with a gun after closing time. Probably didn't figure the girl would be there, or maybe she comes outta the john and surprises him in the act. What's he gonna do? He eliminates the only witness. Musta rattled him 'cuz he takes off without the money. The night's receipts were still in the safe."

"He have a record?" Burch asked.

"Nah. But you know what they say: Those who live by the sword get shot by those who don't."

"He confess?"

Callahan frowned. "Nah. Never did. But we had the son of a bitch by the balls. Found the murder weapon and evidence from the scene in his car. His prints all over it."

"What was it?"

"A drawer from the victim's desk. You won't believe how that went down. One of our crime scene techs is driving back to the station and sees the punk standing on the street next to his car holding a desk drawer. The tech recognizes it as the one missing from the desk he just dusted for prints at the murder scene. He gets on the radio, we swoop down and find the murder weapon, a stolen gun, in the car as well.

"Why would he take the drawer?" Nazario said.

"Probably looking for his wallet and ID." Callahan shrugged. "We found 'em later, in the bouncer's locker."

Burch frowned. "He leave prints at the scene?"

"Nah. Probably wore gloves. Jury only took twenty minutes to convict 'im."

"Where's he at now?" Burch asked.

"Excellent question." Callahan's wide grin exposed a crooked row of tobacco-stained teeth.

"We might want to talk to him," Burch said.

"Good luck. Punk got two death sentences—too bad they could only kill him once. They shot him fulla the juice last year."

As they trudged silently across hot sand to the car, Nazario paused for another look at the puny craft on the beach.

"Things must be pretty bad where he came from," Burch said. "Think they'll ever identify him?"

Nazario shook his head. "I hope he knows he made it."

CHAPTER FOURTEEN

"How do I look, Kath?"

Jo Salazar peered over her shoulder for a rear view of her navy blue suit in the restroom mirror. "I bought these new pantyhose. They flatten your tummy but padding in the back gives you a rounder, higher, curvier butt. What do you think?"

She did an exaggerated model's spin as Riley stepped back for a better look.

"You sure you didn't put them on backward?"

"Bitch! I'll wash your mouth out!" Jo squirted liquid soap from a dispenser onto a paper towel and took a menacing step forward.

"Drop it, Salazar, or I'll handcuff you to the plumbing!"

Still laughing, they burst out of the restroom into the crowded lobby and the path of Craig Burch.

"Glad you're enjoying this." He wondered how long it had been since he'd seen her laugh. "I'm worried about Stone. The kid blows it and we all look like shit."

Riley tossed her head in that feisty way she always had. "Have faith, Sergeant. He's your detective, he won't let us down."

•   •   •

Sam Stone stared numbly through the glass window of Joe Padron's office.

"We got CNN, we got Fox News, we got Court TV, we got the NBC,

CBS, ABC affiliates, and we got Telemundo," Padron crowed. "The *Herald,* the *News,* and the *Sun Sentinel* are all sending reporters and photographers."

Stone saw Burch and Nazario and breathed a sigh of relief. "Where the hell have you two been?"

"Trust me. You don't wanna know right now. We'll bring you up to speed later," Burch said.

"You think you're bummed, shoulda been with us." Nazario sighed.

"Think the lieutenant will change her mind?" Stone said.

Camera crews were positioning their lights. "Too late now," Burch said. "It would be like trying to call back a bullet after you pull the trigger."

They huddled in the small office as Padron stepped out to meet and greet the working press.

"You have the right to remain silent," Burch warned Stone. "Anything you say will be misquoted and used against you."

"Look at the bright side," Nazario said. "The FBI didn't catch Ted Kaczynski, the Unabomber, for years. Didn't have a clue. They finally go public, publish his writing in the newspaper, and his own brother recognizes his wacky shit and drops a dime. Maybe this guy has a brother who'll blow the whistle."

"Yeah. Sometimes the press can work in your favor," Burch said. " 'Member how it helped us in the Ricky Lee Chance case? Ya just have to be smart about it."

"Is that reporter here?" Stone hoped for a friendly face.

"Nah, haven't seen her since McDonald."

"She took it hard," Nazario said.

"Not the only one," Burch said.

"He had a way with the ladies," Nazario said.

"Beats me," Burch said. "Personally, I liked McDonald. He was one helluva a cop. But the guy would screw a snake. All these women carrying on like it's the end of the world? I don't get it."

"Who knows what women want? But wait till they get a load of you on the tube." Nazario nudged Stone's shoulder. "You'll be answering fan mail."

Padron came back and hustled the other two out.

"Looking good," he told Stone, brushing an invisible speck off his lapel. "We got a full house. Remember, the average schmo can't get a letter to the editor published. And forget TV. But that crowd out there wants to hear every word you say and repeat it to the world. The power of the press. It's all yours. A politician would kill for this. Just remember, be yourself, address each individual who has a question, except the guy in the green shirt from the *New Times*. They're always busting our balls."

Hell, Stone thought. I can do this.

"Excuse me a sec," he said, suddenly energized. "I need to make a quick call."

"Make it brief, the chief just got here." Padron rushed out to greet his boss.

"Gran," Stone said into the phone, "I'm gonna be on TV. You remember how to use the VCR?"

"Show time." Padron was back, checking his watch. "Here, fasten this button. I'll get it. Look straight into the camera. Be strong, forceful. Make us proud. Break a leg."

CHAPTER FIFTEEN

SIX HOURS LATER

The cat playfully bats my hand with his paws as I fast-click the remote from station to station.

Stone appears on every freaking channel, including CNN and MSNBC. He is flanked by the flags of Florida and the USA, the huge city crest embossed on the wall behind him.

Jockeying for position on the dais are all the brass and a number of dignitaries. Even Miami City Commissioner Victor Sanchez. He represents the district where Virginia Meadows was murdered. She is still one of his constituents. Never mind that she's been dead for twenty-four years.

His loyalty is not unusual. Given the state of Miami politics, Virginia Meadows has probably voted in every city election since her demise.

The cat has abandoned the toys I bought him, his squeaky mouse, his sparkly ball, and his feathered bird, to watch TV news with me. That's more than Max the sheepdog ever did.

I bought a sandbox and set it up in a bathroom corner. Better to keep him safe inside until his owners' return. I don't want to have to explain how their beloved pet disappeared on my watch. I have enough to explain—to my wife, my bosses, my detectives, and myself.

"He works for me," I tell the cat, as Stone's face reappears. His words echo as I surf the channels. Earnest, indignant, and dedicated, he is the voice of justice closing in on evil.

Intense and clear-eyed, hands gripping the sides of the podium, he comes on like gangbusters, fielding questions with grace and aplomb. He does the dance. Revealing few details—God forbid anybody should guess how few there are—just enough to work the media into a lather.

Even the chief looks impressed.

The best sound bite, replayed over and over, is his response to a reporter who asks what he has to say to the killer.

"You think you're getting away with it. Well, your worst bad dream is about to come true. Keep looking over your shoulder," Stone said, gesturing for emphasis, as if his words needed any. "Because we're coming for you."

I envision thousands, maybe millions of viewers, all thinking: *I wouldn't want that guy looking for me.*

"We know more about the killer than he realizes," Stone is saying on screen. "We're cataloging his travel and his behavior."

I wish to hell it was all true.

A reporter asks how close we are to an arrest.

"Every day brings us another day closer," Stone says confidently.

Where does the Meadows case go from here? And what about Terrell?

If only those charred jawbones in a box at the medical examiner's office could talk. Who were you? We know who you weren't. In the morning we start pulling old missing persons reports filed around the time of the fire.

Somebody's still missing. Somebody with bad teeth and a fatty liver. What the hell does Natasha know? The faces of Terrell's kids haunt me. How can he not be dead? How could he be alive all this time and never contact them? If he really is alive and well, somebody should shoot him.

What about my kids, my wife?

I continue to channel surf, flicking the remote long after the cat tires of the game. We lie on the bed and listen to this huge old empty house creak, groan, and settle in the dark.

By the time the press conference ended and we brought Stone up to speed, it was too late to run by Downtown Automotive to pick up the Blazer, so I managed to score a take-home car from the motor pool, a beige Ford Taurus.

I miss my family and wonder what they're doing right now. Then I realize that, though the Blazer would be a dead giveaway, nobody would spot me in a beige Taurus.

So I grab the keys and skulk off under cover of darkness to spy on my family like a stalker. The familiar drive home to Kendall comforts me. I crack open another beer from the six-pack beside me on the seat of the Taurus and start to feel better. Maybe this will again soon be my daily commute. I am optimistic because Connie hasn't called the station since noon. She is simmering down, I can feel it in my bones. Or is that just wishful thinking?

Maybe it's ominous. She may have lost interest, found somebody else. Even negative attention from her is better than no attention at all. I miss her rubbing my shoulders and giggling at my jokes as she lies beside me in our bed.

I can deal well with chaos on the job when my personal life is good, and vice versa. It's hard to handle when both turn to shit at the same time. Nirvana is when both are in sync. That's heaven. I didn't appreciate it enough the few, rare times I was that lucky. I'll know better next time. If there is one.

I slow down to turn onto our street, watching stealthily for neighbors and family members. Our house is all lit up. I roll by slowly. The grass needs cutting and the ficus hedge looks out of control. Damn. If it isn't kept trimmed its invasive roots will infiltrate the septic tank's drain field for sure.

Through the kitchen window, I see Connie's silhouette at the kitchen sink. My heart flipflops. Since when did seeing her rinse dishes make me sentimental? The light is on in Craig Junior's room. He's probably listening to music or accessing who knows what crap on the Internet. Hopefully he's cracked one of the books on his summer reading list.

A dancing pixie figure hops and spins past the living room picture window. Annie, the youngest, who always rests her little head on my shoulder when we watch TV together. Shouldn't she be in bed by now?

Where is Jennifer? She must be driving Connie's Saturn, which is missing from the driveway. Or out on a date with some adolescent, pimply-faced, sex-crazed teenage pervert who probably smirked when he didn't have to shake hands and hear rules laid down by her father.

Down the street, I pull over to call her cell phone number and am relieved when she answers on the first ring.

"Hi, honey."

"Daddy?"

"Wanted to say I miss you, honey."

"Miss you, too, Daddy. But Mom is, like, really unglued."

"Still?"

"Daddy, Melissa's having a coed sleepover at her house Friday night, but Mom won't let me go. Is it okay with you if I do?"

"Coed?" What are parents thinking? "No way."

"Melissa's mother and stepdad will be there."

"If Mom said no, it's no."

"You never let me do anything!"

I tell myself that at least she hasn't hung up on me.

"What you doing now, honey?"

"I'm at work." She pouted.

"What work? Did you get a summer job?"

"The volunteer job, Daddy. Remember? I told you about it. Helping out at the homeless shelter, folding donated clothes, unpacking and sorting food donations."

"But you didn't say it meant night work. It's after ten o'clock."

"That's only once a week and then Father Jeffries takes us all out for pizza. We're almost ready to go now. I'll be home by eleven-thirty."

"Be careful driving, honey. Don't forget to fasten your seat belt." The thought of her driving home alone late at night makes me sick. What is Connie thinking?

"I love you, Daddy. Miss you."

"Same here, sweetheart. See you soon. "

I hang up, feeling empty, wishing we had talked more. The homeless shelter is down near St. Luke's Church, not the best neighborhood. She's so young. Driving alone.

I pull out from the curb, roll slowly by the house again, and turn north, back to my temporary home. But a little detour and I find myself near St. Luke's. The closest pizzeria is only a few blocks away. I see them inside through the plate-glass windows, half a dozen girls and two skinny boys along with Father Jeffries. Who the hell is he really?

I take his tag number when he leaves and make a mental note to check on whether he has a rap sheet. I hold my breath as Jenny and three other noisy kids pile into Connie's car. Teens with teen passengers are among the highest-risk drivers. I am glad to see Jenny fasten her seat belt. I trail them as she drives the other kids home.

I spot her on her cell phone as she's driving. She knows that's forbidden. She rolls through a stop sign, head turned, talking to the kids in the backseat, and I cringe.

I'm about to slap the blue light on the dash and pull her over myself but can't risk blowing my cover.

I follow her from house to house as she drops off her friends, then home. I watch from half a block away as she locks the car and darts inside. She disappears so quickly that I wonder if the front door was even locked. Maybe Connie heard the car in the driveway and opened it. Max never did bark. He's worthless, useless, no protection.

I watch the house for more than an hour until, one by one, the lights go out and it's dark.

I drive away thinking of Joy Terrell's sad, sweet smile. Death was Charles Terrell's perfect excuse for not being a good dad. What, I wonder, is my excuse?

CHAPTER SIXTEEN

"The French have a saying for it: Life has a way of always getting fucked up." Martin Asher's laugh had a melancholy ring as he described his past with Natasha.

The man was not what Burch expected. Still another unlikely match for Natasha. It seemed they all were. Short, swarthy, and pudgy, Asher wore what appeared to be a permanent five o'clock shadow and an expensive suit that looked as though he'd slept in it.

His office was in a modern ten-story building, one of a dozen in a busy light-industrial complex sprawled around a huge man-made lake stocked with tropical fish and swans. Employees could stroll, jog, or simply take in the view during breaks and lunch hours from promenades and park benches along the water.

A plain, pale-haired woman smiled from a family photo prominently displayed on Asher's desk. Two small children were enfolded in her arms. A teenage girl sat next to them, her head on her mother's shoulder. All resembled each other. Behind them stood a beautiful dark-haired girl who resembled none of them. Age nine or ten, she was a miniature version of Natasha, complete with attitude and a built-in pout. She stared at the camera with sly amusement.

Lots of luck with that one, Burch thought.

"The family?" He assumed that the Asher children were his, hers, and theirs.

Asher nodded. "The one in the back is Natasha's and mine."

"I can see the resemblance."

"Ah, so you've met Natasha. We don't communicate much anymore. She recently remarried. Again," he said with regret.

He, too, had seemed apprehensive about a visit from a detective—until he learned what it was about.

"Hadn't thought of Charles in years. Poor bastard. Loved the guy, loved to hang out with him. The man was a regular chick magnet. Take him to lunch, dinner, or for a drink and we'd have waitresses, barmaids, and cocktail waitresses all over us. And the guy didn't even drink."

"You and his widow got married pretty quick after the fire," Burch noted.

"I was afraid she'd change her mind. Look at me," he said, pudgy arms outstretched. "You've seen her!"

"So you two must have had a little something going on the side before her husband's untimely demise."

Asher paused and licked his lips, as though debating how much to reveal. He leaned forward, his face grave. "Look, they had problems. It never would've lasted. Natasha requires a lot of attention, time, and care, like some exotic flower, and Charles . . . Well, Charles had other interests. She felt neglected."

"So she naturally turned to you for comfort and advice?"

"Exactly!" Asher seemed pleased that the detective understood. "So after he died, it seemed only natural that we—"

"Where were you when Terrell was killed?"

"Look, I prefer to keep this between us." His eyes darted furtively to the family photo, as though fearing that it might conceal a hidden microphone that would broadcast his words to those pictured there.

He lowered his voice. "At a motel on U.S. One down near Dadeland . . ."

"With . . . ?"

"Natasha," he whispered. "And the baby. I stayed for a couple hours after she left, watched a movie. Room was paid for, I figured I might as well. Look"—his voice took on a pleading quality—"I didn't know she was gonna bring the kid. We used to get together there once or twice a week."

"Did your pal Charles know?"

"No, but if he did, he wouldn't have cared. He was doing his own thing."

"So that made banging your buddy's wife okay?" Burch asked mildly.

"Charles was serious about somebody he was seeing. I thought he was crazy. To have a wife like Natasha and be chasing some redhead, a stripper—I told him he was nuts."

"Who was the redhead?"

Asher shrugged. "Can't remember her name off the top of my head. You know, they never use real names anyway. They use stage names. I forget hers. But he called her Big Red. Tall, statuesque, beautiful woman, but a stripper, for God's sake. And she was older than Natasha, in her thirties. Been around the block a few times. Did an act with a snake. I think it was a python, or a boa constrictor." He grimaced. "Huge. Grotesque. The thing would wrap itself around her body.

"Big Red had legs up to here and a beautiful face, but kinda hard, brassy, laughed too loud. People would turn around and stare."

If his description even approached accurate, Burch thought, it probably wasn't her laugh that made people stare.

"Charles, he got a big kick out of her. Liked to show her off. Took me to see her dance, introduced us."

"Where was that?" Burch leaned forward.

"Ummm, mighta been Heavenly Bodies, that big club used to be on Biscayne Boulevard at a hundred and sixty-third. But I couldn't swear to it. She played the circuit, Fort Lauderdale, Key West, Miami Beach, all the strip joints."

"Miami Beach?"

"Yeah. She was a headliner, I remember, at the Place Montmartre over on the beach. You know the one, used to have that huge sign on top, that big, blond reclining woman."

"I remember it." The hair on Burch's arms stiffened and stood on end. "What became of Big Red once Charles was gone?"

Asher's face scrunched into a horsey frown. "Haven't heard a word about her in years. She wasn't at the funeral. I'da noticed if she was there. It woulda been pretty brazen of 'er to show up."

"Hey, a gal who strips on stage with a boa constrictor, or even a python, ain't no shrinking violet. If she'da wanted to pay her respects, a SWAT team probably couldn'ta kept her away."

Asher shrugged. "She was crazy about him."

"How stressed out was Charles about that wrongful death suit against the weight-loss clinics? He upset enough to want to disappear?"

"A terrible thing." Asher averted his eyes and straightened the blotter on his desk. "The widower took aim at the wrong targets. Who could blame him? But it wasn't our fault. Our lawyers had it under control. We took a financial beating, going bankrupt and all, but it coulda been a helluva lot worse."

"Hypothetical question," Burch said. "If Terrell hadn't died, if the man was alive today, where do you think he'd be, Marty? What would Charles be doing?"

Asher's padded shoulders rose nearly to his ears. "Who can say? Charles liked the good life, beautiful women, nice cars. The man never looked back or had any regrets, as far as I knew. *Carpe diem.* Seize the day. A guy like him, who knows? What do any of us know?"

"How true," the detective said.

"You're wasting your time, Sergeant. The fire was a tragic accident, plain and simple. He wasn't the kind of guy anybody would kill. Nobody murdered Charles Terrell."

"I think you're right," Burch said. He paused for another look at the family portrait before leaving. "Nice family. You're a lucky man."

"Damn straight. I'm the luckiest man on earth that she took me back. The woman has a heart of gold. Believe me."

"Took you back?"

"Oh yeah, Esther and I were married, with one kid, the oldest girl there, when Charles died . . . I had to fly down to Mexico for a quickie divorce so me and Natasha could get married.

"Two years later, Natasha and I crashed and burned when she found somebody else. My life was in the crapper and Esther took me back. Don't know what I ever did to deserve a woman like her. Believe me, she's salt of the earth. But"—his voice dropped and his eyes changed—"between you and me, after all she did to me, if Natasha walked in that door right now and said, 'Hey, Marty, let's go . . .' "

He heaved a deep sigh. "God help me . . ."

CHAPTER SEVENTEEN

"I hated the guy, I hated them all. I would have killed them with my bare hands if I could have," Sal Vasquez told Nazario.

"My Celia never did a bad thing in her life." He sat in the back room of his shoe-repair shop, surrounded by shelves of luggage, shoes, and handbags all brought in for repair.

"We had three little kids, five, three, and one. It killed me. If it wasn't for those kids, I'da done it. I would have killed them."

"Who could blame you? You lost so much," Nazario said.

"She had trouble losing weight after the last one. She was in his store, checking out the over-the-counter diet pills, when Terrell touts his program to her. She comes home all excited. Said she wanted to give me a size-six wife for our anniversary. Her goal was to lose twenty pounds by September fourteenth.

"She almost did it. She lost sixteen pounds by the middle of August, but she wasn't feeling so good. I told her forget it. Stop the pills. You look great. But she wanted to stay on the program and meet her goal. She always kept her word. She thought I liked her the way she was when we met. I did. But I loved her the way she was, no matter how much she weighed.

"It was horrible. She went to bed that night right after the kids went to sleep. That was unusual, I shoulda known something was wrong, 'cuz we always stayed up to watch the late news together, then Johnny Carson's monologue on *The Tonight Show.*

"She was sound asleep, like an angel, when I came to bed. I was careful not to wake her up. Something woke me about three A.M., a noise she was making, breathing funny, like snoring real loud. I turned on the light and asked if she was all right. I tried to help her sit up. Her eyes were open, she just looked at me but she couldn't talk. Some foamy stuff came outta her mouth and nose. I was looking for the address book, for her doctor's number, when she stopped breathing. Stopped. Just like that.

"I started yelling and screaming, trying to call nine-one-one. It woke up the kids and they were screaming. It was only a few minutes but it seemed like forever. Nobody came. I tried to give her CPR, then I just picked her up and carried her down to the car, screaming for the next-door neighbors to watch my kids. I took her to Baptist.

"I musta been driving eighty miles an hour, screaming all the way for Celia to wake up. I was crazy, scared I'd get lost in the dark and miss the turn to the hospital.

"The rescue squad arrived right after I left. My neighbors told them I'd taken off for the hospital. I nearly crashed into the emergency room entrance. The squad had called ahead and people were waiting. Medics came running out. They worked on her for forty-five minutes. Nothing. She was twenty-eight.

"I wanted them to pay, to keep them from killing anybody else. I hired a lawyer, but they had a better one and it didn't work out for us."

"Did you ever do anything else to retaliate against Charles Terrell, or anybody, for what happened?" Nazario asked.

"No," Vasquez said. "No, I take that back. I did. I prayed to God for justice. I couldn't forgive. When I saw in the newspaper that Terrell was killed, that the fires of hell had consumed him, I was glad. I would have lit the match gladly, but I didn't have to, God did it for me."

. . .

"He's not lying," Nazario told Stone and Burch at La Esquina de Tejas. "Guy lost his wife, hates Terrell and Asher, but he had nothing to do with it. Scratch him off the list."

"The stripper," Burch said, "she's the key. If the son of a bitch is alive, what do you want to bet Big Red is with him or knows right where he's at? I ran Big Red through known aliases but came up with nothing."

"Probably just a pet name," Nazario said. "I have a CI, a stripper. From when I worked narcotics. I'll see if she's got a line on Red. Those girls, they all know each other."

"Good. And we've gotta pull up missing persons reports from 'ninety-two and look for one who mighta had a connection to Terrell. That's gonna be tedious as shit."

"Right," Stone said. "I hate it when people are so quick to report somebody missing but forget to tell us when the happy wanderer turns up wearing a sheepish grin."

"We can forget the missing finger." Burch sighed. "If Terrell did fake his own death, he sure as hell wasn't lucky enough to find a candidate who matched his general description and also happened to be missing the same finger."

"You know what that means," Stone said.

"He hacked it off himself, before burning up the body," Nazario said. "A cold, scary guy. Wonder why he and Natasha didn't work out? They seem so perfect for each other."

Burch turned to Stone. "How's Meadows coming?"

"How the hell can I even work on the case with all the media shit?" Stone said. "I thought we do it and that's it. I show up today galvanized, energized. Dozens of messages waiting, but none are tips in my case. They're all requests for more interviews! You believe that?"

"A star is born." Nazario sipped his *cortadito*.

"Padron is lining up more radio and print interviews with reporters from the cities where there were killings. I can't shake the guy."

"Your new best friend," Nazario said.

"I feel so phony, it's a non-story—there's no new developments," Stone said. "The papers all say we're closing in on the killer."

"In Miami you can tell a lie at breakfast and it's true by dinner," Burch said. "Don't worry about it."

"It's the price of fame," Nazario said. "Before you got here, Sarge, you shoulda seen, a buncha customers stood up and applauded when Stone came back from the men's room."

"Thought my fly was open," Stone said. He grinned and leaned back in his chair.

His picture, with the chief and prominent politicians clearly in the background, was splashed five columns across the front of the morning paper displayed in big yellow news racks on every street corner.

"Your fifteen minutes won't come cheap," Burch said. "When they run in a pack, reporters go into a frenzy. They want your time, your attention, your whole goddamn life. And they raise holy hell if they don't get it. Then they'll turn on you, all of a sudden. Slam you for not accomplishing anything. The best way to deal with the press is to find a good reporter you can trust, build a relationship with that one, and avoid the pack."

Stone sighed. "I tried ducking Padron. Didn't answer his messages, but then he griped to the chief, who called Riley. She said to cooperate with PIO as long as it doesn't compromise the case. Isn't it compromised when I'm not working on it?

"The chief catches me in the lobby today, shakes my hand, and says, 'Nice job.' The man didn't know I was alive until yesterday. Riley said he's impressed."

"You bet your ass he's impressed," Burch said. "You got your picture and his in the newspapers—without robbing, raping, or shooting anybody. You didn't get arrested. You came across like a goddamn eagle scout. That's a breath of fresh air in this outfit."

Their cell phones sounded almost simultaneously.

"Uh-oh, Padron," Stone said, and answered his.

"I feel left out," Nazario said.

"Who the hell is this?" Burch was saying into his. "What are you, some kind of freak? You son of a bitch. You got the wrong goddamn number." He hung up and shook his head. "Second one today. Musta got their lines crossed."

He drained his coffee cup and pushed his chair back. "Gotta make a pit stop before we go get the Blazer."

"Wait," Nazario put a restraining hand on his arm. "Don't go in there, Sarge."

"What the hell you talking about?" Burch said.

"Hold on," Stone told Padron. "I wouldn't go in there if I were you," he said, one hand over the mouthpiece.

"You crazy? What's going on?"

. . .

"Must be that permanent Magic Marker," Stone said.

"I spoke to the owner," Nazario said. "They're gonna paint over it after the lunch hour."

Burch stared in dismay at the graffiti on the men's room wall:

MIAMI POLICE SGT. CRAIG BURCH WEARS PANTYHOSE.

"I hear from Cookie, the cute waitress, the little one with the big butt, that the same thing's on the wall in the ladies' room," Nazario said.

. . .

"I thought she'd mellowed out," Burch said.

Horns blared as they hurtled across NW Twelfth Avenue, Nazario at the wheel. "Maybe somebody else did it. You arrest anybody who knows you eat there? Maybe somebody with a grudge just got outta jail."

"Nah. Connie knows it's my favorite place. That other cops go there. Trying to embarrass me. And I can recognize her printing. Dotting the i with that little heart is a dead giveaway. It's gotta be her."

"Shoulda sent her flowers or something. Sure your car is ready?"

"They said it was."

. . .

Leon wiped his hands on a rag, shoved it in his back pocket, and squinted through his thick, grimy glasses. "Never had this before," he said. "Come 'ere, I wanna show you something."

"When a mechanic says that," Nazario muttered, "it's never good news."

The Blazer sat in the dusty lot outside, the hood up.

Leon displayed the source of the problem.

"What the hell?" Burch said. "Is that what . . ."

"Oh, Jesus," Nazario said.

"Somebody had to put it in the gas tank," Leon said. "Dang thing expanded, eventually worked its way into the fuel line, plugged it up." He regarded them solemnly, his pale eyes questioning. "Hell of a thing. Couldn't have been an accident. Sorry the bill is so high, but this was a tough one."

"Holy shit," Burch said, as Leon disappeared with his credit card. "Do you really think that Connie . . . ?"

"Face it, Sarge. Who else would drop a Tampax in your gas tank?"

CHAPTER EIGHTEEN

The mountain of messages had grown prodigiously in the hour he'd been gone. A stack of new leads had come in from Crime Stoppers, and his phone rang incessantly. As he spoke to callers, Stone tried to organize. He set aside an alarming number of messages from other law enforcement agencies nationwide, all with unsolved murders they hoped to link to the same serial killer. He'd return those calls later. He eliminated tips from psychics and those from callers who named suspects too young to be linked to a series of murders that began twenty-five years ago.

"I'm sure it's not your son-in-law," he assured a fearful woman. "He's only twenty-seven now."

A tearful elderly woman whimpered that she was so relieved to hear his voice. A man had stared at her in the supermarket, she said. Former President Richard Nixon was the killer, swore a man with a shaky voice. His television set had told him so.

A man who insisted on remaining anonymous whispered that the murders were a CIA conspiracy designed to "thin out the herd. There are too many people in the world now. They're starting to eliminate the sick and the weak."

"The killer is living under the Sunny Isles Bridge disguised as a pirate," a caller said.

"Thank you, Lieutenant Riley," Stone muttered bitterly. His phone rang again.

"You're the one who was on television. In the newspapers. You know nothing. It's all a sham. For publicity. What can you know about him?" the caller asked persistently.

"More than he thinks," Stone said, irritated.

"Such as?"

"I can't divulge specifics at this point in the investigation," he said, as Emma, the secretary, handed him another fistful of messages. "But we're moving forward."

"Tell me one thing . . ." the man persisted.

Stone felt almost relieved to see Padron arrive, to spirit him away for more prearranged interviews.

"Have to go now. There's a new development. Thanks for calling." He hung up.

The interviews were phoners with out-of-state media. Stone sat in Padron's comfortably padded leather chair growing increasingly uncomfortable with each telephone encounter. He hated repeating himself over and over to each one. Every reporter he spoke to tried to elicit a promise that Stone would tip him or her off exclusively when he broke the case. As if his top priority, he thought disdainfully, would be to dial a total stranger in New Jersey or Ohio. He soon stopped remembering their names.

Stone thought about Burch's warnings regarding the press. It reminded him of the time Gran took him to a petting zoo. He was nine years old, happily feeding the goats and llamas sacks of food pellets from a vending machine. Then his grandmother had no more quarters for the machine. The animals were friendly, cuddly and cute, until he ran out of food. Then they rushed him, pushy and demanding until he lost his balance and fell. A huge llama stepped on his foot, holding him in place as it ripped the empty food sack from his hands with huge yellow teeth. He screamed until his grandmother rescued him.

Padron was still feeding the llama. How long, Stone wondered, would it stay friendly?

The PIO officer bounced back into his office with word that Nell Hunter, a reporter for the morning paper, wanted to write a profile on Stone.

Stone remembered her from the press conference. A small, nicely built girl with blond hair and a friendly smile. She'd worn a peasant skirt and sandals and asked her questions in a chirpy little voice that reminded him of a cartoon character. He hadn't heard any of the guys gripe about her. Burch was right about developing a relationship with a trusted reporter. Maybe she was the one. He'd liked that savvy female reporter who'd worked on the Ricky Chance case. Females are more sensitive to victims, he thought, and way more interesting to talk to. They also smell better.

Most male reporters, except for the slick TV guys who wore makeup, appeared nerdy and uninteresting. The one from the *News* sprayed saliva when he talked, had crumbs in his beard, and never let anybody finish an answer before blurting out another question.

He called Nell Hunter and set up an appointment.

As he left PIO, Detective Ron Diaz was putting together a brief press release on his case, the elderly widow's brutal murder.

"Got 'em," he told Stone with a grin. "Just booked the guy."

"Good deal, who was it?"

"The handyman. Paroled six weeks ago on a sexual battery conviction. Did a day's work for the victim last week. She was nice enough to fix him a sandwich for lunch. Well, no good deed goes unpunished. He asks to use the bathroom and while he's in there, he steals her antique watch. She misses it after he leaves, calls and tells him that if he doesn't bring it back, her next call is to the cops. It's already pawned and he's on parole. So he goes back there the other morning. Says he knocked but she didn't answer the door. Musta been in the bathroom with the water running. He gets into the house and one thing leads to another. Patrol pulled him over. He was driving her car."

"Nice work."

"Thanks, but no rest for the weary. Just caught another one. Bar shooting in Little Havana. A crazy thing. Guy leans over a pool table to line up his shot and all the other players see his underwear. He's wearing pink boxer shorts. Believe that? They all start hooting, cracking jokes, ragging on the guy. Insults fly. He goes out to the car for his gun and walks back in shooting. Kills one, wounds two. Who'da thought pink underwear 'ud get three people shot, one an innocent bystander."

· · ·

Stone had never been to the newspaper office before. When he stepped off the elevator she was waiting, big brown eyes and a smattering of freckles across her nose. He sat next to her desk while she asked him questions and typed his answers into a computer terminal.

He balked at certain personal questions. Yes, he was single. He listed the schools he'd attended, revealed that his grandmother had raised him. Nell laughed a lot. She seemed to take no offense when he said, "I'm not answering that, it's too personal," as when she asked about his parents.

She listened to his war stories from patrol. He waxed enthusiastic about police work, cold cases, and how he had persistently applied until he landed a berth on the squad.

She pried for more details about the Meadows investigation but he refused to elaborate. When they took a break and went to the employee cafeteria for coffee and oatmeal cookies, she insisted on paying.

She was from Long Island, she said, had worked on two other newspapers, and had won an award while working in Akron, Ohio, for a series on abused women.

They took the elevator back to the newsroom. It wasn't what he had expected. He had imagined it noisier, more crowded and convivial. Instead, each reporter labored alone in a little gray-walled cubicle with a telephone and a computer terminal. It was much like police headquarters, but unlike headquarters, this seemed to be a very boring place to work.

She had brightened her drab cubicle with photos, cartoons, and a pink paper flower in a plastic vase.

"Will your story be in tomorrow's newspaper?" he asked.

She laughed heartily, as though he'd told a joke.

"No, silly." Her shiny little white teeth flashed. "I have lots more work to do. Maybe it'll run next weekend, or maybe not." Feature writers, she explained, had more time to work on stories than reporters who cover breaking news.

They talked easily and she seemed enthusiastic when he hinted at possible collaboration in the future. What was it that Burch said? One hand washes the other. That's when it occurred to him to ask the favor.

Maybe she could help out his team, he said. He explained that they were trying to identify a corpse in an old case. The man was a drinker, between thirty-five and forty-five years of age, and approximately six feet tall. He had been missing since 1992. There might have been something in the newspaper then. Was there a way to look it up?

"Sure," she said lightly, and demonstrated.

The paper's information retrieval system fascinated him. Type in a word or a phrase, pick a year, and the computer would instantly spit out a list of all the stories in which that word or phrase appeared.

"It only goes back as far as 1981, the year our library system—formerly known as the morgue—was computerized," she said cheerfully. "For stories prior to that we have to pull the old files and search the hard clips by hand, but everything since then is in the system."

She typed in "missing man," then selected a year, 1992. The archives reported forty-seven stories. Stone noted the names of men who fit Terrell's general description and had vanished during the right time period. Nell typed them into the system to see if they had been reported as found in later stories. Time-consuming, but faster and more all-encompassing than could be done through Miami police records. No wonder reporters often can get ahead of detectives, he thought.

The disappearance of the man whose identity they were seeking may not have been immediately reported, Stone told her. If he vanished after a move to Miami or arriving in South Florida on vacation, he might not have been missed for some time.

Stone would have liked to continue searching the system—in fact, his fingers itched to command the keyboard—but Nell insisted on continuing their interview, to the point of silliness, he thought.

What sports did he play in high school? Who was his prom date? His favorite foods? "You're not going to put that in the story," he objected.

"I won't know until I write it," she said. "Too much information is better than not enough."

She walked him down to the lobby when he was leaving, and promised she'd continue the computer search for his missing man later.

"I have to tell you," she said. "Your description is so vague it fits half the population. I mean, you didn't even give me the hair or eye color. What about scars, birthmarks, tattoos, clothes, jewelry, or other identifying characteristics?"

"Sorry, that's all we've got."

"What you're saying is that he's just bones. He must be a skeleton you found."

"I didn't say that."

"Mr. Bones." She winked mischievously. "Sure you don't want to tell me everything?"

"Help me out on this," he promised, "and you'll be the first to know." He meant it. He gave her his number.

Did she like him? he wondered. Was she this flirtatious with everybody?

.   .   .

He told Padron, who'd beeped him twice, that he was still tied up at the newspaper, then drove to Miami Beach. The big house across from the golf course on Chase Avenue was just the way he remembered it, a new generation of children playing in the yard.

"Samuel!" Mordechai Waldman greeted him from behind the cluttered desk in his study. "It is wonderful to see you. I've been reading about you in the newspapers! I knew you would grow up to be a force for good, just like your grandmother. How is she?"

"The same, but older."

"Like all of us, if we are fortunate." He was dressed in black, wore a beard and a yarmulke, the corners of his fringed undershirt showing beneath his dark vest.

"I need your help, Rabbi."

"Whatever I can do, Samuel. Anything."

He told the rabbi everything, there in that comfortable study where Waldman's wife, Chani, served tea and cake.

The rabbi listened gravely. Dubious at first, he shook his head. Then he became thoughtful.

"When death comes, the eyes and mouth are traditionally closed by the firstborn son," he said. "The body is washed with warm water and the hair and nails are trimmed. Then the loved one is covered with a clean white sheet or wrapped in a white linen shroud. The dead are never left alone. A *shomer* stays with the body, reading from the Psalms until burial. The mourners eat hard-boiled eggs and bread for the first meal afterward. I concede that these traditions bear some similarities to what you have observed, but America is known for its ritual murders and serial killers. That doesn't mean—"

"But, Rabbi, in ritual murders investigators find behavior that is not necessary to commit the crime but gratifies the emotional needs of the killer. Isn't it true that the emotional needs of many people are rooted in religion or perhaps in a deluded perversion of religion?"

The rabbi sighed, his gaze wandering to the children at play outside his study window. "The world today is such a dark place. Summer will be gone soon," he said, as though thinking aloud. "Yom Kippur is coming. The Day of Atonement."

"One thing I don't get," Stone said, "is the dirt. A small amount of soil, apparently a teaspoon or so, has been found beneath the victims' heads. The scenes are otherwise immaculate. It has to be put there deliberately."

The rabbi's eyes flicked away from the children and back to his. "You're sure of this?"

"It's consistent at every scene, all nine."

The rabbi leaned forward, speaking carefully.

"A small sack of soil from Israel may be placed under the head because when the messiah comes, those buried in Israel's earth will be resurrected first."

Stone felt an adrenaline rush.

"You may be right, Samuel. But you say that most of these poor women were not of the Jewish faith." He paced his study, his narrow shoulders hunched. "Could it be someone of the faith, unbalanced, forever trying to atone for some prior sin?"

He turned to the detective. "Is this what you meant when you told the press that you knew more about him than he realizes?"

"I wasn't sure, then. What do you think could take him to all of those cities? Is he a musician? A truck driver? What job? What profession?"

"Who can say? How does he travel? In comfort to a preplanned destination? Or is he a hobo, a lost soul who wanders the road and finds himself wherever he happens to be?"

"Hard to say whether he's well financed or a nomadic wanderer, but my guess is that he has specific destinations because his pattern may be repeating. The first was in Paterson, New Jersey. So was the last. Miami was the second. And, Rabbi, I have a strong suspicion that he's here. I can't explain it, but I can feel it my bones."

"Never discount your instincts, Samuel. If you are right he has probably heard your voice, seen your face. That leaves you at a disadvantage. You haven't seen his. If he is unbalanced he may be quite agitated by what you said. Be well. Be careful."

He walked Stone out to his car.

"Above all," he said, "trust your instincts, Samuel. Trust your instincts."

The detective watched him enter the house, pausing for a moment to touch the *mezuzah* on the door post before going inside.

Stone went back to the station, up the rear elevator to Homicide, but was still ambushed by Padron, eager to learn how his interview had gone.

Stone fielded some calls and listened to his voice mail. One caller left no name, just three words: "You know nothing."

"You're right," he muttered. He played it again. Weren't those the same words an earlier caller used? Was it the same voice? Only three words. It was hard to tell.

He spoke to several elderly ladies who had nothing to offer but were eager to chat.

A roiling sky exploded into a pounding rain as he drove home. Heavy rain depressed him. It always did. He opened the door to his darkened apartment. The red light on his message machine was flashing. The tape was full. Most were messages from old friends, neighbors, and school-mates who had seen him on television or in the newspaper.

One was from Nell Hunter.

He stretched out wearily on his bed in the semidarkness and called her.

"A couple of possibilities on Mr. Bones," she said in that chirpy way she talked.

"You still at the paper?" he asked. "You always work such long hours?"

"It keeps me out of trouble, off the street." She laughed. "I don't know many people in town yet."

"You won't meet them at the office," he said.

"*Au contraire,*" she said softly. "I've met some pretty interesting people here. Like today."

Is she coming on to me? he wondered.

"Okay," she said, suddenly brisk and all business, as though she'd read his mind. "Here's what I've got so far. A couple gets married in Canada. Big family wedding. The happy newlyweds drive south for a three-week honeymoon. No official itinerary. Maybe headed as far as Miami. Maybe not. Probably depended on how many motel stops they made along the way," she said slyly. "The couple is never heard from again. The car never found. Credit cards unused, bank accounts untouched. Gone.

"The stories don't say if he was a drinker. He was thirty-four, she was twenty-seven. First marriage for both. Knew each other for seven years. The endless honeymoon remains a mystery."

"They're still in the car," he said quietly, "probably underwater." He remembered the scoop-neck blouse Nell was wearing and how beneath it her breasts looked as perky as her little voice sounded. "They ran off an unfamiliar road into water, or somebody killed them and ran the car into the water with their bodies inside."

The wind-driven rain lashed against his windows. His room suddenly seemed unbearably lonely, with the only light and warmth at the other end of the telephone line.

"Anything else?"

"Yeah. A romantic stranger, approximately forty, disappears after marrying a lonely, well-to-do, and somewhat older Boca Raton widow. Her money and jewelry disappear with him. Lots of it. Police investigate, and guess what they find? More abandoned brides! In Fort Lauderdale and Key West, they all have the same story. He used a different name each time. Each wife reported him missing before realizing he'd ripped them off. Far as I can tell, he's never turned up. The Boca cops might know."

Stone frowned. "What else?"

"Don't you ever get enough?" Her voice dropped to a sultry purr.

He chuckled. "Never."

"Okay. Two years ago we ran a story about a college girl from Wyandotte, Missouri. She was on a mission to Miami looking for her long-lost father.

"Dad was a drinker, a loser who abandoned the family when she was seven. But he kept in periodic touch, with Christmas and birthday cards, occasional weepy phone calls—most likely collect. Said he loved them, missed them, and wanted to come home, but wouldn't do it while he was still down and out. He didn't want them to see him until he was clean and sober with a job and money in his pockets.

"Last time she heard from him was a letter from Miami, postmarked May eighteenth, 1992. He loved them, missed them, realized how much his family meant to him, yada yada yada."

Stone smiled at Nell's cynical take and her oddly upbeat delivery of a sad story.

"Said he finally got a break, blah, blah, blah, blah, was getting his life together, coming home in style, planned to start a business. Promised to make everything up to her and her mother. He'd be there in a few weeks. So every time the bus stops or a phone or a doorbell rings, the poor kid, then eleven or twelve, expects it to be Daddy Dearest.

"But they never hear from him again. No more cards, no more letters, and no phone calls.

"So, two years ago, a now grown-up twenty-two years old, she takes a vacation to Miami to find her father. Thought he might still be here.

Wanted to tell him money didn't matter, she just wanted to see him again. She hit every homeless shelter, every bar, every jail and flophouse. Some vacation. A reporter did a nice little heart-tugger. We ran a picture of her holding her dad's photo. I couldn't find a follow-up, so looks like she was unsuccessful."

Stone had stopped smiling.

"When was that last letter postmarked?"

"Let's see. May eighteenth, 1992."

Stone sat up and reached for the notebook beside his bed.

"Where she from again? What's her name?"

"What will you give me if I tell you?" she teased.

"What do you want?" His mind raced. Had he already heard enough to find the story without Nell's help?

"I'll have to think about that. Let me see now, what do I—"

"Nell," he said. "Tell me the name."

"Donna Hastings. Dad is Michael Hastings, age thirty-seven when last heard from. He'd be forty-nine now."

"Can you print me out a copy of that story?" He gave her the fax number.

"Sure, you think it's anything?"

"Probably not." He tried to sound casual. "But it's worth checking out."

CHAPTER NINETEEN

The relentless rain drowned out all other sounds until he opened the door to the club and the driving beat of the music washed over him. The first thing Nazario saw was Floria, up on stage, her body gyrating, her tawny skin glistening.

He settled at the bar and ordered a Cuba Libre. The place wasn't crowded. It was still early, the rain probably keeping people away.

Floria's legs looked long from where he sat, though she was actually petite, with high, full breasts, not big bosomed, but perfectly proportioned for her frame. Natural, not siliconed, implanted, or man-made. She seemed a little thinner than when he last saw her. Floria was not a trained dancer. She had a style of her own, a delicate, almost ladylike way of prancing, twirling, and spiraling to the beat of the music as she peeled down to a G-string and red high heels. Her hair was shorter now, a mass of tight dark ringlets with auburn streaks and golden highlights that shone and shimmered in the spotlight.

Their eyes connected as he ordered his drink. Her lips curled into an arch smile and her hips waggled in his direction with a little bump of recognition. He felt a slight sting of embarrassment as a dark-shirted man at the bar turned to look at him.

She finished her performance, scampered offstage, tied on a shirt to cover her breasts, and, grinning like a schoolgirl, trotted to where he sat.

"Like a migratory bird, you always come back," she trilled. She rested one hand on his shoulder as she climbed onto the stool next to his. "I knew you couldn't stay away forever."

There was a smattering of applause as a blonde waving a tiny American flag skipped on stage in a skimpy little blue-and-white sailor suit and saluted.

The heavyset bartender frowned at Floria as he meandered toward them. She introduced Nazario as an old friend.

She didn't want anything to drink. "I just want to drink you up with my eyes," she said.

They adjourned to a tiny table in a dark corner.

He looked at her glistening skin, then deep into her golden eyes, and inhaled her scent. *She is a trap,* a voice inside told him, repeating the words, the mantra that would save him.

"Where have you been, baby?" She leaned forward, lips parted, as though eager for his answer.

"Are you okay?" he asked. "Staying on the program?"

She smiled, eyes guarded in the dim light. "I'm fine. Let's talk about you, honey."

He knew why she didn't answer his question. Floria never lied to him.

"How much do you weigh now?" Was it even a hundred pounds? "Are you eating, taking care of yourself?"

She playfully shrugged away his questions. "Let's go outside for some air," she said.

"It's raining."

She lightly caressed his hand. "We can sit in your car."

She is a trap, the voice echoed.

"I need a cigarette," she said.

He stepped to the door to check. The rain had let up a little.

"Come on," he said.

She signaled the bartender that she'd be right back. "Where's your car?"

"No. Not the car," he said. "We can talk over here."

They huddled together beneath an overhang at the corner of the building, protected by walls on three sides. He held the match as she lit her cigarette. A kaleidoscope of lights reflected on the dark, slick wet street as traffic rolled by. Floria fit neatly under his protective arm.

"I need some information, *chica*. Hoped you could help us out."

She exhaled. Smoke from her cigarette spiraled into the soggy night.

"I thought you looked me up because you missed me." Her voice sounded small.

"I do. I think about you all the time." He was telling the truth. "But you know how it is with us."

"How is it with us?" she asked mournfully. "Tell me again."

"You know. I don't want to go out on a call someday and find out that the body in the street is you."

"That's not fair."

She flipped her cigarette into the drenched parking lot, where it sputtered and died in an inky puddle.

"I'd live with the same fear because you're a cop. Look at McDonald. You worked with him. One of the girls here lost it when he was killed. Couldn't work for weeks. She's still not over it. She knew him a long time."

"Tell me about it," he said. "He had a way with the ladies."

"So do you." She turned easily into his arms, raised her face to his, and kissed him.

He turned her back to the wall, pressed against her, and kissed her again.

"Where's your car?"

He couldn't catch his breath. Hand in hand, they ran to his car.

He couldn't wait to touch her everywhere. She was unbuckling his belt. The car windows steamed up and fresh torrents of rain pounded on the car roof.

.   .   .

"This isn't why I came here, Floria," he told her later.

"That's the hell of it," she murmured, curled up beside him, her bare right knee nestled in his crotch.

"Is that time right?" She sounded drowsy, squinting at the dashboard clock. "I've got to go back soon."

He told her what he was looking for.

"I remember the redhead with the snake. They called her Desiree. Hadn't seen or heard a word about her in years. Thought she left town to get married. She knew how to dance, but that snake. It gave me the creeps. She talked to it like it was a baby. Fed it mice and rats, live ones." Floria shuddered and lit a cigarette.

"Ran with a rough crowd." She inhaled, licked her lips, and cracked open the passenger-side window. "Danced at the Place Montmartre, on the Beach. Some mobbed-up guy owned it until he got wasted. Then the place shut down."

"You see her after that?"

Floria shrugged. "She must have left around that time."

"I need her real name, age, where she's at now, if she had family here, or friends she mighta stayed in touch with."

"I know somebody who knew her. Come by tomorrow night?" She smiled. "I can have something for you by then."

"How about if you call me?" he said.

She stared at the floor for a long moment.

"Okay," she said wistfully.

They went back inside. A dark-haired girl in long braids and an abbreviated Indian costume was on stage.

"God, I'm on next. I've gotta go." Floria kissed his cheek. "Don't stay away so long next time, Pete."

He went to the men's room and surprised the man in the dark shirt masturbating.

His spine stiffened as he flashed back to the first time the tall priest took him to his office. He was eight years old, and it was the first time he had ever seen an adult with an erection. He caught his reflection in the bathroom mirror. For a moment he didn't recognize himself as he tried to remember. Was that the orphanage in New Jersey or the one in New Orleans? As if it mattered.

Stomach churning, he returned to the bar and waited until Floria reappeared on stage. He watched her, then left near the end of her act. He paused at the door for one more look. The lights backlit her hair, her soft skin glistened as she moved, and her golden eyes met his. The club was noisier now and more crowded. It was a relief to plunge out into the sweltering night and leave it behind.

CHAPTER TWENTY

"I think I've got something for you," said Dan Powers from the Forensic Video Unit.

"I love it when you talk to me like that," Burch said. "We're on the way."

"Powers wants to show off the enhanced video," he told the detectives. Lieutenant Riley joined them.

. . .

"Here we have the original." Powers rolled a computer-enhanced image: a chubby boy tying a balloon to the collar of a golden retriever. Children milling about as a white blur passes in the background.

"The videotape actually picks up more than you can see," he said. "All machines crop the tape on playback. But the bigger picture is really available, with more pixels.

"Here we go. See, with frame averaging you can pull out more detail." He locked in on the blur.

"A van." Stone peered at the image. "Looks like a white Chevy van."

"Right," Powers said. "A 'ninety, or 'ninety-one model."

The van slowed to a crawl in front of the Terrell home, stopped for a moment or two, then moved out of the frame.

"As you see, the tag was never visible."

"That's it?" Burch said. "We wanted you to zoom in on the driver's back pocket, pull out his license, and blow it up on screen."

"I may have something almost as good," Powers said. "The van moves out of frame for ninety-two seconds. Probably the time it took to drive around the block. When it comes back, you can see it's clearly the same vehicle; note the little sticker in the back of the side window. Probably a parking permit or club validation.

"The next shot is from a more favorable vantage point, better lighting and fewer obstructions."

Joan Walker, still operating the camera, had moved in order to focus more closely on HoHo and his magic.

Powers worked his own. The van slowed again, then stopped briefly at the far corner of the Terrell house. "You stabilize the video and the image becomes rock solid. Look. There." A figure, a fleeting image, blocked by the van itself, scrambled into the passenger side.

"No way to see the passenger any better. But you can see the driver's profile."

"Looks like a woman," Stone said.

The van drove out of the frame. "Gone, a full three minutes before fire begins to erupt from the garage."

He brought up the driver's image again.

"Not good enough for a positive ID, but that hair's got to help. Unless, of course, it's a red wig."

"Big Red," Burch said. "She was there."

"Charles Terrell is back from the dead," Nazario said.

"What do you mean back? The son of a bitch never went. That's the hell of it," Burch said.

"The camera never blinks," Powers said happily. "The camera never blinks."

.   .   .

"My entire career as a cop," Burch said in the elevator, "the part I hated most was breaking hearts. Telling strangers that their sons or daughters, husbands, wives, or fathers wouldn't be home again. Ever.

"You'd knock on a door and they'd answer, without a clue that their life was about to change forever. Some would scream or start to cry before you could spit it out. They'd look at your face and know. And I'd know I was gonna be part of their worst bad memory forever."

"We've all felt that, Sarge," Stone said. "Only a sicko wouldn't."

"Yeah, but now I'm looking at something even worse. Breaking the bad news to April Terrell and her kids. 'Sorry, but your dad *isn't* dead. Nope, he's one son of a bitch, kids, a cold stone killer. But if we can just hunt him down, we'll try to have the state do the job. And this time we can make sure he's dead.' How the hell you think that's gonna go over?"

"Maybe it's still premature, Sarge," Nazario said.

"No," Riley said. "If you're sure they have no guilty knowledge, it's only fair to give them a heads-up. I'd hate like hell to have them find out some other way and think we kept it from them. Just swear them to secrecy until it's resolved."

"Uh-oh," Stone said, as the elevator doors opened. Padron was waiting, with a stranger.

"There you are!" Padron greeted them. "I was wondering where everybody went. What's happening? Anything I should know?"

"Not a thing," Riley said. "Just a routine meeting."

The balding stranger wore glasses and a bulky vest with multiple pockets. Several cameras swung from leather straps around his neck.

"I'm here to shoot Stone," he cheerfully announced. He was the photographer assigned to Nell's story.

"Do what you'd normally be doing. Pretend I'm not here," he told the embarrassed detective.

"Say cheese." Burch grinned and waggled his fingers at Stone.

"A star in the making." Nazario rolled his eyes. "A matinee idol."

"Don't forget, we want autographed copies," Corso said.

Stone noticed that even Riley, whose crazy idea was responsible for all this, retreated to her office.

"Don't disturb me," she said, closing her door, "unless he really shoots Stone."

"Listen," Stone told the photographer. "We're all a team here. We work together. You can shoot pictures of all of us, the whole crew."

The photographer checked his assignment card. "That's not what it says here. You're the subject."

"Did you talk to Nell Hunter?" Stone asked irritably, aware he'd be razzed unmercifully by the others. "She said she was sending me a fax."

"Oh yeah." The photographer patted his pockets. "She said to give you this."

He pulled an eight-by-ten manila envelope from an inside pocket of his vest.

It contained a copy of a news story, along with the picture published with it. An earnest-looking college girl with hopeful brown eyes holding a family photo of her runaway father, the long-lost Michael Hastings. He sat laughing on a wooden front porch, elbows resting on his knees. He wore jeans and a work shirt and was holding a stick out to a spotted puppy.

On the back was a penciled phone number in Wyandotte, Missouri, and a Post-it note from Nell.

"Dear Sam Spade, Photos don't fax so well, so I'll send this with Hal. Hope you get lucky and he's your Mr. Bones. You owe me. Nell."

Stone called Missouri himself. The number was still valid. The mother answered and gave him another number for her daughter.

He caught Donna Hastings at work.

"I don't believe this!" she said, when he told her he was calling about her father. She sounded almost giddy with excitement. "I'm getting married next month. Finding him would be such a great wedding present! I've always dreamed of my dad walking me down the aisle. Do you know where he is?"

"Sorry," Stone apologized. "I didn't mean to give you false hopes. This is just routine. A follow-up. I saw the old news story about your search for your dad. Have you heard from him since that May 1992 letter?"

"No." She sounded crestfallen. "Nothing. But I'm glad the police haven't forgotten him. I came to your headquarters when I was in Miami looking for him."

Stone's discomfort was exacerbated by a blinding flash. He'd forgotten the photographer, now crouched several feet away, shooting candid shots of him on the phone.

Donna Hastings said that the big "break" her dad had written about and the money he'd promised to bring home had probably fallen through.

"He was probably too embarrassed to come back and face us. But we—"

"The reason I called," Stone said, still blinking at the spots before his eyes, "is to locate his dental records. Do you know where they're located?"

She gasped.

"It's strictly routine," he lied, "to complete the file."

"I don't know," she said uncertainly. "I'll ask my mother."

"And that photo you were holding in the newspaper picture, could you send me a copy? And any other good pictures you might have of your dad."

She hesitated. "I'll FedEx them this afternoon."

"Great." He gave her the street address.

"To the Missing Persons Bureau?"

"No." He couldn't bring himself to say Homicide. "Just make it to the Cold Case Squad, fifth floor."

. . .

"That's impossible," April Terrell said. "It can't be. It just can't." Tears filled her eyes.

"Nothing is certain," Burch said. "But that's the direction this thing is moving in, and I thought—the lieutenant thought—you should know."

They sat at a table in the coffee shop of the high-rise building housing the law firm where April Terrell worked as office manager.

Her tears spilled over.

Nazario handed her his handkerchief.

"How can I tell the children?" She dabbed at her eyes.

"Don't," Burch said. "Not yet. We'll let you know when the time is right."

"Does Natasha know?"

"We're not sure what, or how much, she knows. It's important to keep this just between us right now."

She nodded, sniffled into the handkerchief, then blew her nose. "I'm sorry. But the kids, they idolize his memory."

"Kids are resilient. They're strong. You did a good job with yours," Burch said.

"You probably regret now that you ever came to us," Nazario said.

She looked up at them quizzically, eyes swimming. "No. Not at all. If it is true, it means someone else is dead. Someone else's husband, or father. You have to find out the truth. Please, promise me you won't stop until you know what it is."

. . .

The message was waiting when Nazario got back to the office.

He called Floria back.

She'd outdone herself. She always did, he thought, in every way. His pulse quickened as he took notes. Was it the information she gave him, or her voice?

"When am I going to see you?" she said at the end. She sounded like a little girl.

"We're up to our asses in alligators right now. Maybe after we wrap up this case."

"Okay," she whispered.

He sat staring at the phone for a moment after they said goodbye.

Stupidity, he told himself yet again, is repeating the same behavior and expecting a different outcome.

"S'matter, Naz?" Burch said. "Bad news?"

"No. It's good." He stood up, clutching his notes. "Wait till you hear this. My CI came through."

Big Red's real name was Linda Pickett, aka Desiree. Last seen in South Florida headlining the show at the Place Montmartre.

When the club shuttered after owner Chris Martelli and a young dancer were murdered, Linda Pickett had apparently packed up her python and left town.

Most people assumed she'd married the boyfriend she'd been involved with and retired from the business. Nobody had heard from her since. A local relative, an aunt, lived in North Bay Village. Linda had often stayed with the woman while performing at Beach clubs.

The aunt's name, also Pickett. "First name maybe Sara or Saundra, something with an S."

"Hope she's still around," Burch said. "Good work."

"But that ain't the half of it, Sarge."

Desiree, Big Red, was more than an employee. She'd known Chris for years. "She was a former squeeze who apparently stayed friendly with the guy even after he moved on to younger girls."

The murdered club owner had been the dark prince of Miami Beach nightlife. Into more than just booze and strippers, he was deeply involved in drug trafficking, loan sharking, prostitution, and all the other shady businesses that thrive in South Beach.

Some had believed that Chris kept the bank for all those operations stashed in a bookcase safe at the club. Big bucks. The money had reportedly vanished with the killer.

Burch and Nazario locked eyes.

"A night's receipts were small change compared to what was in that safe. Word on the street at the time was that nobody was sure if the killer stole the big cash, or if the cops who showed up took it, or even if the cops killed him for it."

"What about Scheck, the guy they busted?"

"My CI says that the Miami Beach cops were happy as hell to close the case in a hurry. Some were on the take, some worked for the dead guy. The last thing the department wanted was outsiders looking at their high-profile investigation."

"Shit," Burch whispered. "Scheck is dead. What the hell are we into here?"

"*¡Dios mío!*" Nazario said. "The State of Florida executed the wrong man."

CHAPTER TWENTY-ONE

Nazario was on the telephone when Burch's cell rang again.

This time Burch sent it sailing through the air. It clattered to the floor, skittering between their desks.

"Hey, hey," Nazario protested. "Bet it's busted now."

"You heard it," Burch said. "Damn piece of crap's been ringing non-stop all day. Wrong numbers, every one of 'em weird guys, sickos, perverts. This some kind of joke? What the hell's going on?"

"Let's see the thing. Hope you didn't kill it," Stone said. "I'll answer it next time it rings."

"You're not in for a long wait," Burch warned. "I'm telling you, you don't want to talk to these guys. There it is again."

Stone reached under the desk, retrieved the phone, and answered it.

"No, he's not here right now, but I can take a message."

Burch tried not to listen to the conversation, which went on for some time.

"You wanna do what?"

Burch nodded grimly, his expression saying *I told you so.*

"Yeah, I see, and what would the date on that be? Sure thing, I'll check it out. It's a mistake. Do me a favor and don't call this one again. No. Not me either. You're wasting your time. Okay, if you insist." He jotted down a number. "Thanks.

"Be right back, Sarge. I gotta go get a copy of the *South Beach Times*. Padron must have one down in PIO with all the others."

He returned a few minutes later with the tabloid open to a back page.

"Okay, Sarge, solved your mystery." Stone looked pleased. "Just remember, lay off my problems with Padron, PIO, and the press. They're not my fault. And I presume—I hope—that your present problem is not your fault. At least directly."

"What're you talking about? Spit it out, Sam."

"You're in the classifieds, Sarge. The personals to be exact. Under 'Men Seeking Men.'"

"Let me see that." Burch snatched the paper. "Which one?"

"The one that says 'Boy Toy.' Listen to this." He read the ad aloud. "'I have a smooth, toned body, a tight butt, and strong hands. Seeking an older male to help bring out the feminine side of me for fun, games, and a possible LTR.'"

"What the hell is an LTR?" Nazario asked.

"Long-term relationship, something you ain't familiar with," Stone said.

Nazario picked up the paper. "Look at these. Whoa! You see the ones under 'Women Seeking Women'?"

"Connie," Burch said grimly. "She thinks this is funny. Well, it ain't. Enough is enough."

"The guy insisted on leaving his number," Stone said. "In case you change your mind and want to give him a call."

The cell phone rang again.

"Let me get it." Nazario answered. His expectant grin faded. "Hold on a minute. He's here."

Burch shook his head, frantically signaling no.

"Sarge. She says it's Maureen Hartley."

Burch took the phone back to his desk.

"Uh-oh. You know who that was," Nazario told Stone.

"The other woman. The mother of the girl, the surviving victim in the Chance case," Stone said.

"Right. When she surfaces, it's trouble for the sarge."

"When are he and Connie gonna stop the games and realize they're meant for each other?"

"Maureen, what's wrong?" Burch was saying into the phone. "Calm down. Okay. Okay."

His stomach churned. She was weeping. "What the hell's going on?"

"I'm sorry, Craig, I'm so sorry. I don't have anybody else to turn to. Donald and I quarreled. He pushed me against the wall. I'm leaving. But I have nowhere to go."

"Maureen, Maureen," he said helplessly, running his hand through his hair.

"Look, I can come and take you to a shelter for battered women, or to your daughter's place. But, hon, I'm in a world of trouble at home myself right now. There's no way I can—"

"I'm sorry, I'm sorry." She sounded on the verge of hysteria. "I tried to reach you at your office an hour or so ago. You weren't there. Your cell phone was busy every time I tried to call. So I called your home number . . ."

He felt suddenly deflated as though something had just sucked the air out of his lungs.

"Oh, jeez. You didn't . . ."

"Your wife answered. She was very rude. I told her it was an emergency. But you wouldn't believe the things she said to me . . ."

"From the look on the sarge's face," Nazario told Stone, "the news ain't good."

"Want me to call your daughter?" Burch asked.

"You said you'd always be there for me."

He sighed. "I'll be right there."

"I gotta go out for about an hour," Burch told the detectives.

Emma, the secretary, called after him as he left.

"Sergeant Burch, your wife is on line four."

Burch kept walking.

He still looked grim when he returned ninety minutes later.

"Good news and bad news," Nazario greeted him. "I got a line on Big Red. Never arrested. But the Beach used to require city ID cards on all nightclub employees. Showed her date of birth as January fourteenth of 'fifty-five, and a name and address for next of kin. Sylvia Pickett, the aunt in North Bay Village. I'm heading up there now."

"What's the bad news?"

"Connie's been calling every five minutes. She's really steamed. Had Emma in tears, and even Riley can't do that."

"Christ. Let's get out of here and go find the aunt."

·   ·   ·

They drove north on the boulevard, then east on the Seventy-ninth Street Causeway to North Bay Village, three man-made islands dredged out of Biscayne Bay in the 1940s.

The quaint waterfront village, only two miles long, was a sin city from the sixties to the early eighties. All-night bars, strip joints, and restaurants, known havens for hoodlums, hookers, and assorted shady characters, including the local politicians, lined the causeway strip.

The area had since settled into a tranquil residential community but was about to explode in a major upheaval. A dozen new high-rise tower projects were under construction or in the planning. The once-quaint village was about to double its population and blossom into a towering urban skyline on the causeway between Miami and Miami Beach.

"I hate to pry, Sarge. But your thing with the little woman—"

"Look, I took Maureen to stay with a friend, another former model, in Bal Harbour," Burch said, as they crawled through traffic behind a slow-moving cement mixer. "I don't know what I'm gonna do."

"Connie's really on your case. You shoulda heard her on the phone."

"Maureen's timing sucks. She called my house today and Connie apparently blew a gasket."

"That explains a lot." Nazario whistled. "If you want to make things right with your wife, you've got to do some serious work. You're gonna need more than a couple a Hail Marys and Our Fathers. More than candy and flowers. You're gonna need a priest, a rabbi, and an exorcist. Your wife is hunting your ass down, and you're about to become road pizza."

·   ·   ·

Sylvia Pickett didn't live in the small apartment house on Treasure Island anymore. The manager of the building, a new hire, wasn't familiar with her name. He said he'd check with someone else in the office.

He came back shaking his head. "She hasn't been here for more than three years. Apparently had a fall, broke a hip—"

"Please don't tell us she's dead," Burch said.

"I won't. She moved out to Winslow Park, that assisted-living center that the Methodist Church runs for the elderly. Hear it's a pretty nice place. A couple of friends here still stay in touch with her."

They drove west on the Palmetto Expressway.

"I hate visiting old-age homes," Burch muttered. "They're too depressing, smell like urine and bleach. The forecast of things to come, the place your kids are gonna dump you someday."

They turned into the complex.

"This is not your typical old-age home," Nazario said. "Look at this place. God bless America."

Charming vine-covered town houses were lined up like spokes radiating out from a large circular community center. There was a pool, deck chairs, a gymnasium, a recreation hall, a library, and a craft center.

On the south side was the golf course and to the north, tennis courts. Bright flower beds bloomed everywhere.

Residents drove golf carts along paved pathways.

"I want to live here when I grow up," Nazario said. "Think my pension will cover it?"

They circled the community center, then stopped an elderly man for directions. He was driving a golf cart with two women passengers. "Tell Sylvia that her boyfriend Bob said hello." He adjusted his jaunty cap and pointed the way. "She'll know who I am."

Sylvia Pickett answered the door. Her short silver hair was stiff and freshly sprayed as though she'd just left the beauty parlor. She appeared to be in her seventies. An ornate cane stood unused near the door. Her linen slacks and matching silk blouse were the same shade of pastel blue.

Inside, the furniture was mostly antique, with a blue velvet settee and two china cabinets displaying Hummel figurines. Her kitchen looked as though it had never been used. Meals were available in the community center dining room or could be delivered, she told them.

Bob was right. She knew who he was. "The man's in his second childhood," she sniffed. "Absolutely girl crazy."

"He did have two of them with him," Nazario said.

Sylvia asked questions. She wanted to know what his companions looked like. Which way their cart had been headed.

The woman appeared sprightly, talkative and active, her eyes bright and birdlike, until they mentioned her niece Linda.

Sylvia Pickett slumped a bit in her chair, suddenly less animated.

"We need her current address."

The woman shook her head slowly as though trying to remember. "Linda? I have no idea. Haven't seen that girl for years and years."

"She used to dance, right?" Burch said.

"Beautiful, a beautiful little girl," Sylvia said slowly. "Started when she was five years old, or maybe it was six. Classically trained. Would have been a ballerina but she grew too tall. Ballet dancers have to be petite so they can be lifted and carried.

"You should have see her in *Nutcracker* when she was just seven or eight. I think it might have been 1962, or was it '63? Prettiest, daintiest little thing you ever saw."

"You have pictures?" Burch asked.

She shifted in her comfortable chair, shoulders drooping into a hunch. Sylvia Pickett seemed to be aging rapidly before their very eyes. "Must have lost them when I moved, I guess."

"Where does she live now?"

She closed her eyes. "Who knows?" She sounded lost and forlorn.

"When did you last hear from her?"

"So many years ago . . ." Her voice trailed off. "Ten? Twenty? Who can remember?"

"Where did she tell you she was going when she left town?"

"At my age, my memory is not what it used to be. Could you hand me my cane, please?" She pointed to it with a shaky finger.

"Going somewhere?" Burch said.

"No." Her voice trembled. "I'm just lost without it."

Nazario fetched the walking stick from beside the door.

Sylvia Pickett held it across her lap, hands resting on it, as though for support.

"Is she married now, or still single with the same last name?"

"Who?" The bird eyes widened, as though bewildered.

"Your niece. Desiree, Linda, Big Red," Burch said impatiently.

"Linda." She smiled dreamily. "I used to take her to dance class. She'd wear these cute little tutus. Adorable, just adorable."

"Where'd you say she lives now?" Nazario asked.

The woman shrank, as though trying to make herself smaller, like a tiny animal surrounded by predators.

"Time for my nap," she murmured. "Doctor's orders. I have to take a nap every afternoon."

· · ·

"Her niece ain't the only one in show biz," Burch said outside. "This one could win an Academy Award."

"She's lying," Nazario said.

"You didn't need your built-in shit detector for that one."

· · ·

"Sylvia, of course," said the smiling young woman in the administration building. Blond and deeply tanned, she wore white shorts and a Winslow Park T-shirt.

"She's doing very nicely. Came back completely from a hip fracture. That's unusual at her age. She's got lots of stamina. You should see her at the weekly dances. She's cut a wide swath among the gentlemen here. A heartbreaker if there ever was one.

"This place," she whispered, with a grin, "is an absolute hotbed of romance, jealousy, and passion."

"Something to look forward to," Burch said.

"Can I fill out my application now?" Nazario asked.

She giggled.

"Sylvia have lots of visitors?" Burch asked. "Family?"

"No immediate family that I know of."

"What about Linda, her niece?"

"What a wonderful woman! She made all the arrangements for Sylvia to be here. Pays all the bills, but she's out of state. Can't get away long enough to visit. But's she's so-o-o devoted. Stays in touch with her aunt and writes us every month to check on Sylvia."

"You have her phone number, or an address?"

The girl paused. "I guess it wouldn't hurt."

She checked a file cabinet. "Here's her last letter. I understand she has a very demanding job."

"What job is that?"

The girl shrugged. "Some sort of business consultant, I think. Must be lucrative. It's not cheap to live here." She handed Nazario the envelope bearing a return address. "She used to be in show business, a dancer. I bet Sylvia showed you all the pictures. I've seen them a hundred times. She's got scrapbooks full."

Linda Ballard, 1432 Greenway Dr., Portland, Maine.

. . .

"Hey, lookit that," Nazario said, as they drove out of the complex. "Short nap."

Sylvia Pickett was scurrying down the path toward the community center.

"Musta forgot her cane," Burch said.

CHAPTER TWENTY-TWO

Nelson found a vacant bright yellow stool at the red Formica counter, ordered a cup of strong, black Cuban coffee, and downed it in one shot.

Nearly every stool was occupied in the noisy Little Havana cafeteria. Neon signs flashed and the counter space was elbow-room only. Most customers were men in work clothes, blue jeans, and baseball caps, or uniforms.

He had to think about what to do next. He already had a bid from the used-furniture dealer on the contents of the apartment. He had to smuggle the man inside when Lourdes and the children were not at home. The offer was very small. Even when Nelson included the stove and refrigerator, which belonged to the landlord. Like life, used furniture is cheap in Miami, where restless residents are always on the move. The money was nowhere near enough. The smuggler, that bastard who brought Lourdes and the children to Miami, had the *cojones* to ask for just as much money to return them.

And Nelson had not yet informed the man of possible problems, because they would not go willingly. He had tested his wife's reaction. He had turned off the TV and for hours spoke lovingly of their homeland, its special landmarks and memories, the music, good friends, and close relatives he knew she missed. Then he had suggested their possible return, without mentioning he would not be accompanying them. Lourdes had laughed in his face and called him *loco*. Then had turned on the TV, loud, so that she would not have to listen to his foolish talk.

He would need handcuffs. He could buy them for a discount at the police supply store on Twenty-seventh Avenue. How difficult, he wondered, would it be to obtain chloroform? One of his customers, the one with the vast green lawn on Sunset Island, was a doctor. The doctor had given him one hundred dollars last Christmas and said his lawn had never looked better. Perhaps he would be willing to provide a small amount of chloroform if Nelson explained he needed it for a family emergency. A more serious problem was money. The smuggler demanded full payment, in advance this time. How could he raise so much cash? He had only one possible source. The time had come for he and Natasha to begin their future life, together. Her husband must be told. The old man had to be told the truth at once. He must leave so that their love would no longer be denied. Then he could ask her for the money. She had so much, but obviously did not realize how little he himself had. Normally he would not want her to know this. His pride would not allow him to ask her for money, not even for his labors on the landscaping at her home. But this time was different. She loved him. She wanted him to be happy. Happy with her, forever. *Para siempre.* He could see that in all of the things she did when they were alone. Just the thought of her writhing in passion made his blood pulsate in concert with the flashing neon signs. Natasha would understand. Only a loan. She would not miss it. The price of just one of her shiny bracelets would more than pay for the one-way journey that would help insure their future happiness together. A small price to pay for love. And he would repay her every cent.

They must do it, he thought. Her husband must be told. Nelson had never asked Natasha for anything. But she would understand. He would deliver the cash she gave him directly to the man in Hialeah and then arrange to take Lourdes and the children to Marathon, to the dock from which they would depart. He would take them in his truck. The children would do as they were told and could ride up front with him. But Lourdes . . .

He could roll her up inside a tarp in the back of the truck with his lawn mower and tools. But the children might object. Perhaps he could trick them, say he was taking them fishing. He knew that at the last minute they would recognize the men and their boat. Lourdes would never forget them. She and the children had been seasick through rough weather all the way across the Florida Straits. But by then it would be too late.

The stool beside him became vacant and one of the B-girls at the café sidled up, sat down next to him, and pinched his thigh. Her name was Tonya. An illegal from Nicaragua, she wore a skimpy midriff top, a miniskirt, and big hoop earrings. He had liked her, before Natasha. After dark, the lights went down and the café became even busier as "waitresses" fraternized with the customers for money. In exchange for a series of escalating fees, the girls would sit, talk, and flirt with the customers, dance with them, fondle them. Sometimes even accompany them into a tiny back room.

But who would be interested in a woman like Tonya, with her pockmarked complexion, big frizzy hair, and bigger behind, when a goddess like Natasha awaited him? He could not believe his good fortune. That soon they would be together. Forever.

He looked at Tonya's chipped-tooth smile, smelled her cheap perfume, and knew he was doing the right thing. Natasha would give him the money. He would demand it. Content that he had made the right decision, he ordered a *palomilla* steak and *frijoles negros*. He had to shout to be heard over the din.

CHAPTER **TWENTY-THREE**

TWO HOURS LATER

I'm numb as I drive home. The Blazer is handling perfectly at last. My cell phone is turned off. Maureen sat there beside me this afternoon, as lovely as ever. Her tear-filled eyes haunt me. She begged to stay with me. It was hard to say no. I yearned to bring her back with me to my quiet, private place with its secret gardens and shaded courtyard patios. But what if she and her husband never tire of that sick game they play with each other's heads? If some people can make themselves miserable, they will. You can count on it. I care for her. I always will, even if she continues her slam dance with him. But what about my family? Nazario's words repeat like a warning drum beat in my head.

"Your wife is hunting your ass down and you're about to become road pizza." Nice. I feel like one of the settlers waiting for the Indian attack.

I can't wait to pack a bag, get out of town, and head for Maine. We're hot on the trail. I'm totally focused and hope to achieve some satisfaction there. Make somebody proud, even if it is only myself.

The authorization for travel money won't come till Monday. I hate red tape, warned Riley that Big Red could run. I'm sure her aunt, the one with instant amnesia, tipped her off. When we saw her last, she had to be beating feet to the nearest pay phone. Big Red had probably warned her to never call from home.

Maybe she was just sniffing for the trail of Bob, the boyfriend. Would she ever stoop to advertising him under "Men Seeking Men" in the personals?

Being away will give Connie a little more time to cool off. I'll be out of range, too distant a target, and then, when I come back, I'll try to figure out this whole mess between us. I can't believe Connie had all those guys calling me.

We'll be gone just a day or two at most. I bought a feeder to funnel a constant supply of cat food into his bowl till I get back. Stone will come by to check the house while I'm gone.

I pull into the driveway, grateful to be home. I think about Maureen and how nice it would be to have company in that lonely room upstairs tonight. To stroll with someone in that scented garden amid the splashing fountains. I fight temptation. Maureen needs time to think about her future as well. I focus on Big Red and Charles Terrell instead. Do they sense change? Do chills run up and down their spines? Does something tell them that we're coming, at last, that after twelve years somebody knows what they've done?

The driveway is dark and shadowy. I pick up my dry cleaning and the bag from the supermarket as the cat streaks out from behind the hibiscus to greet me. Uh-oh. I left him inside. Locked in. What is this? I reach for my gun.

No other cars here. I didn't notice the action out on the street before pulling into the driveway. Damn. I wasn't paying attention. Was that a Saturn parked halfway down the block? Shit. Connie must have made me! Found out where I'm staying. She's damn good. That woman would make a hell of a detective. Nazario was right. She probably followed me the other night. Whew! Close call. Thank God I didn't weaken and bring Maureen Hartley home with me. What a mistake that would have been! I lock my gun in the glove compartment for safekeeping. God forbid Connie gets her dainty little paws on a loaded weapon.

The cat looks agitated. What happened? I ask him. She must have scared him. He doesn't know her.

He doesn't wind himself around my leg as usual. He paces between me and the house. Stay outta the way. There could be fireworks, I say, and carry the bag and clean shirts up the stairs. I leave the packages on the landing and try the door. Locked. I unlock it as quietly as possible.

It's dark and hushed inside. But somebody is, or has been, here.

The drawers in my bedroom have been opened and disturbed.

I think I hear a distant sound. Damn, did she go into the big house? Sure enough, the door at the top of the stairs is ajar.

This could be good, I begin to think. We're alone. We can argue, talk it out. Without the kids, no distractions, I can explain. Win her over. This could wind up cozy, maybe even romantic. I'm glad I made the bed this morning. Connie hates a messy room. I'm thinking romance here.

"I know you're in there," I shout down the stairs. "Come on out. Let's talk."

Something hits the floor and breaks. Shatters, like glass.

Shit, the place is full of valuables. I can't let her trash the house.

"Don't do that, Con! Stop what you're doing. Right now! Talk to me."

All I hear are footsteps. Running. Shit!

"Con, listen to me." I descend the stairs. "We can work this out." My voice echoes through vast empty space.

More running.

"Con," I bellow, losing my temper. "You're exhibiting an antisocial personality!"

Scrambling, more running footsteps.

She wants to play games? Okay, I can play, too. I'm a helluva lot faster than she is.

I sprint through the kitchen. My shoes crunch through broken glass on the floor. Meanwhile, a stray thought nags at my subconscious, just as the questions begin to surface: What happened to the alarm system? How did she manage not to set it off? I stumble against something. Something that shouldn't be there. Things that shouldn't be there.

In the dining room, stacked beside French doors that open out into the garden, is a mountain of items. Heavy wooden silverware chests, TVs, stereos, statues, binoculars. Everything but the kitchen sink.

I grab for my gun. It isn't there.

I see movement out of the corner of my eye just before he tackles me. We grapple, then hit the floor rolling. I smack the side of my forehead, hard, on a corner table as we thrash around. I think I'm bleeding.

Now I'm furious. The dumb son of a bitch let the cat out and now he's stealing the stuff I get free rent to guard.

"Goddammit." I whack him in the face with my elbow and grab him in a choke hold. Meanwhile, more footsteps. He's not alone. I let go of him, scramble to my feet, and give him a swift kick to the groin to keep him down as his buddy comes through the door. I grab something, a television remote, from the stacked loot and fake it.

"Miami Police, don't move or I'll shoot!

I point it at him in the shadows, I'm praying the son of a bitch doesn't hit a light switch. And that he doesn't have a real gun. Shit, I think, everybody in Miami has a gun. You can count on it. "Police!" I yell again. "Drop the gun or I'll fire! Son of a bitch. I'll drop you right there!" I'm so good I almost convince myself I've got a gun. The guy on the floor makes a sound and tries to roll over. I give him a quick kick to the side of the head. He cries out in pain.

"Drop it now!"

The one in the doorway drops something that clatters heavily to the floor. My God, he had a gun.

"Hands in the air. Higher! Now kick it over here." The gun slides toward me across the marble floor in the dark. "Turn around!" I yell, madder than ever. Does the guy on the floor have one, too? He gurgles as I put my foot on his Adam's apple and press. "Hands on the wall," I tell the other one. "Now!"

Thank God he listens. I quickly pat down the one on the floor. All he's packing is a screwdriver and a flashlight. I take a step and snatch up the gun. A .357, fully loaded, one in the chamber.

Not until both are cuffed and staring sullenly from the backseat of a Miami Beach police car do I stop to think about how badly this all could have turned out.

The Beach cops are a little surly to see that I have this great housing deal in their city, but they become more friendly fast.

The suspects are pros. Been giving them fits, hitting dozens of homes since spring. They had managed to dismantle the alarm system, part of their MO. They turn out to be known offenders, ex-convicts, both on parole. Their car was parked around the corner. Once they accumulated all the loot, they would have checked that the coast was clear, then brought the car up to the house for loading.

Between the multiple burglaries and parole violations, assault on a police officer, and gun charges, they're looking at some hard time. Not a bad night's work.

One of 'em even asked a Beach detective how I knew who they were, that they were "cons." I'm just lucky the guy surrendered at the point of a TV remote. There ain't no cure for stupid.

Somebody notified the city that I was involved in an off-duty situation on the Beach. Next thing I know, Riley shows up, just as the ER doc at Mount Sinai is taking a coupla stitches in my head. In blue jeans and a T-shirt, all pale with no lipstick, she looks worried, wants to make sure I'm all right.

"Think you'll be good to travel on Monday?" she said.

"Absolutely," I say. "Wouldn't miss it for anything. I'm on a roll."

Then somebody hands me a phone. Padron wants to talk to me, wants to write a press release.

This ain't a story I want told. I'm embarrassed. I was stupid. I walked right into it. Unarmed.

Too late. A Channel Seven news crew descends. I don't want them to catch me in my bloodstained shirt. My wife and kids might see it. I tell Padron he better come to run interference.

I realize it's okay. Padron can make anybody look like a hero. For the second time tonight I am so grateful that I didn't invite Maureen Hartley home with me. Maybe virtue is its own reward. I call Adair to say his house is okay and everything's under control. It's the middle of the night here, but in Italy, the sun is shining.

Then I call home. Jennifer says her mom had a bad day and is asleep. "Don't wake her," I say. "Just tell her I called to say I'm okay."

"Why, Daddy? What happened?"

"Nothing. I arrested a couple a guys. Got a little bump on the head. I just wanted you to know I'm fine in case they have something on the news."

"Where are you, Daddy?"

"At the ER, over at Mount Sinai."

"The hospital?" Bless her heart, the kid starts to bawl. "In the hospital?"

"No, no, I'm not, sweetheart. I'm leaving right now. Just got a little iodine and a Band-Aid. A scratch. It's nothing. Get some sleep now. I miss you all. Nighty-nite, honey."

Somebody loves me after all, I think.

CHAPTER TWENTY-FOUR

Stone ran late all morning. Though it was Saturday, he went by the station for the FedEx package sent by Donna Hastings.

She had enclosed the photograph of her father on the front porch, and a few others. The only dentist her mother remembered him seeing had died years ago and no records were available, her note said. In his pictures, Hastings looked like a happy-go-lucky loser who laughed a lot. Excellent, Stone thought. He checked his mail and messages, phoned Burch to hear firsthand about his exploits the night before, then took the photos to the medical examiner's office.

By the time he finished his shopping at Home Depot and arrived at his grandmother's cottage, it was nearly noon.

She was drying her hands on a dish towel, music playing on a small radio in the kitchen.

"Thought you were comin' for breakfast." She hugged him. "It's a little late for that now."

"I'd still love some eggs and grits." He carried his heavy yellow toolbox into the kitchen. He'd bought a brand-new inch-and-a-half dead bolt for her back door and some bolts to secure a shaky porch railing.

"A lightbulb in the bedroom ceilin' needs changin', if you got time, Sonny."

He grinned at her. "I got time."

As he went through the living room to check the bulb, he noticed something missing.

The frame that had always held his parents' smiling photo stood empty. The frame next to it, which held the childhood picture of him in front of the TV in his little blue suit, lay facedown on the shelf. He stood it up. It, too, was empty.

"Gran, where are the pictures?"

"Oh, Sonny, the girl took them."

"What girl?"

"You know, Nell."

"Nell Hunter?"

His grandmother smiled. "Nice girl. I think she likes you."

He stared at her, speechless for a moment, still holding the empty frame.

"Nell was here?"

"All afternoon on Thursday. Talkin' 'bout you, askin' questions. Borrowed the pictures to put in the newspaper." His grandmother saw his eyes and grew serious. "She promised she'd bring 'em back. Said it was all right, she talked to you first."

"Oh no," he muttered. "She can't do this. Gran, you never should have let her have those pictures. You shouldn't have let her in the house. Never should have talked to her. You should have asked me first."

"I did call you," she said in a small voice. "I left a message."

"Damn." He sat in the armchair and tried to think. He'd seen her message and hadn't answered. He'd assumed she just wanted to ask what time he'd be there. This was all his fault.

"How would she know to come out here, Sonny, if you didn't tell her where I'm at? Said she's writin' your profile. What's wrong? She's from the newspaper. Isn't she? The one that put your picture on the front page?"

"What did she ask you about, Gran? Did you say anything about what happened to Mama and Daddy?"

"She knew all about it. Was askin' me questions."

This was too personal. Way too personal.

"Sonny?" His grandmother sat down on the sofa across from him. "The photographer came with her. A man with a lotta cameras. They took my picture, too. Is that bad?"

"Oh, Jesus," he said. "Where?"

"Here. In the backyard. Out on the front porch."

Stone sprang to his feet and began to pace.

"Did I do something wrong, Sonny?"

"No. It was me, Gran. My fault," he said. "But I'll fix it. I'll stop her."

"I was gonna fuss at you for not tellin' me she was comin'. I coulda fixed my hair up and put on my Sunday dress. I didn't want you to be ashamed of me."

He swallowed hard. "I could never be ashamed of you, Gran." He sat down next to her, put his arm around her shoulders. "I just don't like you being exposed, or put in any danger because of my job."

"Oh, she wouldn't do that, Sonny. Seems like a real nice girl, really friendly."

"Gran, remember when I was little and you took me to the petting zoo? Remember the llama?"

. . .

Stone was furious. Nell wasn't at the paper. He'd left messages on her voice mail. There was probably plenty of time to clarify what she would and would not include in her story. But he had to be sure. He kept calling.

No one seemed to be in the whole damn place. Didn't newspapers operate twenty-four hours a day, like police departments? He hated voice mail. Finally he reached a human on the city desk and said it was urgent.

They would not divulge Nell's number but said they'd have her call him. She didn't.

He worked furiously, more angry at himself than anyone else. He should have known better. He'd seen how reporters can access information. She had simply typed his name into the system. What was he thinking? She had taken advantage. He wanted those pictures back. He wanted them now.

He called the city desk every half hour.

At five-thirty he was mowing the yard, shirtless, sweaty, and out of breath, when his cell phone rang.

"Hey, Sam Spade," she said lightly. "You rang?"

"Nell." He tried to sound calm. He just wanted the pictures back. He just wanted her to cooperate. He'd bargain if he had to. He carried the cell phone onto the shade of the porch, where his half-empty glass of iced tea stood.

"Nell, I have to say I'm upset because you came out to see my grandmother without telling me."

"Silly, that's what reporters do. *Good* reporters. You don't write a decent profile without talking to a lot of people familiar with your subject. That's the difference between an interview and a profile. I spoke to your boss, your high school coach, and your homeroom teacher, too. You upset about that?"

"I'm not happy about it," he said. "But I'm downright alarmed about my grandmother. You saw her. She lives alone. And I'm involved in a high-profile hunt for a serial killer who preys on elderly women. You can't put Gran's name, her picture, or her address in the newspaper. That would be dangerous. It could compromise her safety. I don't want strangers to even know I have a grandmother."

Nell was silent for a long moment, then came back feisty. "You mean you actually think that this killer, who could be, God knows, anywhere, might really stalk your grandmother? Now, that's pretty paranoid. Plus, he's only killed white women."

He tried to control his temper. "Stranger things have happened, Nell. And I can't risk it. It isn't just him. As a policeman I've arrested a lot of people that I wouldn't want to have my family's home address."

"Her address isn't in there. Just a description of the house and that it's in Overtown."

Dread overwhelmed him. "You mean you already wrote it?"

"Right. It's a good story. Some of my best work. You'll like it."

"I won't if my gran's name or picture is in it. And I want my parents' picture back. Right away. Tonight. I can come pick it up. You didn't mention in the story what happened to them, did you?"

He knew the answer by her silence. "You can't use that, Nell. It's really private. The people I work with don't even know."

"But that's what makes the story." She sounded exasperated, as though explaining simple logic to a child. "It makes you seem human, vulnerable, and gives the piece a real edge. Small boy whose parents are killed in an unsolved murder grows up to be a detective specializing in unsolved murders. What's more dramatic or heart-wrenching than that? Great story."

"Take it out, Nell. You have to. It would mean a lot to me. Please."

She didn't answer.

"You're violating my privacy."

"What privacy?" she asked coolly. "You gave that up at the press conference. You can't have it both ways. You can't ask for publicity on one hand, then try to stop it when you don't like where it goes. That's not how it works."

"This is different. I'm no politician or celebrity, I'm just a cop. It was part of my job, I had to do it. Nell," he pleaded, "take it out. We can stay friends, I'll tip you off on other stories. You'll be the first to know when we close a big case. Just take my grandmother and my parents out of it. Please."

"It's too late."

"Why? You can just tell your editors that—"

"It's in tomorrow's newspaper. The early edition is already out on the street."

CHAPTER TWENTY-FIVE

"What's the other guy look like?" Stone asked Monday morning as Burch walked into the office, a Band-Aid over the stitches in his head.

"Two guys. There was two of 'em," Nazario crowed. "And he captured 'em both with a TV remote. That's our sarge."

"Yeah," Burch said. "Between the two of us, we're keeping Padron busy. *Too* busy."

Stone nodded grimly. The story that ran on the front page of Sunday's paper had included a photo of his grandmother, age seventy-eight, seated on her front porch, smiling proudly, the house number clearly visible on the wall behind her.

"How the hell did you let that happen?" Burch said.

"I didn't. That reporter burned me, sneaked behind my back. When I found out she'd been to see my grandmother, I called in time to stop the story. She got my messages, had to know why I was calling, but didn't get back to me until it was too late. That had to be deliberate."

He looked sick. "She didn't care. All they care about is a good story."

"And why the hell didn't we know about your folks' case?" Burch said, his voice lowered. "Why'd we have to read about it in the newspaper along with the rest of the world? Jesus Christ, a double murder, a police officer's parents. I mighta seen it once when I was rummaging through old files. From what I remember, it didn't look promising. Nothing new in years. But that ain't stopping us from taking a run at it. You couldn't be the lead officially, but we can work it, see what we find." He shook his head. "You work side by side. You think you know somebody. Why didn't you tell us?"

"I was gonna bring it up at some point," Stone said, "but I want to prove myself in this unit first."

"Hell, Stone. You did that a long time ago."

"What about your grandmother?" Nazario asked.

"Yeah, is she relocated?" Burch asked.

"No," Stone said. "I wanted to move her to my place. But she's stubborn, independent. Always has been. Says that nothing or nobody can make her leave her home. I spent all day yesterday arguing with her and securing the house. Her neighbors said they'd keep an eye on her and I gave her a cell phone, though she didn't want it."

"We'll have patrol put a watch order on her place," Burch said. "The zone cars can keep tabs on her. Damn it. Didn't I warn you about reporters?"

.   .   .

At Nazario's request, police in Portland, Maine, discreetly checked and found that Big Red, Linda Pickett, apparently lived alone at the Greenway address, a high-rent condominium apartment house, under the name Linda Ballard. She'd been seen there within the last twenty-four hours.

"Looks like it's a go," Riley told them.

"Wonder where the hell Terrell is," Burch worried. "How come he isn't with her?"

"We'll find out soon," Nazario said. "I'm psyched."

They conferred with Assistant State Attorney Jo Salazar before their noon flight to Maine.

"Maybe I should go with you," the prosecutor said. "Don't make her any promises, but obviously, he's the one we want. Find out how much she knows, what she has to offer. Maybe we can deal her. If you need me, I'll come up."

They stopped at Bob Hope Road. The chief medical examiner had been poring over the file.

"Your victim, whoever he was, had a hemoglobin saturation of fifty percent carbon monoxide. At that time, investigators believed that the victim's high concentration of carbon monoxide meant he was alive at the time of the fire and died from smoke inhalation. Such high levels are common in fatal house fires, but recent studies show that they are not in gasoline-fueled flash fires. Those victims die so quickly that the carbon monoxide content remains low.

"He must have been overcome by carbon monoxide in some other fashion—such as from automobile exhaust. He was dead from carbon monoxide poisoning before the fire. Then the fire itself was set, possibly with paper trailers later consumed by the flames. That would leave no evidence of arson and allow the perpetrator enough time to escape before the fire was noticed."

"So Terrell must have left him either unconscious or tied up in the garage with the car engine running," Nazario said. "Not bad. He almost got away with it."

"He did get away with it, for twelve years," Burch said. "I wonder if the victim was already dead, or still alive when Terrell dropped the car on him and took off his finger."

The doctor shrugged. "That would be speculation. If you find him, maybe he'll tell us."

"We had no luck on dental records for Hastings," Burch said. "But you've got the photos the daughter sent. And we're leaving you a good shot of Terrell. Think they might be enough?"

"We should know soon," the chief said. "Dr. Wyatt plans to look at them today."

They made copies and took pictures of both men with them, picked up their overnight bags at headquarters, and were about to leave for the airport when Lieutenant Riley hailed them from her office.

"Uh-oh," Burch said. "Here she comes. Look at her face. Something's up."

"We shoulda beat it out of here while we had the chance," Nazario said. "We're cutting it close."

"Guess who's missing in action?" Riley said breathlessly.

"I'm afraid you're about to tell us," Burch said.

"Natasha Ross. She's disappeared."

"What the hell . . . ?" Burch said.

The detectives stared at each other.

"Can it be related?" Burch said.

"How can it not be? What's going on?" Nazario frowned and checked his watch.

"When's your flight?" Riley said.

"Noon." Burch sighed in frustration, eyes uncertain.

"Hell. You don't have much time. Go! Go!" She hustled them in the direction of the elevator. "I'll head out to the Ross place. Stay in touch. Now go!"

CHAPTER TWENTY-SIX

Nelson leaped into his truck, slammed the door, and burned rubber as he raced away from the towering high-rise building. He did not look back. The tall green van swayed, the lawn equipment inside shifting, as he swerved through traffic, took corners too fast, and raced onto Southwest Eighth Street, Calle Ocho.

Heartsick and furious, his pride wounded, he pounded his steering wheel in frustration. To threaten his manhood! To laugh at his love! How could Natasha treat him so? How could she turn on him? After all they had been to each other. Did she not see the sacrifices he had made for her? He tried to calm himself. Women do such things and later they are sorry, he thought.

Spirited and passionate. Her fiery nature was so like his own. They were more alike than she realized. Soul mates. When they were next together, he would take control. He would become a strong man who dominated her. That's what she wants, he told himself. Women love a strong, virile man who can give them many children. Not an old man with white hair, shriveled *cojones*, and a limp, lifeless penis. She must be dominated.

He must be stronger. Take charge and claim what is his. He nearly turned to rush back to the San Souci Towers to take what was his. To transform her into a more docile and understanding mate.

But what if she continued to hide and elude him? He would appear foolish and weak in her eyes. No, she must now come to him. This was a good lesson after what she had done. She must make her own way home. But he had her dress. He wrinkled his brow.

Uncertain, he lifted his foot from the accelerator, then floored it again at the memory of how she had menaced his very manhood with his own razor-sharp pruning shears. He had missed disaster by only a fraction of an inch, then stumbled, struggling to pull on his pants as she ran away from him.

Miami Police Officer Fermin Santiago clocked the landscape truck at sixty-five in a thirty-mile-an-hour zone as it rattled by him. He flipped on his blue flasher.

This was the debut of the new and improved Officer Fermin Santiago, his first day back on patrol after three weeks in fucking sensitivity / anger management training. Due to his short fuse and multiple use-of-force complaints, he'd had little choice. It was either train or be suspended. His most recent bad luck had been his worst yet. How could he know that smart-assed motorist, so slow to step out of her fancy convertible, was a rich lawyer's wife? How could he know that when he grabbed one of her fancy high-heeled boots to yank her out of the vehicle that she'd bump her head on the pavement? Twice.

His sergeant said he had worked too long on midnights in the inner city and had forgotten how to treat civilized people. Santiago was bitter. He had no anger management problem. Sleep deprivation was his real problem. If that bitch Andrea would just muzzle the fucking kids and let him sleep, he'd be fine. The twins had howled all night again and Andrea, puffy-eyed and sleep deprived herself, had told him just this morning to fix his own damn breakfast.

In spite of it all, Santiago was in good spirits, back in control, back on patrol. Sure, it was the day shift, where he would endure close scrutiny by his supervisors, but they could watch all they liked, he thought. They would be nothing but impressed. Fresh out of the classroom, he had spent days learning, absorbing, and practicing verbal judo. Being accustomed to constant action out on patrol, he had found it difficult to stay awake. The talky sessions were mind-numbing, fall-asleep boring, but he had regrouped, applied himself, and had the drill down pat.

The chief was a believer in verbal judo, so verbal judo it would be. He'd win the goddamn fucking Olympic gold medal in verbal judo, if such a thing existed. If that's what it took to stay out of trouble and boost his ass onto the sergeant's list, he would follow the rules to a T.

Verbal judo classes would soon be SOP for the whole department, the chief had said. In Savannah, they had reduced use-of-force reports, injuries, and civilian lawsuits by 30 percent.

Santiago fell in behind the green landscape truck, blue light flashing. The driver ignored him and accelerated.

"Pull over. Driver of the green van, pull over to the curb," Santiago calmly instructed over the PA. The dispatcher had reported back that the license tag was valid. The van was not reported stolen. This guy was acting like an asshole for no good reason.

Motorists in the stream of traffic around them hit their brakes. But the driver of the green landscape truck pounded his steering wheel. Then he floored it.

"Goddammit." Santiago switched on his siren. Miami police policy forbids the high-speed pursuit of traffic violators. Orders are to let errant motorists escape rather than risk a crash.

They had taken all the fun out of police work, Santiago thought bitterly.

Luckily, the inevitable traffic jam loomed up ahead. Moments later the landscape van was pinned in by traffic.

• • •

Nelson knew he was in trouble. That woman! Damn Natasha. She had called the police! Now they would handcuff him, drag him to jail, treat him like a common criminal, all for love!

Filled with helpless rage, he knew he had done nothing wrong. Every man knows what it is like to have a woman make you crazy, drive you insane, and force you to do things you would never otherwise do.

Hands on the steering wheel, he ignored the policeman who approached his van.

He would not be humiliated again.

His window was halfway down. The policeman asked for his driver's license and registration. Nelson ignored the request and continued to stare straight ahead.

Was he being tested? Santiago wondered. Was this a setup? Was the green van a plant arranged by internal affairs detectives who were out to get him? He'd show them.

This was his first opportunity to apply his newly acquired expertise in verbal judo in real life, on the street.

He had already taken the first of the five steps. *Just ask them what you want them to do.*

Santiago smoothly segued into Step Two: *Explain why you have asked them to do it.*

"Sir, I need to see your driver's license and registration just to check and make sure that they are, indeed, valid and up-to-date."

Nelson stared at him contemptuously.

The old Fermin Santiago would have had this mope facedown on the pavement by now, handcuffed and bleeding.

The reformed Officer Santiago refused to take this motorist's recalcitrance personally.

Step Three: *Give the citizen positive and negative reinforcement. Make them think it is their idea to cooperate. Allow them to surrender with dignity. Give them a choice.*

"It will be beneficial for you and good for me if you decide to cooperate," Santiago said carefully, wondering if Internal Affairs had this mope wired. "We're both working men and you are probably having a bad day. We all do from time to time. You'll be on your way shortly if you show me your driver's license and registration. Otherwise, I might have to tow away your nice green truck. I'd hate all that paperwork. I'm sure you don't need the hassle either. How about it?"

"She lied," Nelson said, with a sneer.

Shit, Santiago thought, woman trouble. He knew how that was. He put on his most sincere face and launched into Step Four. "Sir, is there anything I can say that will persuade you to cooperate with what I've asked you to do? If so, can you share it with me now?"

Nelson glared.

"Anything at all?" Santiago sighed. He had done the best he could, by the book. Time for Step Five: *Get reaaaady to rumble.*

He radioed for backup. The van door burst open. Nelson leaped out, his .45 caliber Walther in his hand. Santiago launched himself headlong to the ground behind his patrol car. He took cover as Nelson fired wildly.

Cars screeched around him as Nelson shot the patrol car's radiator, windshield, and right front tire. Then he dove back into his van and hurtled west.

"Fuck!" The old Santiago radioed that he was under fire, leaned over his car, closed one eye, and emptied his eighteen-shot semiautomatic Glock at the fleeing van. One slug shattered the plate-glass front of the Chevrolet dealership across four lanes of traffic. Another bullet ricocheted off an airport shuttle loaded with tourists bound for South Beach, then hit a passing pedestrian in the ankle. The shuttle careened wildly across two lanes, causing a Ford Explorer and a Toyota to collide. The Explorer slammed into a royal palm and rolled over. The huge tree toppled onto Florida Power and Light wires, knocking out the power to the traffic signals.

As brakes squealed, tourists screamed, and cars collided all around him, Santiago's sole, small consolation was that most of his eighteen full-metal-jacket, hollowpoint rounds had found their mark. He'd riddled the back of the now-vanished landscape truck. His euphoria lasted only a split second before the urgent voice of the dispatcher called out his unit number.

"Hold your fire, Three thirty-three. I repeat, do *not* fire at the van. The subject driver may have a white female kidnap victim restrained inside. Do you read me, Three thirty-three? Repeat. Do *not* fire at the van."

CHAPTER TWENTY-SEVEN

Stone sighed in frustration. He'd cross-checked all the names the new tips had generated with the names of witnesses, suspects, and neighbors interviewed twenty-four years ago after Virginia Meadows was murdered. None matched.

He decided to look at the total picture. All the cases took place in cities with thriving Orthodox congregations, synagogues, Jewish cemeteries, kosher markets and restaurants, and what else?

He spoke again to Mordechai Waldman, who suggested religious bookstores, *mikvehs,* the ritual baths, and Judaica shops.

Stone's phone never stopped ringing. Callers were eager to chat about Sunday's newspaper story; some had lost loved ones to murder, others were friends or acquaintances. Nell Hunter had left two messages. Stone tossed hers. A courier from her newspaper had returned the borrowed photographs to his grandmother. He had no reason to talk to Nell again.

• • •

He studied city directories, street maps, and locators on the Internet and, city by city, began the tedious process of creating geographic profiles of each crime scene radiating out from each victim's address. Many didn't drive, they walked or rode buses.

By the end of the day he found that stores that sold Judaica were located within two miles of each victim's home.

He found the small store in Miami filled with books, candles, picture frames, even kosher scouring sponges.

"Most of our merchandise comes from New York and from Israel," the pudgy proprietor said. He wore a yarmulke, gold-rimmed spectacles, and a snowy white shirt under a black vest and tie.

"When a young man becomes engaged to be married, he is given a gold watch and a set of *shas,* books that contain writings from the Torah." He displayed some of the tall, handsome leather-bound volumes, some sets worth as much as twenty thousand dollars.

Brides-to-be receive sterling candlestick holders and a silver challah knife.

There were rows of *mezuzah* cases, each containing a small scroll with a quote from Deuteronomy 6:9: *"And you shall write them on the door posts of your house and on your gates."*

He has seen them fixed in a slanted position on the upper right-hand doorposts of Jewish homes.

Stone was frustrated again to learn that the Judaica stores were independent and family-owned, not part of a national chain.

"Are there salesmen or suppliers who call on you and travel to other stores all over the country?"

"No. We go to New York, to the showrooms, once, twice a year."

"Who among observant Jews working in religious-related fields would travel from city to city?"

He shrugged. "Maybe a chief *mashgiach,* from the National Council. He is the one who oversees the overseers who certify kosher food establishments. He visits, once, twice a year. His job is to inspect and check that all the local *mashgiachim* properly do their jobs, that everything is kept up to par. The laws are very strict. That they don't open on the sabbath or on holidays. That even for Passover, they can't begin to prepare before midnight, that they don't use nonkosher products. There is even kosher Tide detergent. And the flame on the stove must not be lit by a nonobservant Jew. His is an important job."

The proprietor excused himself to help a man carrying a department store garment bag. Price tags still dangled from the suit inside.

The man who bought the suit had come to have it inspected for *shat-niz*. Orthodox Jews are not permitted to mix wool and linen. Stone watched the proprietor use a microscope to carefully examine the suit's fibers. The suit passed. Had the presence of linen fibers been detected, it would have been returned to the store.

Back at headquarters, Stone rechecked his geographic profiles. Kosher restaurants were also located within a two- to three-mile radius of the crime scenes.

He riffled through his messages, found one from the medical examiner's office, and drove to Bob Hope Road.

Dr. Everett Wyatt, the thin, wiry, and intense forensic odontologist, was holding forth in the chief's office.

"Here he is," he greeted Stone.

"We've got some news for you," the chief medical examiner said.

Dr. Wyatt placed a computerized blow-up of the photo of a laughing Charles Terrell beside the jawbones of the man who died in the garage. "Although the victim's upper front teeth are burned and blackened, the protected lower teeth were distinctive. Mr. Terrell's lower teeth, clearly visible in the laughing photo, do not display those same distinctive characteristics.

"These," he said, "are two different men. So now that we know who this fellow wasn't, let's see who he was."

He placed another photo, a computerized enlargement, next to the jaws.

"Now, look at the overall arrangement of the lower teeth," said the fast-talking, ebullient dentist. "See how that left lateral incisor overlaps? And the chipped edge of that right lower central incisor? Voilà! A perfect match! We have our man."

"The victim found dead under the car in Terrell's garage was your fellow from Wyandotte, Missouri," the medical examiner said. "Michael Hastings."

CHAPTER TWENTY-EIGHT

The midday flight was full, packed with the usual cast of characters assembled before any passenger jet can take off. They were all there: the screaming baby, the wheezing, sneezing stranger with a runny nose, and kids who kick the seat backs nonstop.

A large Latino family, parents and an indeterminate number of teenagers, sat inexplicably in distant sections of the plane, then spent the flight shouting back and forth to one another.

"Lucky we didn't plan to take a nap," Burch said.

Nazario cut his eyes at the hacking passenger across the aisle and two rows back.

"This is what I hate about flying. God knows what we'll take off this bird with us. Remember the old days? You catch a cold and you go to bed until you get better. Maybe your family or the guy working next to you catches it. No big deal. Today somebody sick books on a jet from Singapore to London or Seattle. All the way, he's coughing little invisible drops of what's ailing him into the same recirculated air the rest of us are breathing. When the plane lands, a couple hundred passengers fan out, coughing and sneezing, into a whole new unsuspecting population. No place in the world you can't reach in hours. That's how fast a bug can travel.

"Look at AIDS, look at SARS—who the hell knows what's next. We might be inhaling it on this flight right now. Plus, we have to change planes in Atlanta. That doubles our chances."

"Don't do this to me, Naz. Just try not to breathe, okay?"

"They should give everybody a physical before they board."

"Not a bad idea. They already make you take off your shoes."

"Hey, the first AIDS patient was a flight steward who infected people from New York to L.A."

"Yeah, and I'm already suffering from IDS."

"What's that?"

"Income deficiency syndrome. Thank God for that place I'm living. At least I'm not paying rent."

"The guy who owns that spread isn't doing you any favors. He got his money's worth the other night. He owes you. They'da cleaned him out."

"I hope his cat's all right," Burch worried. "Maybe I shoulda boarded him. Hated to leave 'im alone. Anything happens to me, tell Stone to take good care of that cat until Adair comes back."

"Jeez. What brought that on?"

Burch shrugged and went back to an old *Newsweek* he'd plucked from the seat pocket in front of him.

"See this?" He indicated a story about a wildlife photographer and his companion, killed by the Alaskan brown bears they were filming.

"Yeah," Nazario said. "The guy was like a paparazzi."

"What d'ya mean, a paparazzi?"

"They said the guy had been sneaking up on the bears, shooting their pictures for twelve years. The bears had no privacy. They're eating, they're drinking, snoozing, or having sex, and every time they turn around, some guy's creeping through the bushes, shooting their pictures, filming everything they do. A bear can't even take a crap in the woods without this guy and his camera.

"That's exactly what Alec Baldwin and all those other celebrities are always complaining about. They take swings at those photographers, try to run 'em over. Even Jackie O. got a restraining order against one of them. Guy was following her all the time. A bear can't get a restraining order, he doesn't even have a lawyer.

"The bears got tired of it, just wanted some privacy, a little peace and quiet. But here comes the guy again, sneaking around stalking 'em with the camera. Enough is enough. The bears just snapped. So what they do? They shoot the bears. It's a shame.

"Same thing with the big cat in the casino. Wild animals don't belong in a casino."

"Yeah, that was trouble waiting to happen,"said Burch. "The way this little cat I'm baby-sitting plays and pounces is cute, but I'd be in a shitload of trouble if he weighed six hundred pounds instead of six or seven."

．　．　．

They rented a car at the airport in Portland and checked into a Holiday Inn a mile away from Big Red's Greenway Drive apartment.

"Do we go see her now? Or grab something to eat first?" Burch asked, after they checked into their room.

"No time like now. We wait and maybe she's out for the evening."

The Silver Briar, a gabled four-story condo in a fashionable neighborhood, offered private parking for residents and visitors. They found a metered spot on the street instead.

"You think Terrell is here?" Nazario said, as they walked to the building.

"Could be. But if he ain't, Big Red's the key."

"The femme fatale," Nazario mused, "the long-legged, red-headed exotic dancer. She's gotta be something if he dumped Natasha for her. You saw Natasha."

"Wonder if she's still MIA?" Burch said.

"We shoulda told Riley to check out the cabanas. Think she's all right?"

"Somebody like her always lands on her feet."

"Or her back. At least you don't have to look over your shoulder for the little woman while we're here."

"I'm straightening it all out when we get back," Burch said. "One way or the other. Talked to my daughter, the oldest, the other day. She's such a good kid."

A boyish security guard in a blue uniform sat at the lobby desk.

His name tag said Greg Everett.

"Hi, Greg," Burch said. "We're here to see Linda Ballard."

The young guard smiled and reached for the house phone. "Who shall I—"

"We don't want to be announced." Burch flashed his badge.

The guard hesitated, expression uncertain. "Can I see some ID?" he said.

Burch handed over his badge case.

"All the way from Miami, huh? Sorry, Sergeant. The condo association is really strict about the rules. Didn't want to run the risk of losing my job." His wide gray eyes lit up. "How hard is it to get hired down in Miami? I qualified for the police academy here, but there's a waiting list. I just got married and we sure could use the security. I hear the benefits are good."

"Forget Miami," Burch said. "Unless you can shake a Hispanic or two outta your family tree."

Linda Ballard was in apartment 402. "A nice one," the young guard said. "A two-bedroom corner, she's got views of the park and lots of privacy. Owners of the other three units on the floor are all away for the summer."

"She entertain a lot?" Burch asked.

"Once in a while a few of her lady friends come for lunch. They make a lot of noise and laugh a lot. Otherwise she's pretty quiet."

"Ever see this guy around?" Burch handed him Charles Terrell's photo. "He'd be twelve years older than he looks here."

Greg studied it, then frowned. "I don't know. I'm not sure, I've only been on this job for three months."

They left Greg at his post in the pink marble lobby and took the silent, mirrored elevator to the fourth floor.

Nazario rapped three times with the elaborate front door knocker, a gold lion's head.

Big Red opened the door. She was not what they expected.

CHAPTER TWENTY-NINE

Norma the maid said that Nelson's truck had been in the driveway. Mrs. Ross had stepped outside to speak to him.

Then she and the truck were gone. Vanished.

A single, impossibly high-heeled Jimmy Choo sandal lay broken in the driveway.

How could she walk in a shoe like that? K. C. Riley wondered. Surely she couldn't run.

"Something's happened to her," Milo Ross said gravely. "Natasha wouldn't just disappear. There has been no ransom demand. I'll offer a substantial reward if you think it might help."

"That might be premature." Riley wondered how much Ross knew about his wife and Nelson the landscaper. "What do you think the man's motive might be?"

"Natasha fired him," Ross said. "I should have done it myself, but she insisted on taking care of it. She hated the way he'd pruned the royal poincianas, said it looked like they'd been attacked by vandals with chainsaws. Actually it looked like they'd grow back fine and the fellow did an otherwise outstanding job. But my wife's a perfectionist. She called him Nelson the tree slayer and said he had to go."

The retired tycoon kept files on all household employees, including copies of their driver's licenses.

Life would be so much simpler if all homeowners were so thorough,

Riley thought, radioing dispatch to broadcast a BOLO for Nelson's van. "Homicide needs to talk to him about a possible missing person."

Moments later she was startled when the dispatcher reported the van involved in a traffic stop.

"They've got him pulled over," she told Ross.

Riley was about to ask that the driver be detained until she got there, but her radio emitted a long, high-pitched emergency signal. Transmissions were halted. The air cleared. Staccato reports of an exchange of gunfire. Unit 333 breathlessly requesting backup.

"Tell him to hold his fire!" Riley broke in. "There may be a kidnap victim in that van! All units hold your fire!"

Responding officers had spotted the van. A chase was now in progress, headed due west. Patrol was cautioned to use restraint because of the possible hostage.

"I'm going with you!" Ross insisted.

"Sir." Riley touched him arm. "It would be best if you wait here. If she's not with him, Mrs. Ross may call or come home. You want to be here if she does. If we find her, I promise I'll send someone for you."

Tears in his eyes, Ross nodded, unable to speak.

Riley literally ran to her car.

A police helicopter had picked up the van headed out the Tamiami Trail.

He would drive across the entire state, to the Gulf of Mexico, if he had to, Nelson thought. He was alone, against all odds, all for love. He would show them a real man. He would show Natasha. She would see he was willing to die for love. She would beg him to come back to her.

Half a dozen patrol cars trailed behind him, their numbers growing, lights flashing, sirens wailing. But nobody was shooting at him.

A good sign. They knew he was not at fault. He was no criminal. Perhaps Natasha had already told them that. The slow-speed chase crossed Krome Avenue headed west. The city began to fall away. Endless sky stretched out across the Everglades on either side. The brightness hurt his eyes. He could almost hear the asphalt sizzle as it withered in the heat from a relentless sun. It was then that he noticed, as he approached the Miccosukee Indian village, that his gas gauge read empty.

Impossible. It had been three-quarters full. One of that policeman's gunshots must have hit the gas tank.

Why now? Why, Natasha? Why? He wept aloud, then gritted his teeth. More choppers beat the air overhead. He wondered if they would drop bombs on him from the sky.

This was war. He was a soldier of love, he would never surrender. They would never stop him. A combination gas station, souvenir stand, and convenience store lay up ahead. He saw signs for airboat rides into the Everglades.

Empty airboats were parked alongside the convenience store. He could steal one and flee deep into the Glades, where they would never find him. Like an Indian, he could outwit, outwait, and outsmart them. He was unafraid of darkness, alligators, or snakes. But, he thought, it is mosquito season. The swampy sawgrass swarmed with dense clouds of small, ferocious Everglades mosquitoes.

He would take the convenience store instead, hold hostages until they brought his Natasha to him, to beg him for forgiveness. The police were ridiculously slow, he thought. They were afraid. They knew what they were up against, that the forces of true love cannot be denied. They seemed so slow that had his gas tank not been leaking, he would have had time enough to roll up to the pumps, fill the tank, and be gone. But not quite. As the van sputtered and slowed down, they began to close in like hawks cornering a rabbit. The van died. It rolled to a stop about two hundred feet from the store.

Nelson did not hesitate. He leaped out, gun in hand. Ignoring the sirens, the lights, and the shouts to stop, he sprinted into the store.

The few customers inside scattered. He intended to hold them all hostage, but they showed no respect. They ran away, scrambling out the front door when they saw his gun.

All but Trudy Tiger, standing behind the counter in her authentic, colorful native Indian costume.

She'd been showing a schoolteacher from Chicago a pair of beaded moccasins and a rubber alligator made in Taiwan when her would-be customer fled.

Trudy blinked. Six months' pregnant, hormones raging, she felt depressed, bloated, and sleepy.

Nelson ordered her not to move.

Stoic, she said nothing.

"I am a man!" Nelson raged. He ranted, pacing back and forth, stopping only to glare out the plate-glass windows at the police. He pounded his chest at the TV cameras and hoped Natasha was watching.

Trudy frowned.

Television choppers and mobile news vans had joined the chase. The SWAT team had already mobilized and was on the way.

Riley's unmarked car arrived just behind Channel Seven. She strapped her bulletproof vest on over her blouse.

"Keep the press back!" she ordered. The van stood within shooting distance of the store. The small, dark puddle beneath it appeared to be gasoline. But if Natasha Ross was inside that van, wounded by police bullets, there was no time to waste.

"Cover me," she told two young patrolmen. "He comes out with the gun in his hand, drop him." She and a young cop named Victor darted to the back of Nelson's van and forced open the dented, bullet-riddled doors. Riley took a deep breath. Only a wounded lawnmower, a nasty-looking machete, and half a dozen sacks of fertilizer.

And something blue. A silky dress. Torn.

"Where the hell is she?"

They slammed the doors and took cover.

A sergeant reported that all but one of the people in the store had escaped. The lone hostage was the pregnant clerk.

Cops with bullhorns ordered Nelson to come out. He shook his fists in response, spouted insults, and kicked over a display of Miccosukee dolls dressed in authentic costume.

Trudy squinted at the mess.

The SWAT team's armored van arrived, SWAT Captain Billy Clayton in command.

Nelson laughed contemptuously and made rude gestures at them. An army of cowards, hiding behind trucks and cars, behind flak jackets and protective gear. He had the power.

He strutted and preened, performing for the television cameras, hoping Natasha could see him. He imagined what he must look like on camera and tried to emulate Tony Montana, the hero in *Scarface,* his favorite movie.

The phone rang.

"Bring Natasha here," he demanded. "I must see her."

After Nelson laughed at the hostage negotiator and hung up the telephone, Captain Clayton discussed a tear gas attack.

"The woman clerk is pregnant," Riley protested, as half a dozen Miccosukee police officers appeared, accompanied by several tribal elders.

"We don't need any help." Captain Clayton waved them away. "Just step over there with the press, fellows, and stay out of the line of fire—"

"Take your people. Leave now," the Miccosukee police chief said.

"Say again?" Captain Clayton cocked his head and grinned. Half a dozen more Miccosukee officers noisily arrived in airboats. Two pickup trucks pulled up with even more.

"You have no jurisdiction here," the Indian said. "You must take your people and leave."

"We have an armed fugitive inside. He's holding a hostage," Clayton sputtered.

"We will take care of it."

"Like hell. This little powwow is over," Clayton replied. "End of discussion."

"We need to arrest the gunman unharmed," Riley told the Miccosukee police chief. "He may be the only person who knows the whereabouts of a kidnap victim. She may still be alive."

The chief nodded solemnly. "We will take care of it."

"But—"

"This," one of the elders announced gravely, "is the sovereign Miccosukee nation. Your laws do not apply here. You were told to leave. Now you are criminally trespassing."

Clayton quarreled with them as Riley stepped away to make a call.

"We have a situation here," she told Leo Nathan, the city's legal adviser.

"They're absolutely right," Nathan said. "The Miccosukee Reservation is exclusively federal jurisdiction. Nonfederal agents have no right to be there. If you can't negotiate a quick and peaceful settlement, I'd advise you to leave."

"Captain Clayton will not back down," she whispered.

"Sit tight, I'll notify Chief Granados."

Riley rejoined Clayton, who pointed a warning finger at the Miccosukee elder. "Outta my way, Chief," he said. "We're going in."

"Arrest them," the dignified elder said calmly. He had had enough. His tribe was still immersed in long-standing feuds and lawsuits with outside government. The state had not lived up to its legal agreement to reduce Everglades pollution levels. A new U.S. Army Corps of Engineers crusade to protect the Cape Sable seaside sparrow by diverting the freshwater flow was sure to doom the roseate spoonbill, a dazzling pink wading bird, and the Everglades kite and harm all of northeastern Florida Bay. Weeks earlier construction workers digging trenches for state power lines had unearthed an Indian burial ground. Legally, a work stoppage is required so archaeologists can investigate and protect the site. Instead, the contractor had his men hastily pour cement over the human bones, skulls, and artifacts and continue their work. Now this . . .

"You and your officers are under arrest for criminal trespass," the Miccosukee police chief informed Clayton.

"No! *You're* under arrest for obstructing justice!" Clayton roared, as TV cameras rolled.

Nelson shouted insults, paced, waved his arms, and made obscene gestures, as the situation outside escalated. He sensed he was losing his audience. If only he had a TV set, he would know what was happening.

Riley talked to Nathan again. "Do something," she whispered. "The Miccosukee police and the SWAT team are arresting each other."

"The cavalry's on the way," he said.

K. C. Riley's heart sank. This wouldn't help find Natasha.

Nelson found Trudy Tiger's transistor radio behind the counter. According to the all-news station, Miami's mayor, the city manager, the police chief, his PIO officer, and their legal advisers were all racing to the scene of a tense standoff at the Miccosukee Indian Reservation.

Nelson screamed in triumph. The mayor himself would bring Natasha to him! He did a macho strut back and forth in plain view of the police. He felt invincible. Arms raised in victory, he shouted triumphantly at them, challenging them to send their best and bravest to try to take him. He did bumps and grinds in their direction, humiliating them in front of the cameras, laughing aloud at his own bravado.

But, as Miami police and the Miccosukee Nation faced off outside, Trudy Tiger grew tired of waiting.

She grasped the ballpeen hammer she kept beneath the counter for just such an occasion and plodded up behind Nelson. He bellowed at police, flapping his arms like a chicken and making chicken noises at them.

Clutching the hammer in both hands, Trudy swung and slammed the side of his head so hard that brain matter hit the wall. Irritated by the mess, she swung and hit him again as he fell.

. . .

"Slow everybody down. It's resolved," Riley radioed, as medics bundled Nelson into a rescue helicopter. She flew with him to the Ryder Trauma Center and held his hand, hoping, even though he was bleeding from the ears, nose, and mouth, to ask him a question.

CHAPTER THIRTY

He watched from his car across the street as she knelt in the yard beside the wooden cottage snipping leaves from an herb garden.

Look how stiffly she moves, he thought, watching her struggle to stand when she had finished. She was one of them. Alone, aged, and lonely. He had seen her speak to strangers at the market and buy only enough food that she could comfortably carry.

Ending her pain by providing the final passage that returned her to dust would serve two purposes. Perhaps this time he would do it perfectly and his mother would forgive him when the messiah came. At last *mechilah*, forgiveness.

He would try again to atone for what he had failed to do when he was called upon. And it would bring bad *mazel* to the detective, for all he had said and done, the lies he told on television and in the newspaper, the lack of respect, when he knew nothing. Detective Stone had brought the evil eye upon himself. But is it truly deserved? he asked himself, trying to remain objective. Or was it because something about Stone's arrogance had awakened the *yetzer hara*, the evil impulse, in him?

He watched the old woman cling to the railing as she slowly climbed the stairs. Her life had not been easy. But neither had his. After his humiliation, his loss, and the ridicule he endured, he had studied and studied, read the Torah, worked hard. He still did. So diligent was he that he now held a position of trust and importance. The chief *mashgiach*, the overseer of the overseers, he demanded excellence and exacting enforcement of all the rituals. Religious laws must not be broken. The other, lesser *mashgiachim* feared his inspections, cringed at his reports, chafed at his demands. But they must be perfect in their observance of the rules, the laws, the rituals. Nothing less than perfection was acceptable.

If those from whom he demanded so much knew of his humiliation, knew that he himself had failed to perform the greatest *mitzvah*, the one the recipient can never return in kind . . .

If he could only do it perfectly this time, his mother would forgive him when they met again after the coming of the messiah. The sting of his shame was as painful now as it was then, so many years ago.

She had been sick for so long. Had lost weight, had found it increasingly difficult to walk. His younger siblings did not remember how their mother had looked before she was ill. Doctors came and went. His older sisters had whispered and wept. By six months after his bar mitzvah his mother had become someone he scarcely recognized.

The night they said she was a *goses,* a person at the brink of death, they called him to her room. It is a *mitzvah* to be present at the very end of a life. The room was crowded with relatives, the air so thick with grief and impending death that he could not breathe. The smells, the weeping of his sisters and his grandmother repelled him.

He hid trembling in the hallway, knowing what lay ahead.

He heard wailing and then the prayers.

Barukh atah Adonai, Dayan ha-emet.

His father came for him then, ushered him into the room, to the bedside. Unable to speak, he could not resist.

He was the firstborn son. His duty was clear.

He was to touch his mother, to close her blank eyes and gaping mouth.

He had never seen death up close before. She stared at the ceiling, her skin gray, her tiny body like a bundle of rags in a huge bed. He did not recognize her, could not bring himself to touch this dead stranger. His father lifted his hand, to place it gently over her eyes. Violently, he recoiled. He screamed and screamed, high-pitched cries like a woman, even though he was now a man. He rushed wildly from the room, shrieking down the stairs, hurling people and objects out of his path. Still shrieking out the front door and down the street. He ran and ran until his body was numb, his lungs bursting, and he no longer knew where he was. Then he fell to the ground and cried like a child. He finally returned home long after midnight only because he was alone, afraid, and had no other place to go.

He had spent his life from that day forward atoning for his failure, but he could never do enough, never do it right. His mother had demanded perfection from her firstborn son. That much she deserved. All he had wanted was to please her. He could never forget the pain, the stigma, the stares, and the knowing looks that his weakness, his cowardice had brought upon him. If only he could do it over, relive the moment. He had tried, for the last twenty-five years, he had tried.

He watched the woman open her screen door and thought about her bedroom, where this time he would perform as required. He would do it all. He could close her eyes and mouth, recite the prayers, wash her naked body with warm water, cut her hair and nails. Beside him on the seat he had the fresh white linen sheet with which to cover her.

In his pocket, a small bag of earth from Israel. To be placed beneath her head, so when the messiah came and she was among the first to be resurrected, she and the others who had been alone with no one to perform these services would intervene with his mother, proving he had made *teshuvah*, repentance.

As he watched, the grandson arrived. He saw the detective look around, up and down the street. He knows nothing. No one could see him behind the tinted windows of the old station wagon. Again with the yellow toolbox. Out on the porch repairing a window frame. His constant repairs would not be enough to keep anyone out. But perhaps she did have someone to do for her. Perhaps the Angel of Death should pass her by. No, for him, she would open the door. And he would return her to dust.

CHAPTER THIRTY-ONE

Milo Ross and Norma the maid identified the silky blue garment found in Nelson's van as the dress Natasha was last seen wearing. But where was she?

There seemed little chance that Nelson, comatose and in intensive care, would be able to tell them anything. Ever.

"Think positive," Riley told Ross. "The only thing Nelson said to the hostage negotiator was that he wanted to talk to Natasha. If he was telling the truth, she may be safe somewhere."

"That animal," Ross said bitterly. "If he's harmed her . . . I want to offer a reward for her safe return. Do you think a hundred thousand dollars is enough?"

"That should get everybody's attention," Riley said.

"How do I announce it to the media?"

"The department has someone who can help you with that." She called Padron.

•   •   •

The SWAT team battered down the door and swarmed Nelson's Little Havana apartment. It was strangely empty. Even the furniture was gone. Neighbors had not seen his wife and children for at least two days.

Using the work schedules and logs found in his van, Riley marked the locations of all the landscaper's regular jobs on the big wall map in Homicide. Then she flagged the intersection where he'd been spotted by Officer Santiago.

Despite the wounded pedestrian, the shattered windows, and a dozen car crashes, Joe Padron had issued a press release identifying Fermin Santiago as an alert and heroic cop nearly killed in a single-handed attempt to abort the kidnaping of a multimillionaire's wife.

Santiago, that screw-up, Riley thought in disgust, would probably make officer of the month.

Computing times and distances, she concluded that if Nelson had taken Natasha to a job site, it was probably the San Souci Towers. Information had a listing, but it was only a sales office.

The huge, nearly finished high-rise was empty, with no crews working. Riley reached the architect and the contractor, who gave their permission to search. The contractor met police at the site with elevator remotes that would allow them access to all floors. No sign of Natasha.

"Check every closet, every storage space, every garbage chute," Riley told half a dozen cops. "Don't forget the elevator shafts. Start at the bottom, work your way up. I'll start at the top and meet you in the middle."

In a fortieth-floor penthouse garden, she found a discarded pair of pruning shears and Natasha's other high-heeled sandal.

Riley called her name. Her voice echoed in the emptiness.

The unoccupied structure was otherwise silent except for the eerie wind off the water.

Riley took the staircase to the roof and ran across along the south side. Nothing.

The wind whistled and picked up. The view was spectacular from the top. To the south she could see halfway to Homestead; the bay sparkled to the east, as did the azure sea and a panoramic vista of city skyline sprawled out to the west.

Riley trotted along a wide wraparound terrace near the empty shell of a rooftop pool.

"Natasha! Natasha! Can you hear me?"

Riley stepped to the edge to check the ground, the construction equipment below, and the roofs of smaller ancillary buildings. Nothing. Where the hell could she be without her dress?

Kathleen Constance Riley tasted the sweet summer wind, drank in the reddening horizon, and forgot Natasha for a moment. Instead, she stood poised at the edge, thinking how glorious it would feel to step off to ride the wind currents like a lonely bird in a vast blue sky. She took a deep breath.

Someone called out her name. A stranger holding an elevator remote waved from the far side of the roof. He'd emerged from the same stairwell she had used. Fit and trim, with prematurely gray hair, he wore a neatly pressed gray suit and once-shiny shoes now coated with construction dust.

She stood and watched him approach.

"Conrad Douglas, FBI," he said. "Any word on Natasha Ross?"

"Where were you when we needed you, out at the reservation? Now I know how General Custer felt."

"I hear it was more a standoff than a massacre."

"Only because the hostage saved herself. She was too efficient," Riley said wistfully. "I would have liked to have talked to the man."

"What are his chances?"

She shook her head. "They'll do another scan in twenty-four hours, but initial neurological testing showed no brain activity."

"From what I hear, that was this guy's normal condition."

She grinned in spite of herself. They stood silhouetted against the open sky high above the city, the wind riffling through their hair.

"What's your interest? There's no evidence she's been taken across state lines and there's been no ransom demand."

"Between us for now?" he said.

She nodded.

"We first became aware of Natasha Ross about a year and a half ago. She'd called immigration to turn in a household worker she wanted deported for pissing her off. A savvy agent there took a harder look at her and called us. We've had her under loose surveillance ever since."

"Must have been extremely loose or we wouldn't be here."

"We only checked intermittently on whether she appeared to be in contact with her father."

"You know where her parents are?" Riley said, interested.

"Not exactly. But we'd like to."

"She told my detectives she was born in Iowa, but we couldn't find any record of her there. Where *is* she from?"

The FBI agent smiled. "Croatia."

"Get out, as in Yugoslavia?"

"Istria actually. On the northern Adriatic in northwest Yugoslavia. That's where she was born.

"After the Russians and before Milosevic, a lot of bad things happened in the former Yugoslavia. Her father was responsible for the majority of them. He was in charge of the military, left a lot of corpses behind in mass graves. Torture, rape, you name it, he did it. He bailed out when the regime changed and left a lot of people looking for him. He, his wife, and their daughter, Natasha, age two at the time, made it to this country using false passports. They moved around a lot, but did eventually settle in Iowa, of all places. Fourteen years ago Croatian agents, still hunting him after all these years, got a line on his whereabouts. They wanted him arrested, extradited, and tried for war crimes. But before that could happen he disappeared again. The family had relocated in the past when investigators got too close. But this time Natasha was nineteen and chose not to go with them. Guess she didn't see much future in it. She changed her name, took off on her own, and wound up in Miami."

"Where she met Charles Terrell," Riley said.

"Husband number one, who may, or may not, be dead."

"Right, we're thinking not. So what's her real name?"

"Dubravko," he said. "Gabriella."

"Does Milo Ross know?"

"Apparently not."

"Looks like the apple doesn't fall far from the tree," Riley said. "Think she's in touch with her parents? That it might have something to do with all this?"

"Not as far as we can tell. This caper looks strictly domestic."

Douglas smiled at Riley, then flung his arms open wide to the pink and gold sunset across the Everglades. "I love it! Only in Miami could a pregnant Miccosukee Indian cave in the skull of a Cuban exile wanted for snatching a native of Croatia. By God, I love this place!"

His words echoed in the wind around them.

CHAPTER THIRTY-TWO

Big Red's hair was shot with gray. She'd put on pounds, lots of pounds. Her thick face looked jowly beneath heavy makeup and her tortoise-shell eyeglasses and comfortable slippers gave her a matronly appearance. Linda Pickett, aka Linda Ballard, Desiree, and Big Red, was age thirty-seven when she left Miami; she was close to fifty now and looked every day of it.

She studied them speculatively, a drink in her hand.

Burch flashed his badge.

"From Miami, right?" She smiled. "What the hell took you boys so long? I've been expecting you for a good ten years."

"We've been busy, Linda," Burch said.

"Call me Desiree. That was my stage name."

She had a sultry Mae West delivery and her double-wide hips still had a sexy twitch as she led them into her parlor. But she was hardly the heartbreaker, the seductress, the bombshell sweetheart and companion in crime they had expected.

"So, Desiree, anybody else here?" Burch's eyes roved the premises as they followed her into a white-carpeted room, its windows framed by lush layers of velvet drapes with fringed gold-tasseled valances.

"So, Sergeant, who were you expecting?" She cocked her head coyly.

"I think you know."

"It's just little ol' me," she said, "and my bottle of good scotch." The ice tinkled in her glass as she sipped. "Care to join me?"

"Thanks, but we'll pass for now. We're here on business."

She settled in a mauve lounge chair, crossed her fleshy legs, and waved them toward an overstuffed couch.

"So am I busted?" Her posture was casual and there was an earthy bravado to her voice, but the eyes behind her glasses looked resigned and weary.

"In a matter of speaking," Burch said.

"How bad is it?" She shook a cigarette loose from a pack on a small marble-topped table beside her and lit it with a ceramic table lighter. Her hands were steady. "How much trouble am I in?"

"That's entirely up to you," Burch said. "Where is he?"

She thoughtfully smoked her cigarette, as though she hadn't heard.

"You know who I'm talking about. When did you last see Charles Terrell?"

"Didn't you hear? He died. A long time ago, back in Miami."

"We know better."

"To tell you the truth," she said, smiling gently, "I haven't seen Buddy for years."

"Buddy?"

"His nickname growing up. You didn't know that? His childhood friends and high school chums all called him Buddy. That's how he was introduced to me. I met him through one of them."

"So you two were pretty tight."

"We had our thing, but came to a parting of the ways. Too hot not to cool down. Like the song says. You know how it is." The pain in her eyes looked real.

"How long, exactly, since you've seen him?"

She shrugged. "Four, maybe five years. Seems a lot longer in this burg. I miss Miami. A lot. Hear the nightlife's hot these days."

"Your Aunt Sylvia tipped you off that we might be paying you a visit, didn't she?" Nazario said.

Desiree snorted in derision and sipped her drink, leaving a crimson lipstick smear on the rim. "Actually, she thought she had you snowed. Thought you believed her. But I knew better. If you went to the trouble to find her, you wouldn't buy it. You have to give Syl credit for trying. How is she? How'd she look? I miss that crazy old broad. Closest thing to a mother I ever had."

"Living the good life, thanks to you," Nazario said. "Doesn't use her cane anymore. I think she's got a boyfriend."

"Too bad she's going to jail," Burch said.

"What do you mean?" Startled, Desiree sat up straight. "She had nothing to do with anything."

"She lied to us," he said. "And she's an accessory."

"No way." She set her drink down on the marble-top table with a loud *crack* and got to her feet. "She's an old lady. Had a tough life. Don't drag her into anything."

The detectives exchanged glances as she paced.

"Maybe we should talk," Burch said casually. "See what we can work out."

"You could be in a world of trouble," Nazario said.

"I know." She stood at the window, her back to them. "I'da been a helluva lot happier to meet you boys three years down the road."

"You studying law?" Nazario said.

"I miss Florida. I'm lonely here." She hugged herself as though chilled. "I wanted to go back. So I bought a sit-down with a local lawyer a couple of years ago to check out my options. There is no statute of limitations on murder. But he said if I was charged as an accessory, which would be likely, there's a fifteen-year statute of limitations. Three more years and I'da been home free."

"Unless the charge was homicide."

"I didn't kill anybody." She returned to her chair and drained her drink. "Sure you boys don't want to join me?"

"No thanks, but you go ahead," Burch said. "Enjoy it while you can."

They joined her at a small bar in a far corner and watched her fix a drink, light on the ice, heavy on the scotch.

"We know the Place Montmartre murders are connected," Burch said.

She paused. "I wasn't there that night. I didn't know anybody would get hurt."

"But you were at Terrell's house just before the garage went up."

"Like hell."

"See, Desiree, that's what's going to make things difficult between us," Burch said. "Nobody ever got a sweetheart deal by lying to us."

Nazario nodded. "We've got you on tape."

Her eyes widened. "Tape? You're bullshitting me."

"Remember the kid's birthday party across the street?" Burch said. "Somebody videotaped it. We got the tape and, what do you know, there you are, plain as day, across the street behind the wheel of that van.

"Lie to me one more time, Linda, and you sleep in the local lockup tonight and every night until you're extradited to Florida. And I make a phone call that says Aunt Sylvia sleeps in the Dade County Jail tonight."

Tears flashed in her eyes. She jerked off her glasses and dabbed at them with a paper bar napkin, smearing her mascara.

"It's not fair." She sniffed. "I was almost glad to see you. I want to go home to Florida."

"If you don't like it here," Nazario said, "how come you never packed up and left?"

"It's not that easy. Buddy's a control freak. Always has to be in charge. I gave up my career for him. Don't smirk, Sergeant. I made damn good money. Then, when I'm past my prime, he finds somebody younger. What kind of work could I get now? This apartment, my car, everything, it's all in Buddy's name. He doles out the money."

"So you do know where he is."

"No. Enough cash to support me and pay Sylvia's bills is wired to my checking account once a month. The deal is, if I leave town or take off on my own, the money stops. I can't sell this place or even take out a loan on it. For his protection, he said. He was afraid I'd go back to Florida and blow his cover.

"The man likes being legally dead."

"So your bank records would track back to him?"

She shook her head. "A third party, a lawyer I think, wires the money.

Buddy's a very careful person. I don't have a dime that he doesn't know about and he could cut off in a heartbeat. Even if I landed a job that could support me, which ain't easy at my age, what about Sylvia? That place she lives in costs a bundle. Her income from Social Security is only about five hundred a month. She'd be out on the street. So would I."

Burch frowned. He thought he'd been clever, using Aunt Sylvia to pressure Desiree. But Charles Terrell had thought of it first.

"Look, Desiree. You're not our prime target. Nobody wants to see you in prison for the rest of your life. He's the one we want. We'd need your cooperation for a successful prosecution. You have strong cards you haven't even played. Tell us what you can offer. We'll pass it along to the prosecutor."

"The way I see it, you'd be happier back in Florida instead of alone up here," Nazario said.

"I'd love to see Sylvia and my old friends," she said earnestly. "I thought it would be different with Buddy. He was the one. I was crazy about him. He wasn't happy, in a dead-end situation. Paying child support, in a bad marriage, in over his head financially.

"Chris, who owned the Montmartre, introduced me to Buddy. They went way back together, to high school. I'd known Chris for years. He trusted me. I'd been in his office after hours lots of time. I knew he kept a major stash up there. Money he couldn't deposit in banks for obvious reasons. He was a player, trafficking drugs, into extortion, robbery, and everything else you can do to make a dirty buck. Buddy had pharmaceutical connections and supplied him with pills—Quaaludes and methamphetamines. He and I used to joke about the big bucks Chris kept in the safe. Next thing you know, Buddy wasn't joking. He came up with a scheme. It meant the two of us could start a new life together, far away.

"I didn't think anybody'd get hurt at the Montmartre. Buddy set up a deal to deliver some 'ludes. Instead, he was gonna rob Chris, fake his own death a few hours later, and we'd be out of there. All our troubles behind us. It was foolproof." She shrugged. "Even if Chris sent his goons to the widow to look for his money, she didn't know anything.

"I wasn't a bad person. It's like they say: When you dance with the devil, you don't change the devil, the devil changes you."

"Who was the man who burned up in the garage?" Nazario said.

"I didn't know his name. Only saw him once. Buddy said he was perfect, a wanderer who arrived in Miami alone. Somebody who wouldn't be missed.

"He was a drifter, a drinker, showed up at the drugstore looking for work or a handout. Buddy befriended the guy, said he'd help him get off the booze and make some money. He used him for backup at the Montmartre that night, then set him up in his garage. He was a boozer, no family."

"This the guy?" Burch handed her Michael Hastings's photo.

She squinted at it for a long moment.

"Mighta been." She shrugged. "Not a face you'd remember." She handed it back.

"That day, when I picked Buddy up at his house, I didn't know that Chris and the girl were dead. She was only a kid. When I found out, I was shocked, but I was already in too deep, and I loved him."

"Did you know that another man was convicted of the murders at the Montmartre?" Burch asked.

"No." Her eyes widened. "Are you sure?"

"You expect me to believe that you never heard that somebody else took the fall?"

"Who?"

"Some poor schmuck who got thrown out of the club a couple nights before the murders."

"Jesus. Well, they'll have to let him out now, won't they?"

"A little late for that, Desiree. Regardless of what some people think, wrongful convictions, especially those that lead to wrongful executions, are big deals for prosecutors and for us, very big deals. How is it you never heard the news about the arrest, trial, or conviction? Was it your terrible judgment or a complete lack of morals that stopped you from saving him?"

"I swear to God! I didn't know. The first year we traveled and partied a lot. Buddy knew I hated leaving Miami. He kept saying we had to make it a clean break, put it behind us. He didn't want me to subscribe to a Florida newspaper or listen to the news. I swear I didn't know.

"I guess ignorance was bliss. I thought we had a future. For a while, it was great. Me and Buddy, we'da had gorgeous kids. I was at that age, you know, the old bio clock ticking away. If I was gonna have children, it was then or never. But Buddy didn't want them. Said he'd had enough kids. But hell, it wasn't like he was ever gonna see any of them again. I never understood that."

She sighed.

"You ever see my act?" she asked, fixing herself another drink. "Too bad. Choreographed it myself. I wasn't just some two-bit stripper. I was a classically trained dancer. The snake was my gimmick. The theme was the Garden of Eden. My hair was long, all the way down to my ass. It was artistic. Those were the days."

"You keep the snake?" Burch glanced around the room.

Her big laugh boomed, hoarse and raspy. "Don't worry. Buddy didn't want it around. Hated seeing me feed it. We turned it loose in a park.

"Wish I still had it for company." She downed her drink and fixed another. "It was a great pet.

"Those were the days," she repeated, slightly slurring her words. "There's something about getting naked in the spotlight. Gives a woman a sense of power. You know every man in the place is fantasizing about you. Chris always said that the power of a woman is stronger than an atomic bomb."

"With twice the lethal fallout," Burch said.

"What makes you so cynical, Sergeant? Strip clubs are magic places, full of erotic dreams and fantasies.

"Your partner knows what I'm talking about." She laughed again and winked at Nazario. "I can see it in his eyes."

"Myself, I always considered them perpetual crime scenes, twenty-four seven," Burch said.

"Think about how tough dating is on a man," she coaxed. "A lap dance at a strip club is cheaper. He doesn't have to buy her dinner or promise to call the next day. And he can lie. So can she. Everybody lies. Sure, she's working her way through college, or about to land that big role on Broadway. He can be a movie producer, a dashing foreign diplomat, or a famous writer. A club is a magic place full of naked women. One way or the other, all you boys have to pay for a woman. Spending time at a club is cheaper than dating or marriage. Buddy still feels that way.

"Maybe that's why he never married me. He said he'd had enough wives, too."

"Did Natasha know?" Burch asked.

"No, just me and Buddy, and that ten-foot blonde looking down from the roof of the Montmartre. She always saw everything, and nothing. Nobody else knew. Just us, now you."

"You haven't seen Natasha, have you?" Nazario said.

"When?"

"She recently came up missing."

"No, but funny you should ask. A while back, Buddy thought he saw his ex-wife. Not Natasha. The first one, April. He was into sailing. Took his boat down to Mystic Seaport in Connecticut. On the street, doing a little sightseeing, he thought he saw her and the kids. Freaked him out. When he looked back, she was staring, like she was seeing a ghost. He was gonna track her down, do something about it, but changed his mind, I guess, or lost her in the crowd. Instead, he just got out of Dodge. That was a close one."

"When was that?" Burch asked thoughtfully.

She shrugged. "A while back."

"You're sure you don't know how to reach him?"

"Look, I'm spilling my guts here. You know I'd tell you if I did. Listen, I'll go back to Miami with you right now. I'll cooperate, make a statement, tell everything I know. But I want the best deal I can get. And you have to keep Sylvia out of it."

"We can probably arrange something. Like I said, you're not the one they want."

"Yeah. I didn't have any, what do they call it? Criminal intent. That's it.

I didn't intend to do anything wrong. I just fell in love. There's nobody like Buddy." Her voice dropped to a whisper and she looked teary-eyed. "Never will be."

. . .

Burch used his cell to fill in Assistant State Attorney Jo Salazar. "Terrell did the two at the Montmartre," he told her.

"Christ," she said, in her kitchen, a child crying in the background. "This is big. This is bad. I knew I should have gone up there with you." She tentatively agreed to offer Desiree a plea to reduced charges, or even full immunity, depending on her honesty and level of cooperation.

Desiree spoke to her briefly, agreed to submit to a polygraph test and to return to Miami with the detectives.

"I know it sounds crazy," Desiree told them after hanging up. "But I'm looking forward to it. I may regret it, but I want to see that big sky over Miami again, feel the sun on my shoulders. I even loved the humidity. Does wonders for your skin. When I lived in Miami I never even had to use a moisturizer.

"I have to pack," she said enthusiastically, "settle up a few things. In Miami I bet I can land myself a job. People will remember me. Hell, Gypsy Rose Lee still made appearances at my age. So did Lili St. Cyr. I just need to drop a few pounds, get in shape. If me and Sylvia got a little place together, we could make it."

They agreed to fly back the following afternoon.

"Okay," Burch said, as they left. "I'm warning you, Desiree. Don't screw with us. We're your new best friends. We're looking out for your interests. Don't try to run, don't take a walk and forget to come back, because if you do, Sylvia goes to jail and we issue murder warrants for your arrest. We've got the Portland Police keeping an eye on this place, and you. Got that?"

"I can't believe you're so paranoid." She grinned, eyes alight with relief. "The only place I'm going is Miami."

It was late. The night security guard now manning the desk promised to notify them if Desiree left the building or had visitors.

"Think I should camp outside her door tonight?" Nazario asked, in the rental car. "When she said she doesn't know where Terrell is, she lied."

"You sure?"

"The woman knows."

"Makes no sense," Burch said. "The guy's a cold stone killer. Has her dump her act, her pet snake, her friends and family, life as she knows it, such as it was, then dumps her for somebody else and she's still loyal?"

"She loves him."

"You see how she wrote off the guy killed in the garage?"

"And the execution of an innocent man?"

"Yeah, just starts talking about her act. Terrell sure knew how to pick 'em."

"God makes 'em and God matches 'em," Nazario said. "You hungry?"

They hadn't eaten all day.

"My stomach thinks my throat's been cut."

They found a Denny's restaurant.

"Salazar can have her testify before the grand jury and get three first-degree murder indictments against Terrell," Burch said between forks full of salad. "We can get that artist, the really good one that Stone talks about, to age-enhance his pictures and plaster his mug all over the country, all over the world. Sooner than later, the man is ours."

"She's the next best thing to bringing him back," Nazario agreed, buttering a roll. "When she first opened the door, did you believe it was her?"

"She looked used up," Burch said, as his steak arrived. "But did you see her when we left? She looked ten years younger. Like a weight's been lifted. There is something to be said for coming clean and going home at last. She'll do all right."

CHAPTER THIRTY-THREE

The caller had begun to both interest and irritate Stone. "You call your-self a detective?

"So why don't you solve your own case? Chase your parents' killer. You know nothing." It was the same damn guy.

"Sir, do you have some information to offer? If not, you shouldn't be tying up this line."

"Who would tell you anything? You—"

"Yeah, I heard. I know nothing. Don't be too sure. How will you pre-pare for Yom Kippur, the Day of Atonement? How can you call the peo-ple you have wronged and ask for forgiveness, *mechila?* The dead can't forgive."

The caller gasped and hung up. A sick puppy, or maybe the killer.

Stone stared at the telephone.

It rang two minutes later. "You know nothing. Nothing. What would make you say something like that?"

"It's true," the detective said quietly. "Isn't it?"

The man hung up again.

The phone rang.

No one spoke but he could hear the man's raspy breathing.

"Why don't we meet and talk in person?" Stone said.

"*Kayn aynhoreh.* Do you know what that means?"

"Of course," Stone said. "The evil eye."

"You have brought a *kayn aynhoreh* on yourself. And your grand-mother."

. . .

Downstairs, in PIO, Milo Ross, perspiring and shaky, implored anyone with a clue to his wife's whereabouts to come forward. Flyers bearing Natasha's photograph, her description, and the offer of a $100,000 reward were being distributed to the media and throughout the city.

The former CEO had already hired a small army of private investigators.

"I don't mean to imply that you're not doing enough," Ross explained to K. C. Riley. "But I have to use every possible resource. Time is crucial. She could be in danger. You're still a young woman, Lieutenant. You have no idea what it's like to think you've lost someone you love."

She had no answer.

. . .

"The poor guy is throwing dollars at anybody he thinks might bring her back," Riley said to Agent Conrad Douglas, who stood off to one side as the press conference broke up.

"You here on official business?" she asked.

"If I say no, does that mean I can take you to dinner?"

"No," she said.

"What's wrong with me?" he demanded.

"Not a thing. You're terrific."

"Right. Great guys like me don't come along every day."

"I know. That's probably a good thing. I couldn't handle another one."

. . .

Leads poured in for the next twenty-four hours as the search for Natasha went nationwide. *America's Most Wanted* offered to feature the hunt for the missing woman. And Milo Ross increased the reward to $250,000 for her safe return.

Tips came in, fast and furious. Natasha was "seen" on a yacht on the Intracoastal Waterway, gambling in Vegas, cheering the Fish from the bleachers at a Marlins game, and driving a school bus in Opa-Locka. One of Ross's private detectives immediately jetted to Mexico to investigate a rumor that Nelson was a procurer who kidnaped women for a white slavery ring.

Another caught a transatlantic flight to follow up on reports she'd been seen at Monte Carlo in the company of an elusive international fugitive.

Strangers scheduled a candlelight vigil. Natasha's smoldery eyes and pouting smile were everywhere, on television, in the newspapers, on every pole, and in every storefront.

CHAPTER THIRTY-FOUR

Natasha was not on a yacht, in Monte Carlo, or in Vegas.

While her husband's private detectives trotted the globe, it was business as usual at the county dump. Trucks waited in line to empty the Dumpsters picked up from construction sites.

As one did, a bulldozer driver, assigned to flatten and redistribute the load, spotted a tangled wave of dark hair and long legs amid the falling debris.

The trucker who had delivered an empty container to the San Souci Towers and removed the full one had noticed a foul odor, but people will sometimes leave a dead animal in a Dumpster.

Natasha had been there all along.

When police first searched the San Souci site, an officer had lifted a corner of the lid. All he saw was a clutter of Styrofoam, plastic, and cardboard. They were hoping to find a live woman at the time.

K. C. Riley and the chief medical examiner pieced together what happened.

Nelson took Natasha to the building to talk, hoping for an assignation, or to show off his work on the penthouse gardens. They quarreled, she eluded him and fled. Without a remote device, the elevator would only take her to the lobby. Nelson must have been in close pursuit, on the second elevator, still clutching her dress. She reached the lobby moments before him and hid inside the Dumpster near the large rear double doors.

She pulled a piece of cardboard over herself, remaining silent as he searched. He called her name, pleaded for her to come out.

A witness, a boy passing the site on his bicycle, heard Nelson's shouts. Then saw him storm out to his green truck and speed away.

After everything became quiet, with Nelson gone, Natasha tried to escape the Dumpster. Too late.

Her hiding place was nearly full of flattened cardboard cartons that had contained appliances, Styrofoam packing, and plastic wrapping, but beneath them, at the bottom of the Dumpster, were partially empty cans of paint solvents and heavily saturated rags.

Panting, breathing heavily in the dark after she dropped the lid down over herself, she had quickly become disoriented.

Damage to her manicure, broken fingernails, cuts, and abrasions indicated that in her confusion she had pushed, then clawed at the hinged side of the lid instead of the side that would have opened easily.

"Paint solvent is an anesthetic agent," the medical examiner explained. "She probably thought at first that it was just a funny smell, but she quickly became groggy, then was overcome."

Toxicological tests confirmed the cause of death: asphyxiation due to inhalation of petroleum distillate, mineral spirits used to dilute the high-quality oil-based paint applied to the luxury building's baseboards and cupboards.

"She was in no pain," the medical examiner assured a brokenhearted Milo Ross. "She simply went to sleep."

Her death was ruled accidental.

CHAPTER THIRTY-FIVE

SIX HOURS LATER

I call April Terrell after we get back to the hotel. I hate to wake her, but can't wait.

"Sorry to bother you this late, but I have two questions."

"Sure. Whatever I can do to help." She sounds sleepy.

"When did you and the kids go to Mystic Seaport in Connecticut?"

"How did you know?" she asks. "Last summer I took the children to see the old whaling ships and the historic sites. Mystic has a fully restored 1850s whaling village and a planetarium."

Nazario was right. I should have known. "That recent, just last year?"

"Yes, we'd never been there before."

It explained a lot.

"What's your other question?"

"When you first came to us, you said it was because you'd begun to see Charles wherever you went. How long ago did that start? When was the first time you thought you saw somebody who looked just like him?"

She pauses. I hear her breathing. "Sometime last summer," she says slowly. "I don't remember exactly . . . Oh my God! I think we were on vacation. I didn't mention it to the children. You think he was there? That it was actually him that I saw? Is it possible?"

"Looks that way. That sighting must have triggered something in your subconscious. Soon you thought you were seeing him everywhere. We haven't found him yet. But we will."

"So it is true," she whispers, stunned.

"I wouldn't tell the kids yet, but I'd start choosing my words."

. . .

I know she won't sleep again tonight. I won't, either. I lie in the dark too elated to sleep. It's as if we're at the end of a giant jigsaw puzzle, when even the small pieces begin to fit. My mind races. So much still to do. But it is coming together. Sometimes you can't do anything right no matter how hard you try and other times, like now, the stars align themselves in the universe.

I can't wait to tell Connie, but want to do it in person, when she's lying next to me, in bed.

I want to high-five Nazario, but he's already sleeping like a baby in the other twin bed.

I become paranoid alone in the wee hours and call the night security guard to make sure he's awake, alert, and still on the job in Big Red's lobby. He assures me all is quiet on the western front.

Still wide awake, I turn on the bedside lamp and thumb through a copy of USA Today left outside our door. They print a one-paragraph story from each state on an inside page. I look for Florida's highlight of the day.

The U.S. Coast Guard, it says, arrested several Cuban smugglers attempting to spirit a woman and three children to Miami. They'd been spotted adrift in the Florida Straits after their engine quit. The woman told a wild story, claiming she'd been abducted in Miami and was being taken to Cuba against her will. Inventive minds these Cubans have. The Coast Guard saw through it, of course. She and the kids were repatriated to Cuba. The smugglers, who claimed to be fishermen, were brought back in chains.

Only in Miami. I am anxious to return home to my family in the city that is never boring.

. . .

I call Greg Everett at 7:00 A.M. The daytime security guard at the Silver Briar has arrived on duty. All is cool, he says, trying hard to sound like a real cop.

"Ten-four here, Sergeant. The subject hasn't left the building since you left last night, sir."

I call Big Red a half hour later. I worried that when she sobered up she might change her mind, but she has no regrets about last night. She's chipper, sounds happy to hear from me, and talks a blue streak about Miami.

She has to go to the bank, to the post office to have her mail forwarded to Aunt Sylvia's address, and run a few other errands.

I don't spoil her good mood by bringing up her lies about the last time she saw Terrell. We can wrest the truth out of her back on our turf, in Miami.

I say we'll pick her up at two o'clock, to go to the airport. Nazario has already checked departure times.

Like clockwork, Greg Everett calls breathlessly minutes later. He sounds excited. "Your subject is leaving the building. Said she was going to the post office."

"What's she got with her? Is she carrying anything?"

"Just a purse and a manila envelope."

"Okay, stay on it and ring me the minute she comes back."

"Another thing," he said. "It might be important. She said she's taking a trip, to Miami."

"Excellent. Good work, Greg."

I fight it but can't resist calling Connie.

The answering machine picks up. "Hi, sweetheart," I say. "I'm out of town on a case, but I'll be back in Miami tonight. I miss you, babe. I really do. We'll be snowed under by paperwork and meetings tonight, but let's talk first thing tomorrow. I miss the hell out of you. Can't wait to tell you all about this case. Kiss the kids for me. Love you, honey."

I realize I haven't thought of Maureen since I left Miami. I think of Connie and the kids all the time. Nothing like distance to clarify things. I love my wife. I hope she still loves me.

Full of energy and hope, I shave, shower, and drink coffee.

Greg calls at eleven. Big Red is back. She told him she bought a bathing suit. You can't say the woman isn't talkative. My life would be simpler if all witnesses were so talkative.

Women. They never cease to amaze me. Their priorities boggle my mind. Two cops are about to escort her back to Miami to discuss three homicides, a wrongful execution, and numerous other little escapades, including armed robbery and arson. So how does she cope? She buys a bathing suit.

I call her. She babbles about wanting enough time to have her hair done. "Lots of hairdressers in Miami," I say. She tells me about the bathing suit, too. I can't imagine it being a pretty sight, but she goes on about it being adorable, something about a tank. I don't know if she's describing the suit or what she looks like in it.

She asks about publicity. Thinks it will enhance her plans for a show biz comeback. "You saw *Chicago*, didn't you?" she demands.

I say I don't see many movies but she wheedles out of me a promise that I won't let anybody snap her picture before she sees a good hair colorist. Jo Salazar, the prosecutor, and my lieutenant, also female, I say, will understand completely and guide her in that department.

Nazario is taking Terrell's photo to police headquarters to be copied. I need to buy souvenirs for Connie and the kids, but I can do that at the airport.

"I'll go baby-sit Big Red until we leave," I say. "I don't want her having any second thoughts at the last minute."

He drops me off in front of the Silver Briar.

Something is missing from the pink marble lobby. Greg, the security guard, is not at his post. Goddamn that kid! AWOL, just when I'm about to write him a to-whom-it-may-concern letter recommending he be leapfrogged to the head of the academy's waiting list because of his diligent assistance to out-of-town police officers.

Probably just a bathroom break, but it pisses me off.

I take the slow-moving elevator to floor four.

A loud radio blares from inside Big Red's apartment, but she doesn't answer, despite my hammering with her lion's-head door knocker. Must be in the shower. I should've called first.

I try the knob. The door opens.

I call out her name and step inside.

A trunk and a matched set of expensive leather luggage stand just inside the door, ready to go.

The shower isn't running. "Desiree!"

I turn off the loud radio and step into her bedroom. Clothes are strewn about. Drawers hang open. She packed in a hurry. "Desiree! Linda!"

She's not in the bathroom.

Alarmed, I pull out my cell, hit Nazario's number, and head for the kitchen as it rings. I pass the large gilt-framed oval mirror and in it glimpse a reflection, something terrible behind the bar. A pale, bare foot, her shoe beside it. The once-white carpet now crimson. She's sprawled on the floor, her head resting against the wall. I rush to find a pulse. Her skin is still warm. But half her face is gone.

"Goddamn it!" I shout.

I hear a *click,* turn, and recognize an older Charles Terrell in the instant before he shoots me in the chest. I see the flame and feel the impact before I hear the shot. The force of the bullet knocks the wind out of me. My knees buckle. I reach for my gun as I fall, but he lunges forward and shoots me in the head.

I can't feel my hands or feet. It's as though a red-hot railroad spike has been pounded into my skull between my eyes. Pain impulses travel up and down my spinal cord, relayed from one nerve cell to the next by chemical messengers to the brain. I feel like I have been doused with gasoline and set on fire.

He takes my gun, cell phone, and identification. My eyes stay closed. To open them would only invite another bullet.

I think he is gone and I am alone.

I smell spilled blood and know that it's mine.

She's dead, I think, as I drift away. It's my fault. I'm dying and it's my fault. I was so stupid.

The room is quiet. Blood bubbles up out of my chest. I try to sigh but it is too difficult to breathe.

My future slips away. All behind me now. Here I am in the valley of the shadow. I think of my wife and my children.

CHAPTER THIRTY-SIX

Horns blared and brakes screeched as Nazario accelerated into a U-turn. All he'd heard on the cell phone was Burch's shout and what sounded like gunfire.

Burch didn't answer when he called back. Nazario called local police. He blew three red lights leaning on the horn, abandoned the rental on the sidewalk, and sprinted into the lobby.

He cursed, skidding on the marble floor, when he saw the security post unmanned. The guard must be with Burch. What went wrong?

He punched the elevator button half a dozen times and had turned to take the stairs when it arrived. He burst out on the fourth floor, gun in hand.

The door to Desiree's apartment stood ajar. He kicked it open and proceeded cautiously. "Sarge?" He took another step inside.

"¡Dios mío! ¿Que pasó?"

Eyes darting, gun ready, he knelt beside Burch, whose shirtfront was soaked with blood. So was the carpet beneath him. Blood gushed from a head wound as well. Multiple gunshot wounds. He felt for a pulse. "Sarge! Sarge!"

Burch's eyelids fluttered. He tried to say something. "Tell my wife I love her."

"Son of a bitch, tell her yourself. Hang on. Help is on the way."

He'd left his cell in the car. He dove on the wall phone behind the bar and saw Desiree.

No dial tone, wires cut.

He raced through the apartment, kicking open the doors. No one else there. He dashed out into the hall. The other tenants on the floor were gone, the guard had said. The elevator indicator showed it was in the lobby. Faster to take the stairs.

He charged down the dimly lit stairwell, taking two and three steps at a time. He stumbled over something at the second-floor level and nearly plunged headlong. Greg, the security guard. The kid who wanted to be a cop. His skin already growing cold. Shot in the back of the head.

Nazario hit the pavement running.

"Three down, one is a police officer suffering from multiple gunshot wounds!" He was still shouting into his cell phone when the first Portland squad car pulled up.

. . .

"No. No. No." Nazario tried to deny what he knew was true as he paced the street, cleared of traffic for the rescue helicopter.

Strapped to a backboard, his skin paper white, Burch was brought out of the building by medics. He wore a neck brace and had intravenous lines in his arms.

"I can't go with you, Sarge," Nazario said in his ear. "I'll find Terrell. Then I'll be there. Hang in."

There was no response.

The chopper spiraled into the air, higher and higher, a vanishing speck in a gray sky.

Big Red and Greg Everett would wait for the morgue wagon.

Where is Terrell? He couldn't have struck this quickly if he lived out of town, Nazario reasoned. He had to have been here already. Big Red must have called him. To say goodbye or to warn him.

"¡Que es estúpida!" Surprising Terrell let her live this long. He only had a five-minute head start. Where is he? Burch is dying, Nazario thought. How did he allow this to happen? To Burch. To the kid, the newlywed security guard with ambitions to be a cop. To Big Red, who would never see the Miami sky again. How many victims now? Where is Terrell? Something Big Red said last night. About strip clubs. Strip clubs. He thought of Floria and tears stung his eyes. Big Red said spending time at a club is cheaper than dating or marriage. *Buddy still feels that way.* That's what she said.

Present tense. Present place.

Nazario gave Terrell's general description to the lieutenant in charge of the crime scene.

"Did you see him?" the lieutenant asked.

"No, but it's him."

The lieutenant was furious. Out-of-town cops had no business taking police action on his turf, he said, without being accompanied by one of his own.

"We didn't take any police action," Nazario explained. "We were just talking to a witness. Can you call in somebody from Vice? ASAP? They would know this guy."

"We need to handle this crime scene first. You stay put," the lieutenant ordered. "We'll want to take a statement from you."

Nazario couldn't wait.

"You ever work Vice? This is a twelve-year-old picture. He could look a lot different now." He paced the sidewalk, flashing Terrell's photo at the uniforms.

"Hey, look at this!" a weathered patrolman said. Another peered over his shoulder.

"Sure thing, that's him." The second one nodded.

"Who?"

"Josh Ellis. Owns a restaurant and the Candy Stick Lounge, a strip joint over on the waterfront. First exit before the seaport."

Nazario walked to his car. He gently eased the rental around the block out of sight, then floored it.

Too early for entertainment at the Candy Stick. The big double doors out front were locked, but a side door to the bar was open.

Only one person in sight, a man cleaning up behind the huge

horseshoe-shaped bar. He was thin and acne scarred, with straight black hair worn too long.

"I need to talk to the boss," Nazario said. "Is Josh here?"

"Nope." The bartender pushed his hair out of his eyes and squinted at him. "Hasn't been here today."

He was lying.

"Okay, I'll leave the message with you." Nazario motioned, as though about to whisper something confidential.

When the man leaned forward, Nazario caught him by the neck and shirtfront and dragged him across the bar. He wrestled him into the women's restroom and left him handcuffed to a pipe.

The office marked PRIVATE was at the back, behind a door, sturdy, reinforced, and locked. Nazario heard someone moving about inside, drawers opening and closing.

He returned to a box he'd seen on the wall near the stage, yanked the fire alarm, and took a position beside the office door.

The deafening alarm was overridden by a computerized voice warning patrons to leave the building at once. After a moment or two the sprinkler system sputtered, then kicked in. Water jets sprayed from the ceiling.

A bolt disengaged and a man stepped out of the office. Charles Terrell, aka Josh Ellis, was a few pounds heavier and a dozen years older than in the photo. He had a suitcase in his left hand and a gun in his belt. "Manny!" he shouted. "What the hell's—"

Nazario jammed his gun to the side of Terrell's head.

"*Maricón*," he muttered. "Please reach for your weapon so I can shoot you now."

"What is this, a robbery?" Terrell raised his hands, feigning innocence.

"*Sí*, a robbery. At the Place Montmartre in Miami Beach. You remember it, the one with the ten-foot blonde outside. Put your hands against the wall." Nazario took Terrell's gun. He patted him down, ignoring the cold spray that drenched them both.

"I've never been to Miami. You don't know what you're talking about."

"Then why is my sergeant's badge case in your pocket? *Hijo de puta.*"

Terrell suddenly spun away, darted through the door to his office, and tried to slam it shut. Nazario lunged forward and wedged a foot inside. He slammed his full weight against it as Terrell let go. Nazario stumbled inside, splashing through water over his shoe tops.

Terrell had backed off to snatch another weapon, Burch's gun, off his desk. He pointed it at the detective.

"Gotcha," Terrell cried, eyes bright. "Don't move," he said. "Drop it. Now!"

Nazario stared at him, then dropped it. The gun plopped into the water at his feet.

"I want you to tell me something." Terrell seemed almost preternaturally calm. He wasn't even breathing hard. "Tell me what the hell happened? Why, after all these years? It was foolproof. Perfect. How did you know?"

"Your ex-wife, April, came in. Said she saw you."

"Mystic Seaport! I should've killed the bitch then! I could have. I followed them, saw where they were staying. I should have killed the bitch!"

"Why didn't you?"

"The goddamned kids were there."

"You know there are more coming behind me. A lot more."

"That's why we're taking a boat ride."

He snatched up his suitcase and motioned toward a back exit with the gun.

They had almost reached the door when Nazario tripped over something hidden in the ankle-deep water and fell. Terrell cursed. "Get up, you clumsy son of a bitch. Hurry!"

As he rolled over, Nazario kicked Terrell's legs out from under him. He landed on his back and elbows and dropped the gun.

Nazario piled onto him. They thrashed about in the water until the detective wrestled him to his feet and caught him in a choke hold. His right arm under Terrell's jaw, he turned sideways to avoid the man's flailing arms and applied pressure. He grunted as his bicep cut off the artery on the right side of Terrell's neck. His forearm squeezed the artery on the left, stopping the flow of blood to the brain.

He continued squeezing after Terrell went limp. He debated whether to stop.

He did. Terrell slid, unconscious, to the floor.

Nazario groped in the cascading water for the gun and picked it up. "Son of a whore," he said. *"Si te mueves te mato.* If you move I'll kill you."

Sirens converged as both the fire department and police arrived.

CHAPTER **THIRTY-SEVEN**

Rabbi Mordechai Waldman sounded breathless, speaking rapidly into the phone. "Samuel, I checked with the national rabbinical council, as you asked. The cities where the women were murdered all share the same chief *mashgiach*. For the last twenty-five years he has traveled periodically to each one, to inspect the kosher establishments and instruct the new *mashgiachim*.

"His name is Yitzhak Friedman. His home address is in Fair Lawn, New Jersey, but they say he is here in Miami now.

"Do you think . . . ?"

Stone felt a surge of adrenaline. Friedman's age, fifty, put him in the right age group. He was staying at a small kosher hotel in Miami Beach.

Elated, he called his grandmother. He'd been doing so several times a day since the news story. This morning she hadn't answered. He assumed she was in the yard or with a neighbor. He tried again. No answer.

He called the cell phone he'd given her. Either the battery was dead or the phone was turned off. He had told her to keep it in the charger, but she thought it foolish.

"If somebody wants to call me and I'm not home," she argued, "they can call me later."

She thought that people who used cell phones on the street, in shopping malls, or in their cars were foolish, with delusions of self-importance.

He called her next-door neighbor, who hadn't seen her all day. The neighbor checked and called back. Gran didn't answer the door.

Alarmed, he thought of sending a zone car by, but what if something had happened to her?

He went himself.

Nothing looked unusual as he parked the car. But his chest tightened as he took the front steps two at a time.

He fumbled with his key, then realized it was because the door wasn't locked.

"Gran!" The cottage was silent. Nothing out of place. The kitchen immaculate. The pictures back in their frames.

Heart pounding in his throat, his dread mounting, he went to her bedroom. "Gran."

He stood in the doorway. There was something on her bed. Knees weak and trembling, he leaned on the door frame for support.

She wasn't there. It was a note in unfamiliar block letters.

"See how easy. You know nothing."

Where was she? He tore through the rest of the house, calling her name, checked the yard. No sign of her, or her purse, or the cell phone.

He called Riley, trying to sound calm and keep his voice from trembling.

She issued a BOLO and dispatched the crime lab. She was on the way.

Before they arrived, he drove quickly through the immediate neighborhood, hoping to find someone who had seen his grandmother. Then to the grocery store where she shopped, and past the library.

No luck. Tears stung his eyes. He made a U-turn to join the other units already at the house.

A lumbering Metro bus blocked his lane of traffic, then stopped, belching poisonous clouds of dirty exhaust. Frustrated and panicky, he leaned mercilessly on the horn, then angrily swerved around the bus. A diminutive passenger stepped off.

She carried a shopping bag and wore a wide-brimmed hat to keep the sun off her face.

He hit the brakes, then pulled to the curb. "Gran! Are you all right?"

"Sonny, was that you blowing the horn back there?" She frowned.

"What ever happened to your manners? That's not how I raised you."

He hugged her so hard she complained. "Are you trying to crush my ribs?"

"Where were you, Gran? I was really scared."

"Sonny, you know that on the third Tuesday of the month I always work over at the Baptist church kitchen, making pies for the Wednesday night bake sale. I've been doing it since you were a teenager. I'm worried about you, boy." She frowned again. "Your memory isn't what it used to be."

"Come on." He opened his car door for her.

"I kin walk the rest of the way."

"People are looking for you all over town. I'm embarrassed. Get in the car, please."

. . .

The intruder had placed the note on her bed sometime after 7 A.M. when she left. She swore she'd locked the door. The cell phone was in her purse. She had never turned it on.

The crime lab took the note, printed on lined yellow paper.

Nothing was missing. Despite her protests, Stone packed her a bag and took her to stay at his apartment in North Miami. She hadn't been there in some time.

"Sonny? When did you vacuum and dust this place last?"

"I've been busy, Gran."

Despite her even more vigorous protests, he left her his off-duty gun. "You know how to use it, Gran. Point and shoot. If you do have to use it, don't stop. Empty it."

. . .

Stone was back at the office updating Riley about Yitzak Friedman when Emma interrupted, her expression odd.

"You need to take this call, Lieutenant."

Riley picked up. "Nazario?" Her face changed. "Wait a minute, wait a minute, I can't understand you."

"Something wrong?" Stone said.

"Pete, Pete, slow down," she said.

Nazario was gasping as though he'd been weeping.

"We got Terrell," he said, voice breaking. "But he shot Burch."

She gasped, the color drained from her face.

"How bad? Oh God. Where? Okay, okay." She scribbled notes as he spoke. "All right. All right, I'll handle everything. Hang in. The world is on the way."

She buried her face in her hands for a brief moment, then took a deep breath.

"Burch was shot," she said briskly.

"How bad?" Stone said.

Emma stood whimpering beside them, both hands over her mouth.

"Critical. Took two, in the chest and the head. He's in surgery. I have to report to the chief and go tell Connie. I also have to let April Terrell know that it's time to tell her kids."

"What should I do?" Stone demanded.

"Exactly what you've been doing," she said. "They're in Maine, you're here. You're making headway on an important case. Don't stop."

She pulled on her jacket, then turned, frowning. "There is one thing. Nazario said something about a cat. Burch wanted you to feed it. It's at the place where he's been staying."

"Sure." He was stunned.

The news hit Homicide like a thunderbolt.

A deputy chief, the department's chaplain, a captain, and Jo Salazar arranged to catch the next flight.

· · ·

Connie Burch answered the door.

She had yellow spatters on her T-shirt and jeans and a paintbrush in her hand.

"Hey, K. C." She stepped back and looked around her. "What do you think? They call it Monet yellow. You think it's too bright for the foyer?"

Something she saw in Riley's face made her stop, lips apart. Her eyes widened.

"Connie, I know you and Craig are on the outs and not together right now. But I wanted to tell you myself . . ."

"No." Connie began to shake her head. "No. He's all right. He's coming home tonight."

"No, Connie, he's—"

She dropped the paintbrush and clamped both hands over her ears. She continued shaking her head.

"—been injured. It's very serious. He's critical."

She yelped once, like a frightened puppy. "Where is he?"

"Still in Maine. He was shot."

Connie took a deep breath and wiped her hands on her jeans. "How do I get there?"

"Are you sure?" Riley said, surprised.

"I love him."

"Mom?" Jennifer stood in the hallway.

"Jenny, get the kids, we're going to your dad."

"All right," Riley said. "Let me try to get you on the same flight as the assistant chief, Jo Salazar, and the others."

The flight left in little more than an hour. The airport was half an hour away.

Riley worked the phone. Talked to the chief, to the airline.

"We have to go," she said. They went as they were, with no time to pack anything. Connie had a credit card, but only forty dollars in cash. Riley emptied her wallet, gave Connie what money she had, then piled them into her car. She slapped the blue light on the dashboard and raced toward the airport.

A police escort, sirens screaming, picked them up at the entrance ramp to the Palmetto Expressway.

The last Riley saw of them, they were running down the concourse, hand in hand.

. . .

Riley intercepted April Terrell as she arrived home from work. They talked, seated on stone benches at a shaded round table in the courtyard of the apartment building where she lived.

"I'm so shocked and sorry about Sergeant Burch. He seemed like a wonderful man." April wept. "To think that Charles is alive and did all these monstrous things. The kids . . . It breaks your heart all over again. You don't know what it's like to lose the man you love, first to another woman, then to death, and now to this new nightmare. You have no idea—"

"Actually," Riley said, "I do. We share something in common." She unloaded, blurted out the whole story. "You see, the man I loved didn't love me, or maybe I'll just never know if he did or not because I lost him to another woman, and then he was killed.

"McDonald gave his life," she said at the end, "to save a little kid who will probably grow into a worthless drug user like his father. You've got your children. I have nothing."

"That's not true." April wiped her eyes. "You have something positive to hold on to. You're in a position to be a force for good in that child's life, to help keep him from becoming a bad man like his father. If someone like your McDonald gave up everything to save him, that's exactly what he'd expect you to do."

Riley stared for a long moment. "You're right, April. You're absolutely right."

. . .

The news was too much for Stone to process. Riley had appeared so cool, so professional, while he wanted to break things, to punch out walls. He had to do something. Take action. There was nothing.

Detective Ron Diaz called. "Helluva thing about Burch. He gonna make it?"

"We're waiting on word from the hospital. I just called again and they won't tell us a damn thing."

"You still want a heads-up on the homicides of elderly females found at home in bed?"

"Definitely."

"We just got us one. I'm en route. The uniform at the scene said it's weird. She's laid out on her bed wrapped in a white sheet. Looks like the mortician's already been there. That's what he says."

. . .

The house was a faded peach color and in a state of disrepair.

"She was a nice lady, never bothered anybody," a neighbor was telling a patrolman out front.

Stone knew. When he walked in the door, he knew. His mind flashed on the photographs of previous crime scenes. Interchangeable with this one.

Her faded, neatly trimmed hair was spread out across the pillow. Her nails had been clipped.

Evelyn Symons, eighty-one, a widow, had lived alone for almost two decades.

"This one's mine."

"Be my guest," Diaz said. "Anything you want me to do before I split?"

"I need the chief medical examiner and Ed Baker from the crime lab. Nobody but Baker. Call him at home if you have to."

Stone pulled on a pair of latex gloves. Gently he moved the woman's head to one side. He knew they would be there before he saw the particles of soil in her hair and on the pillow.

Baker, the crime lab chief, arrived, short, silver-haired, and nononsense.

"It's him," Stone said. "The one we talked about."

Baker nodded and went to work. Using a mega brush, without bristles, he lightly dusted the dead woman's bruised throat with magnetic fingerprint powder, then lifted the powder with tape.

"Anything?" Stone asked.

Baker studied the tape, then shook his head. "No ridge detail at all. Just a blurry smudge, the outline of a finger."

Stone sighed. "Like the others. Okay, you know what I want now. We've talked about it enough. This is it. It's time to try. They say it can be done."

"I've been waiting for the chance," Baker said.

He swabbed the dead woman's throat to lift the remaining fingerprint powder.

"It'll take a little time," he told Stone.

"The sooner the better."

He and the crime technicians worked long into the night examining firsthand what Stone had only seen before in photos.

Before going home at dawn, he asked for surveillance on Friedman. "Bring him in," he urged, distributing his photo at roll call. "If he loiters, or lollygags, or spits on the sidewalk, bring him in. Better yet, if he does spit on the sidewalk, collect it and bring it to the lab."

At several food establishments inspected by Friedman, Stone learned the *mashgiach* was not a popular man. Irate owners dreaded his visits. Nothing they did was good enough. He had them jumping through hoops to remain certified. "He finds violations no one else can see," one complained. "You follow his rules and then, *nu?* He sees something else. I wouldn't wish him to inspect my worst enemy."

Stone took copies of Friedman's printed forms and notices to document examiners. They called the printing extremely similar to that on the note left on his grandmother's bed, but the experts could not swear to an absolute certainty that the same man wrote both. The note was brief. Handwriting would have been easier to identify.

Stone studied the surveillance reports and monitored Friedman's habits. Which is what put him in an unmarked car outside a kosher deli on Forty-first Street in Miami Beach. Friedman ate lunch there as usual. He emerged drinking an orange soda. As usual, he dropped the bottle into a Dumpster as he approached the parking garage.

The Dumpster had been emptied that morning.

Friedman stepped into the parking garage elevator.

Stone went Dumpster diving.

He zipped the nearly empty bottle into an evidence bag for Baker, the crime lab genius.

When the results came back, Stone cheered. He handcuffed Friedman at a restaurant he was inspecting.

"What did he do? Take a bribe?" the manager asked. "It wouldn't be the first time."

"No," Stone said, after informing Friedman of his rights. "He murdered ten women."

"Ten?" the manager asked. "Where did he find the time?"

"I've done nothing wrong," Friedman said. "You know nothing. There are certain laws, religious laws . . ."

"How about the one in Exodus: 'Thou shalt not kill.' "

Stone thought he had never felt better, but then came the icing on the cake, a call from Nell Hunter.

"Hey, Sam Spade. Heard you made your big arrest. Cool. Knew you'd do it. What's the real story?"

As chirpy as ever, she sounded cuddly and cute, friendly and warm, then bewildered.

"What did you call me?" she demanded just before he hung up. "A llama?"

CHAPTER THIRTY-EIGHT

WEEKS LATER

I don't mind the crying baby, or the kid kicking my seat back. I could do without the sneezing, coughing passenger blowing his runny nose a couple of rows back. But I love them all. I'm going home, the luckiest man alive.

The slug that slammed into my chest and tore through my lung made a bigger hole when it exited my back. It grazed a rib, which accounted for the burning sensation. The deformed bullet wound up lying on the rug. They said I was smart to drop and play dead. I didn't say I wasn't playing. The immediate ouch took me down for the count.

Terrell's intended coup de grâce, the gunshot to the head, tore a hole in my scalp and actually left a groove in my skull. It bled like hell. A small contusion and some swelling of the brain cleared up. The doctors say that a mere fraction of an inch more, and I would have wound up permanently brain damaged or even more permanently dead. What can I say about trauma centers and their staffs? They are the reason the homicide rate has gone down. They drag people like me back from the brink every day.

Nazario stayed with me, so did Connie and my kids. They flew back to Miami just two days ago to get ready for my homecoming. Home.

"Look at that, Sarge," Nazario says. The pilot is circling out over the ocean to approach the city from the east. I see Miami's vast sprawl and unearthly light as we swoop down through the clouds toward home. Home.

I look for the sun and the shadows fall behind me.

Terrell is fighting extradition and the inevitable. I don't know if he will be tried up in Maine or in Miami first. When they do bring him back, I hope to be part of the welcoming committee.

Life is good. Doctors say I can be back on the job in a matter of weeks. Riley says we're still in the budget, at least until next year's crisis. While I can't wait to hug my kids again and watch them grow, my heart goes out to April Terrell and her children, and Natasha's oldest, a virtual orphan at twelve. What can you say to a boy whose Mom wound up in a Dumpster and whose Dad has appointments on death row in two states, to say nothing of Granddad, the escaped war criminal? Milo Ross, the kid's latest stepfather, has said he'll raise the boy.

I said I didn't want any fuss at the airport, but as Nazario and I walk down the concourse, there they are. Riley, Stone, Corso, even Emma and a dozen others.

I am welcomed by laughter, applause, and Miami's warm, wet kiss. I don't know why of all Terrell's victims, I alone survived. There has to be a reason. Something I'm meant to do. I can't wait to get back on the job.

After a skirmish with Nazario over the car keys, Stone drives me home. First we three swing by the Beach to pick up my stuff.

"So how'd you do it?" I ask. "You solved the Meadows case. Got the guy! I even saw you on the network news. How did you nail it?"

"As you know," Stone says. "fingerprint residue consists of three main substancess that are exuded from glands all over the body. They are the apocrine, eccrine, and sebaceous glands. The sebaceous gland is usually associated with hair follicles and leaves the best residue for latent prints. Suspects pick it up on their hands as they touch their face, hair, beard, whatever, even their arms. And our suspect had a beard and lots of hair. I was worried at first because he washed the bodies, but I read in an article in the *Forensic Journal* that water alone won't destroy fingerprints left by sebaceous residue."

I am distracted, blown away by everything around me. The rapidly moving clouds and water. The familiar skyline I thought I might never see again. The voices of my detectives, the camaraderie.

"Hold on, genius. Gimme the *Reader's Digest* version."

"Yeah, Stone. Sarge's brain is still healing."

"Okay." Stone grins. "Bottom line? You *can* extract DNA from a fingerprint—even an unrecognizable fingerprint. Some people doubted it could be done. They were wrong."

"The mind is like a parachute," I say. "It always works best when it's open."

"Then," Stone says, "it was no problem to compare it to the DNA he left on the soda bottle. Voilà, a match. Simple.

"We got him, although his lawyers are considering an insanity plea based on some teenage trauma. But how can they convince a jury he was insane for decades, all while holding a responsible job?"

"I'd love to see him and Terrell in the same cell," I say, as we turn into the long, shaded driveway.

Stone took good care of everything, including the cat, who runs to greet me. Who says animals have short memories?

Stone carries my stuff down to the car while I call the owner. Adair is still in Italy. I don't know what time it is there, but he sounds wide awake.

I report that everything is swell, including the cat.

"What cat? We don't have a cat," he insists.

In fact, he says, his young wife is allergic to cats.

I stare at the cat, purring on my lap at the moment. Is this a joke? I hand the phone to Nazario, who will be staying here to baby-sit his place because I am going home.

We swing by the nearest animal hospital to see if we have a match for any of the missing, wanted, or reward posters hanging from the waiting room bulletin board. Nothing. I show the cat's puss to the staff, to see if they recognize his mug as somebody's missing pet.

The receptionist lights up. "You've got one of the city cats." She coos at him and scratches his head. "You can tell by the notch in his left ear."

I thought he'd been maimed in a fight.

The city had too many strays, she says. So volunteers trapped them, to put a lid on the population explosion. They were spayed and neutered and put back out on the street to do whatever they were doing before, but without the same results.

"So what do I do with him?" I ask her.

She shrugged. "You can put him back where you found him."

. . .

My heart beats faster as we turn onto my street. The last time I was here I was persona non grata, sneaking in the dark to check on my family.

Today the house is a splash of color. Hung with welcome-home signs and banners made by the kids. They run to meet me. Connie is waiting outside, crying, her arms open. Neighbors are waving and here I am, walking up to the front door under my own steam, carrying the cat carrier, my feet still on the planet, still vertical, the luckiest man alive.

ACKNOWLEDGMENTS

I am deeply grateful to editor Mitchell Ivers, a writer's dream. He inspires, conspires, and swoops out of the sky like a superhero. What a masterful accomplice! I am home at last.

Dr. Joseph H. Davis, the world's most brilliant forensic pathologist, contributed greatly to this book, as did my fabulous friend, Sergeant Joy Gellatly, the pride of the Savannah Police Department. She is the best and the brightest.

William and Karen Sampson, that phenomenal nationally known team of forensic experts, generously shared their genius. I am indebted to my old friends William Venturi and Raul J. Diaz, former homicide investigators, now ace private detectives and soldiers for justice. Between them, they have solved more real life-murders than most police departments ever see!

Lisa Kreeger, senior attorney with the American Prosecutors Research Institute, contributed invaluably to this book. Her razor-sharp mind, love for the law, and keen sense of justice make the world a better place. So does attorney, journalist, and fearless sports-car driver Siobhan Morrissey, who flashes in and out of my life at the speed of light in her big mean red machine.

Alisa Fanbrini is consistently generous with her expertise and knowledge.

The world is more beautiful, thanks to her. I am also grateful for William B. Wolfson, whose words of wit and wisdom live on. Thanks go to my agent, Michael Congdon, and to Asa Boynton, Fire Lieutenant Russell Frank, Amy Brier, Rabbi Sholom Blank, Matthew Lane, the amazing Freddy Walker, my friends Leonard Wolfson, Brooke Engle, Dr. Howard Engle, Dr. Hubert Rosomoff, and the warm and witty Renee Steele Rosomoff. All gave generously of their time and knowledge—as did my veteran co-conspirators Marilyn Lane, Edward Gadinsky, Ann Hughes, Pam Stone Blackwell, the Rev. Garth Thompson, and Dr. Richard Souviron, the world-renowned forensic odontologist.

The brilliant Joel Hirshhorn, president of the American Board of Criminal Lawyers, rescued me, and my sanity. Again and again.

The usual suspects were there, as always, when I needed them: Dr. Ferdie Pacheco, Al Alschuler, Ira Dubitsky, Sol Schreiber, and Patricia Keen, along with the other loyal and stout-hearted Sesquipedelians. Friends are the family we choose. How cool is that?

ABOUT THE AUTHOR

In her life of sentences, Edna Buchanan has covered more crimes than most cops. A Pulitzer Prize–winning *Miami Herald* police reporter and winner of the prestigious George Polk Career Award, she brings a dynamic and steamy Miami to vivid life in all of her novels. She captures both the heartbeat and the hot breath of this restless, exotic, and mercurial city. The author of fourteen books and numerous short stories, she lives in Miami, Florida, with two dogs, a covey of cats, and Bunjamin, a small brown rabbit. Visit Edna on the Web at www.ednabuchanan.com.